PLAYING FOR YOU

A SPORTS ROMANCE

STACY TRAVIS

PLAYING FOR YOU

STACY TRAVIS

Cover Design: Savage Hart Design

Copyediting: Erica Edits

Publicity: Social Butterfly PR

CHAPTER 1

atum

My competitive streak runs hot. Like melted cheddar under a flaming broiler—that kind of hot.

Maybe it derives from birth order, given that I have five older siblings. I always had to compete and chase after them.

Or I just got the racehorse equivalent of serenity in our family gene pool.

Either way, I've never considered it a problem. Good old competitive spirit saw me through calculus and computer science classes with the smart kids in high school. A lot of them were guys. A lot of them held it against me.

I didn't date much in high school.

In college, I found my merry band of fellow strivers and achievers, so no one looked twice when I rode my sputtering, used red moped to campus in the middle of the night to check my lab results and record them in real time. No one found it odd that I ran a bunch of solitary miles at five in the morning to train for sprint distance triathlons—for fun.

Ah, to be a nerd among nerds.

Study dates with electrical engineering and computer science guys almost qualified as actual dates. After we'd finished our problem sets, they wanted to score as much as the frat boys. And missionary style sex lined everything up at nice orderly angles.

Scientific. Unimaginative. Efficient.

Is that all there is? Probably.

It's why I got engaged at age twenty-one to a fellow coder named Warren and broke it off a year later. Story for another time, but let's just say I lost my mind for a minute because of a juicy eggplant and all of the ways it could be savored between algorithms.

It's why now, seven years later, I don't really date. And why all the eggplants I ever see come in the form of baba ghanoush.

Sitting in my programming pod at the Silicon Valley tech campus where I work, I twirl a purple pen and consider the results of my competitiveness. The desire to outdo my peers has landed me here, at an ergonomically designed desk on wheels which can slide around the open-plan office for impromptu meetings with the design pod or the marketing pod. Infinite configurations of potential pod productivity.

Productivity makes me almost as happy as competition. It's its own sort of measurable achievement.

"Hey, I hear we have another challenge," intones a voice behind me. I don't have to turn to know who's speaking—I have exactly two friends at work, and Terrance is one of them. The other is Leila, who caters lunch on Wednesdays, so really . . . just the one. But Terrance carries the weight of ten.

Splaying one hand on the gray surface of my desk, he plucks a browning leaf from my potted ivy plant with the other. His longish brown hair hangs over his forehead and into his eyes, but if it bothers him, he ignores it for the importance of tending to my plant.

"Ooh, yeah? Tell me." I bend my neck trying to see his light brown eyes, whose sparkle tends to mirror the potential prize for the winner of any challenge within the company. He's fixated on my plant, now testing the soil's dampness, so I won't know the magnitude of the challenge bounty until he finishes fussing.

I type a few lines of code and wait. When he still doesn't speak, I press my lips together to buy a little more time before my impatience makes me blurt, "Terrance! Enough with the plant. What's the challenge?"

The company where we work regularly pits us against each other in friendly design or programming challenges in a race against the clock. They keep our adrenaline racing which leads to some creative ideas.

He looks up at me and smirks, cheek dimples popping in his round face that looks like it hasn't seen the sun in a decade. Terrance doesn't run at five in the morning, doesn't stay at work past six at night, and inexplicably, doesn't care about our boss's challenges. He refuses to waste his time on them, but that never stops him from taunting me. "Um, let me try and recall . . . " He stares at the ceiling, his grin betraying how much he enjoys messing with me.

His methodical persistence amazes me sometimes. He works carefully, thoroughly—but so slowly. Unlike me. I approach every assignment and new project like the Tasmanian Devil, bent on coding the hell out of it and demolishing the competition.

And it's working. I've earned pay raises and a better position at a better company, but I still want so much more. Terrance and I couldn't be more different. Maybe that's why we make such good friends. That, and the fact that there's zero spark for either one of us, something we admitted in the early days of our friendship.

A junior programmer, Terrance started with our company,

ViviTech, a year after I did. He should have earned a promotion to senior programmer by now, but he's happy taking orders from other people and seems to be missing the hyperdrive that might get him a better job.

We've talked about it. I sometimes try to give him a push because he's smart and I see his potential, but he's happy doing workaday programming and not stressing about staying late to climb the company ladder.

I have no idea what that feels like.

"Oh, you recall. Just tell me." It's not that I don't have a sense of humor. I can appreciate his game. I just intend to win at it.

Terrance grins like a cat who's got his mouse cornered and is settling in for a nice long session of fuckery. "I don't know exactly. Something related to a pet project of Charlie's, and you know that could be anything . . . " His voice trails off and he looks for something else on my desk to mess with.

But really, he's messing with me.

"That's all you know? Wow, too bad you can't tell me more. I have about three hours of coding busywork and I've been looking for someone to hand it off to." I smile sweetly at him and let him know—not for the first time—that he's about to come out on the losing end of this bluffing game.

I twirl my pen a few times like I have all the patience in the world to wait him out. Really, my stomach acid is threatening to digest all my internal organs, but I smile.

Then I see it, the telltale twitch in his right eye that indicates he has no interest in three extra hours of busywork. He nods. "Fine. It's a virtual reality functionality competition. I didn't hear about the prize, but I know you don't care about that." He waggles his eyebrows, taunting me.

"And you learned this how?" I squint my eyes at him, not willing to let him off the hook with a bum lead or something he made up—yes, he's pulled one of those and only let on after I'd spent an hour on a wild goose chase. Hence the need for me to have reams of busywork at the ready as a threat.

He laughs. "You're such a hardass. I just delivered the code files to Charlie, and he told me himself."

Charlie is the king of ViviTech, the company he created to revolutionize virtual reality so NASA scientists could virtually walk on Mars and examine the planet with all the simulated land conditions that they'd encounter if they were there.

He then made a big bet in gaming, designing VR sets that have become the gold standard. But the technology can do so much more, and that's what gets me excited—the idea of helping people deal with phobias by simulating those environments in therapeutic settings. The applications are endless.

At five feet nine with light brown hair and light brown eyes, Charlie doesn't cut an imposing figure physically. But the second he opens his mouth, the stream of consciousness visions of technology and world building make it obvious he cleared his first billion before age thirty for a reason.

He regularly creates challenges—impossible-seeming designs, programming quests using minimal lines of code, physical products using recycled materials—and rewards the winners with perks like tickets to pro basketball games, sailing lessons, and cases of wine.

Big surprise, I never care as much about the prizes as much as the idea of winning.

I swivel my chair around to face Terrance head-on, dying to know more. Pulling my messy blondish strands out of their pony, I stare a hole into him while I wait for him to give me the rest of the details.

Enjoying his scrap of power, Terrance backs a few steps away. "I believe Charlie will be sending an email about it soon. You should watch your inbox."

"Terrance . . . " I warn, looking around my desk for something to throw at him. Absent something heavy, I use the purple pen. He catches it and pops it into the pocket of his khakis. Now I'm down a pen, and I'm losing patience. I have actual work to finish, after all.

"Yes?" he asks, batting his lashes.

"The lash thing, not a good look for you. Spill." I swivel the mess of my hair up into a bun and glare.

Terrance leans on the corner of my desk and crosses his arms. "Okay, I've had my fun for the day. Here's the deal. Charlie's going to ask for an enhanced avatar model based on a real person. So all the facial expressions and movements have to match exactly."

I narrow my eyes, trying to see something that doesn't exist. "We already do that. It's the whole point of VR, to mimic real people."

He shakes his head. "I'm not explaining it right, then. It's going to be based on specific people, like celebrities or whatever, so you can be that person in the game. That's what I understood him to mean."

"Oh."

Oh.

We'd never done anything like that before. And the idea of getting to move and think like a real known person sets off little thrill bells of excitement ringing in my ears. Even if the idea of studying the expressions and verbal cues of celebrities doesn't float my intellectual boat, the technology piece gets me seriously hot and bothered.

Terrance frowns at me and his lips turn down in disgust. "I don't need to see your O face at work, Tatum."

"What? Jesus, Terrance. I don't have an O face."

"Well, that's another problem altogether. I'm sorry, but maybe we should address that challenge instead of talking about some dumb thing Charlie dreamed up." Now he's winking at me. If I didn't know he was married—adorably, happily married to an adorable, happy high-school sweetheart—the wink might bother me, but on Terrance's baby face, it never does.

I wave a hand at him. "Stop. That's not what I meant."

"I know, but I don't care. Besides, it wouldn't kill you to go on a date occasionally."

"Thanks, Mom. But I don't date, remember?"

"I remember that it's a stupid idea not to date. Let me set you up with someone. I know single people."

"Do you? Really? I thought you had to renounce your single friend membership when you said, 'I do,'" I deadpan.

Maybe I've picked the wrong person to unload on, given that Terrance has his work-life balance finessed perfectly. But he's my closest friend in an office where barely anyone talks to me. Most of the people I work with I consider colleagues, but I'd never invite one over for coffee, and I definitely wouldn't confide in them. Confiding is the kiss of death in a cut-throat business.

So Terrance is my person, even though we diverge when it comes to personal drive.

He grins. "You're so much fun to play with. It makes me really sad that I have to go back to my desk and do actual work."

"I'm sure." Time wasting aside, he's done me a solid with the early heads-up about the competition. Even though his explanation of what Charlie's planning sounded vague, it's enough to start my wheels turning. Plus, now I can work on clearing other tasks, so I'll have time to take on the challenge.

"Thanks for the info, Terrance. If you want to send a chunk of your programming to me, I'll knock it out for you."

He looks at the floor with a guilty smile. He was counting on easing his workload with his insider information, and he knew I'd take the bait. The truth is I can get through the programming he's tasked with in less time than it takes him because I've done so much of it that I've become efficient.

A few minutes later, Terrance sends me some coding, and a

few minutes after that, Charlie sends a company-wide email alerting us that the challenge is on.

CHARLIE'S EMAIL rounds out the information Terrance didn't tell me. It says that ViviTech's newest gaming project will be a sports reality competition where we'll be creating avatars of real athletes. Gamers will become the athletes they choose and simulate competing in their sports.

"Imagine scoring the winning three point shot as Kawhi Leonard or intercepting a pass as Patrick Mahomes," Charlie's email enthuses. "It's next-level gaming, combining a workout, tactical decision-making, and fantasy play with a sports franchise."

I'm all in for that, especially since I've heard rumors that Charlie is planning on having ViviTech become a major sponsor of a football team. He hasn't said anything officially, which is typical Charlie. He fans the flames of rumors on social media with little hints to whip the gaming community into a frenzy, but gives no confirmation until he's ready.

He has a strict policy of announcing company business to his employees at the same time he announces it to shareholders and the media, so no one leaks anything early, and he controls the narrative.

Still, I hope there's something to the rumor.

The idea of studying football players for the sake of game design sounds way more interesting than building avatars in the likeness of violent auto thieves or world-destroying killers armed with knives and grenades.

Been there, done the savage murdering.

As a peace-loving person, I sometimes go home sick to my stomach after testing the coding for those games. They're that real.

I'd much prefer to craft an avatar with every sinewy muscle and intense facial feature of a pro athlete. It hardly feels like work to conduct interviews with the players, getting to know their mannerisms and speech patterns, learning the way they think about the sport.

Plus, I love football. College, pro, doesn't matter. I'll watch pretty much any team play on TV, and I regularly catch Stanford home games since the stadium is less than a mile from where I live in Palo Alto.

My siblings don't know about that part.

With Finn, the oldest, and Sarah, the second-oldest sister, both working at Berkeley, I know better than to advertise attending the games of their biggest rival.

I almost get so sidetracked thinking about a new potential football VR division that I'd give my right arm to run, that I stare at my screen for a full minute without writing a single line of code. Not exactly the way to win a competition.

But my daydreaming has actually given me an idea. I scrap my original plans and pull together a new configuration for the avatar's backend design.

I test it.

I test it again.

It works both times.

And so far, no whoops or hollers have indicated that one of my colleagues has presented a winning design to Charlie. I tee up my model, write a few lines summarizing how it works, and press send.

Not ten minutes later, a text from Charlie blinks at the top of my screen.

Boss Man: Come to my office please

Me: Coming

Sending my chair spinning, I fly from my desk toward Charlie's office, the only one in our shared workspace that has a door. I always appreciate that he says *please*. Charlie has socially awkward quirks and an oddly fascinating brain, but he never lacks for courtesy.

Smoothing my clammy hands down the legs of my worn jeans, I glance around to see if any of my colleagues notice where I'm going—to claim bragging rights for beating them! Not a single person looks my way.

Typical.

Most of what I do at work doesn't merit much attention since most everyone around here regularly hits their projects out of the park like they're scribbling a Sudoku half-asleep. No one's worried about me stealing focus. I'm not flashy, and I let my work speak for itself.

I've also been told I dress like a tech druid—older sisters are nothing if not brutally honest—in baggy jeans and a hoodie most days, with my hair piled on top of my head so it doesn't get in my face while I type. Makeup seems like a waste of time, especially when I spend my days wearing dark-rimmed computer glasses and looking at no one. So again, I make myself practically invisible to everyone except my married best friend.

Unfortunately, the one person immune to my cloak of invisibility seems to have it out for me. "What's the rush, Finley?" Paul Peters jeers, standing up from his desk to block my path. He's my direct supervisor, and he's always up in my business.

"Just walking by, Paul." I use his actual name even though he insists on being called Pauley. He's not a Pauley. Pauley would have a softer approach, and he'd be a team player. He wouldn't wear a windbreaker with a tie and finger it while he leers.

Paul Peters is the worst kind of human to have as a boss—paranoid about being outsmarted and replaced, vindictive toward anyone who has an idea better than his, and quick to take credit for other people's'work. I have the great misfortune of working directly beneath Paul in the company chain of command, and he lords that over me regularly, giving me extra work to do and boasting about his brilliance to Charlie when one of the projects bears fruit.

"You're going to Charlie's?" His accusatory tone tells me he knows exactly why.

I fold my arms over my chest and fight my instinct to tell him to mind his own business. "It would appear so."

"Good luck with that." His eyes assess me, trying to figure out if I really came up with a solution to Charlie's challenge and calculating how he can take the credit for it.

I give him my biggest smile and playfully punch his shoulder, startling him with the affection. "Thank you so much, Paul. You're the best." I leave him reeling, unsure if I meant it.

"Um, sure. You're welcome." He puffs out his chest, willing to take any praise, even the passive-aggressive kind.

As I stride toward the corner glass-walled office, I tuck the stray flyaway strands behind my ears and swallow thickly. Charlie makes me nervous, mostly because I never know what will come out of his mouth.

"Tatum, greetings," he says, standing to shake my hand in the oddly formal way he always says hello, no matter the time of day or whether we've seen each other an hour earlier.

"Hey, Charlie. How are you?" I try to make eye contact, so he'll know I really do want to know about him. I feel like a lot of people work for him because they like the cachet of being at a sought-after tech company, but they don't really like *him*.

I worry that he doesn't seem to have many friends. He always eats lunch alone in his office, and when other tech pioneers around Silicon Valley have their calendars filled with venture capitalists and serial entrepreneurs jockeying for their time, Charlie chooses solitude.

I like understanding people because it helps when programming VR experiences. In his case though, I really want to understand the puzzle that is Charles Walgrove. He's genius-level smart when it comes to understanding what technology people need and how to build it, yet mundane daily tasks trip him up. He'll spend fifteen minutes in front of the vending machine deciding between regular chips and barbecue flavor because he's weighing the electrolyte variables, the number of bags of each kind in the machine, and weight distribution in the machine that will result from choosing one bag over the other.

Case in point, he looks at me, two fingers pinching his lips together, eyes crinkled under a furrowed brow. He tilts to the side as though he's determining something of crucial importance.

I watch him and wait.

"Your hair is different. It was in a . . . " He flips his hands around pantomiming a ponytail. "And now it's up." The man makes over five thousand dollars a minute and he notices that I threw my hair into a bun.

"Sometimes I switch it around."

"Why?"

With some people, I'd shrug and say I don't have a reason. With Charlie, I know he really wants to know. "Sometimes I get a headache, so I pull the band out. Then it gets in my face, and I pull it up again. Maybe a bun, maybe a ponytail. It's an unconscious decision."

His face opens into a grin, as though he's gleaned valuable information he'll use later, and he nods. "Unconscious. Okay."

I wait while Charlie stares off. Shaking his head, he seems to change his mind about exploring my unconscious mind.

"Well, you've completed my task. Kudos. I'd like you to come up with a few other iterations of the algorithm because I have a hunch you can improve on the performance speed. Based on what you submitted, I saw some opportunities for efficiencies. Of course, I wouldn't expect you to address all of those in a competitive environment, so for these purposes I'm prepared to hand over the prize for this particular game."

Everything is a game to Charlie. The wild success of his

company seems to baffle him sometimes because he's just in it for the fun.

I'm playing an entirely different game. I want to run the new VR project.

I've been dying for the chance to prove I can run a division of the company, and if using VR for therapy isn't at the top of Charlie's list, I'll joyously throw my hat in the ring for a sports game. I know football. I can do this job.

I don't get a lot of solo time talking with Charlie in his office. So now feels like the right time to ask for what I want.

"I don't need the prize, but I would like to put myself up for running—"

He cuts me off. "That response confuses me. The offer of a prize was not about need—of course no one needs a prize and if that was your supposition, it's faulty. Needs imply basic human requirements like food, shelter, clothing, family. Though arguably we can create family where it doesn't exist biologically, so I might remove that from the list, but nevertheless, it puzzles me that you'd turn down a prize without knowing what it is."

I swallow hard.

Play his game.

"True. I was getting ahead of myself. I just meant that I didn't compete in this to win a prize. I did it because I'm really interested in—"

He shuts me down again by raising a hand. "I know. I know why you compete in all my little games—you're ambitious and you like to win. But part of winning is enjoying the fruits of your labor." With a nod, he gestures for me to sit in one of the leather club chairs opposite his desk.

I want to tell him that winning is only part of the prize for me. I want more job responsibility. I want to head up a division. But he's trying to make a point, and he won't consider me to run the new project—or even discuss the new project—until I do what he wants.

The furniture in his office reminds of a well-appointed pub—not a dark, messy English pub with beer-sticky floors and dartboards, but a finer place that serves good food. His desk has a glass top, and the walls are lined with hardcover books.

I lean against the arm of a chair, perching like a bird ready to flee instead of sinking into its depths.

"As you know from my email, we're taking VR to the gaming space, starting with a few football clubs whose players have mostly signed on to have their likenesses included in the games. I've invested personally in the Strikers and their jerseys are currently being redesigned with our logo on the front. Donovan Taylor will make this season very interesting indeed—as a fan, this excites me. All of this has allowed me to offer a pretty exciting prize to our competition winner."

My brain crunches through information I don't understand. Did I know he bought a football team? I'm expecting him to present me with a pair of tickets to a game, but now I'm puzzling through what football team he's talking about since I know there isn't an NFL team called the Strikers.

And a player named Donovan Taylor? Never heard of him.

"I hope you're free this evening because there's a banquet in the city to announce the naming rights and they'd like someone from ViviTech to attend. It's being held at the Edmunton Hotel and I'm told they have a Michelin-starred chef. So go, eat some caviar, be affable, geek out over VR, get the people involved with the team excited. I don't do well in these situations—public . . . gatherings . . . I find them very stressful, and I'm an introvert. I'll either clam up or say something that will get me in trouble with the SEC, no telling which . . . "

He looks at the ceiling and grimaces as if recalling a particularly bad instance. "Anyhow, I'm pleased you're the one I can send in my stead because you're very personable. You'll represent us well."

Before I can process half of what he's telling me, Charlie is standing from his desk and herding me to the door like a corgi with a flock of sheep. "Wait, Charlie, I've got a lot of work to finish. I'm not sure I can make it to a . . . banquet . . . "

I cross my arms over my chest, not liking the idea of going to a dinner where I probably won't get through the door in a hoodie, let alone having to make small talk all night with people I don't know, even football players. "I'd be willing to step aside if you'd like to send someone with more experience at these things."

Make it sound like you're taking one for the team.

Charlie has moved me ten feet out the door before he turns and walks back into his office and closes the door without saying goodbye.

With no other options, I get the requisite information on where I need to be and when and shuffle back to my desk so I can google this mysterious football team I've never heard of.

It only takes me about a minute to understand why—the San Francisco Strikers play European football—otherwise known in this country as soccer. I know next to nothing about the sport, save what I remember from playing in a youth league at age eight —ball goes into the net, parents rejoice, trophies are liberally distributed.

That paltry knowledge won't cut it here.

If I want a shot at running the new VR division, I have exactly two hours to learn enough not to embarrass my boss, our company, and myself. Or just two out of three.

CHAPTER 2

onovan

"It's a great honor to play for you, sir. I feel strong, I feel ready, and I'll give everything I have on the field," I tell the three men in the room, keeping my eyes focused like lasers under a tight brow that conveys my seriousness. Really, I'm only talking to one of them—Jeff Hobbes, the man who hired me. He also has the power to make my next three years miserable if he chooses.

He rubs a hand over a full head of dark hair and crosses his arms over his chest, nodding. His pale gray eyes stay fixed on me, but the rest of his face remains expressionless like a marble sculpture.

I haven't said enough, haven't convinced him my problems are behind me.

So I clear my throat, careful to keep my hands on the table so I don't gesture as frantically as I feel. "Since my contract with Man City ended, I've increased my training by ten percent to get even more of an edge without risking injury. So you're getting me at my best, and I can't wait to start working with the team."

He nods, doesn't care about any of that. "I just want assurances you can keep your head in the game."

I swallow hard. "I can. Goes without saying. I'm completely focused."

I shouldn't have to say it. In my fifteen years of playing professional soccer, no one has ever asked me if I can keep my head in the game.

Oh, how the mighty have fallen.

Not like I ever thought of myself as mighty . . . but I was better than this.

Then, in a matter of seconds, one impulsive reaction has me teetering on the edge, risking a fall from the career peak I've worked to build.

I adjust the orange tie which feels tight around my neck, probably because I haven't worn one since leaving my old team and I went overboard tightening the knot. Allowing the thought of my old life to creep into my head doesn't help me maintain composure.

First things first. Breathe.

Once a little more oxygen hits my lungs, I try to calm my heartbeat which ticked up a notch when I walked into the room and now feels like a persistent snare drum in my chest.

Smoothing the tie down the front of my white shirt, I glance down and notice it has tiny penguins on it. *Did I buy this? Why the hell would I?*

When I look up, three pairs of eyes stare back at me. The conference room where we sit at the Strikers headquarters in the Embarcadero Center feels stuffy and a little hot. In addition to Hobbes, my agent and my publicist look at me warily. Each of them leans back from the conference table as though I have a contagious disease they're afraid to catch.

This should be a celebratory moment.

I've been offered a three-year contract to leave my team in England and play for Major League Soccer, a less competitive league where I'll make a shit ton of money and undoubtedly have more fun.

It's like a golden parachute for top players—Beckham, Rooney, Ibrahimović, they've all done it and some of them went back and played again afterward in the Euro leagues. I should get to tilt back in my chair and enjoy the fruits of fifteen years working my ass off to compete at the highest level in global soccer.

Instead, I feel like the object of an inquisition. And it's my own damn fault.

I don't want to tell them the truth, so I'm leaving them with the public perception everyone believes as gospel—which is its own kind of truth.

"Donovan knows his reputation precedes him, and therefore we're asking for a certain level of faith. You're getting the player you paid for, one with world-class skill and focus," intones the deep voice of my agent, Troy Barnett.

Six foot one and barrel-chested, Barnett would have made a good linebacker, but he never played a sport. Not since he joined the chess club in middle school. Yet he knows sports better than a lot of players and can negotiate like the island of Manhattan's sinking and he owns the last life raft.

We've had a great working relationship from the time I signed with the Premier League at nineteen. It kills me to hear him defending me in front of a new boss, even if it's his job to have my back and he's dealt with far worse clients than me.

"I just want to play. Can't want to get on the pitch," I say, taking a sip from the bottle of water in front of me and waiting for the next question. Troy insisted on this meeting so I could lay to rest any lingering doubt my new club has about me or my commitment. "Kill all rumors and suspicions before they turn into fact," he said. And I trust him. He's never steered me wrong.

Hobbes, the President of Operations for the San Francisco Strikers Football Club, nods at me as he's done throughout the meeting. "We're looking at a great season with the talent we have on this roster. I have no doubt you can raise the level of our game. That's never been the issue."

I know what the issue is. He just agreed to pay me nine million dollars a year to play for his team, and he doesn't want to look like he made a mistake.

"Another incident will derail you. And it's not the kind of publicity the team needs after the work we've put into making a comeback," Hobbes says.

I like the guy, and I'd like to erase the stoic, concerned look from his face. "You have my word." I grimace at the word *incident,* wanting to wipe the whole episode from memory.

Two months back, I got into a fight. A three-punch brawl that should have been between me and the guy at the other end of my fist.

But because everyone and their two-year-old has a smartphone, video footage went viral, and all people saw was me knocking a sorry-looking bastard to his knees. No one captured what came before, no one considered what might have provoked me—they only focused on my reaction and my very powerful swing outside a pub in Chester, where my team had gathered to celebrate a big win over Liverpool.

I didn't help matters by refusing to give interviews or explain the context of what happened. To his credit, the guy I hit also refused to talk, but after the derelict asshole skipped town, people had only their assumptions about his side of things.

Like I said, it's no one's business. I expected that by downplaying the whole incident as a one-off nonevent, it would fail to gain traction as anything newsworthy.

I was sorely mistaken.

Not only did the footage continue circulating for weeks, the league penalized me with a fine and a two-game suspension for fighting. Fans unfollowed me all over my social media, and I instantly gained a reputation as soccer's newest bad boy.

I've always had a reputation for being aggressive on the field. I play hard and I play to win. No one had ever faulted me for it. To the contrary, fans celebrated the wins it earned us. But one bar fight somehow signified irrefutable proof that my on-field fire belied a violent side that finally reared its head.

People love a scandal, and I'd handed them a beauty, then let my silence on the matter be my conviction.

Despite my publicist's annoying calls and emails, I did nothing to help him help myself.

In other words, I kept mum about the whole thing and let the rumors fly. I had my reasons, and I wouldn't do anything differently if I had it to do again.

Unfortunately, the whole thing went down just a few weeks after I'd signed the contracts on my rich three-year deal with the Strikers. Everyone went into damage control mode, hoping Hobbes, the coaching staff, or the team owner wouldn't pull the plug.

Thus, here I sit, jet-lagged, wearing a smile I don't feel, offering assurances, and embracing my future. I'd feel a whole lot better with a ball at my feet.

The three pairs of eyes dart around, looking at each other, glancing at me, and playing at a kind of brinksmanship a soccer game doesn't allow for. I only know speed and tactical decision-making on the fly.

But I'm playing their game now.

I use the time they spend sizing up my mental fitness to take in my surroundings—sleek, modern décor, glass conference table, Aeron chairs, and the requisite bar fridge make this look like so many other corporate conference rooms.

The difference here lies outside the floor-to-ceiling windows, where views of the Bay Bridge and an expanse of water drive home my new reality playing for an American team.

No one speaks and I start feeling antsy. We need to clear the air once and for all and start focusing on soccer. I want to talk about the game. So I inhale deeply, look Hobbes in the eye, and try to put the drama to rest once and for all.

"It was a one-time thing and you know my career history. I don't go looking for trouble," I say. Just like I've said to Troy forty times already.

"Then say that. Say something. Anything. By doing what you did and not talking about it, you look like the angry asshole everyone thinks you are." Jordan Tanner, my publicist, has been waiting for a chance to hammer this point. Again.

He's been telling me the same thing like a broken record for a month. He rubs a hand over his dark goatee, and I can't help but wonder why he keeps it. With his small brown eyes, he looks like a distrustful rodent.

I roll my eyes. "It's no one's business."

"You're naïve if you think that," Jordan quickly interjects, a tiny muscle popping in his jaw as he grinds his teeth. "We need to finesse your debut with the Strikers, so the focus is on the now. Everything that happened back in England needs to be overshadowed by the excitement of what's happening here, and I have a great idea how you can do that."

"By playing quality soccer, I assume," I say dryly. It annoys me that we're still talking about this shit a month after it happened. I've seen these sorts of things follow other athletes for eons and I'd really like to get this behind me.

Jordan steeples his fingers on the desk in front of him and taps them against each other. The man needs a Xanax badly. "I'm thinking a girlfriend."

"What?" I fight to keep my voice calm. "Seriously, what?"

He holds a placating hand up and gives me his smarmy weasel smile. "It doesn't even have to be a relationship. Just arm candy, something to get the media excited, so they take pictures and talk about how you're the next Becks and Posh. They'll leave the other story behind in a heartbeat." He looks around the room for approval.

"And you don't think playing good soccer will accomplish that?" I ask in disbelief.

"Not as quickly, no. You're in preseason for weeks. This is different. It's your image. We need people to see you as a lover, not a fighter. A devoted partner. So people forget the other stuff." Jordan presses his lips together, trying to school his expression at the ridiculous image but he still looks smug.

My eyes shift to Troy. Surely he can't think this makes sense. But he seems semi-convinced, bobbing his head from side to side. "I mean, there might be something to it."

"Jesus." My head hurts and I rub my temples to no avail.

"Just consider it," Jordan says, hands extended in a plea. "All I'm asking."

What I consider is whether I can fire him without making things worse for myself. All his handwringing over the past month has only added stress to my life. Sometimes I think he fans the flames of minor drama so he can prove his hefty paycheck.

Hobbes finally smiles, waving a hand at Jordan. "Hey, hey. I think we all get the picture. I don't want to belabor the personal stuff any more than necessary. Let's move on, shall we?" He's staring Jordan down and the little weasel shifts in his chair.

"Fine by me," Jordan squeaks.

"I've heard all I need to as far as assurances, Donovan. I know you're a pro, but I wanted to hear it from you myself so I can convey as much to the team. I know Coach is itching to see you at the training facility. He's optimistic about the team's chances this year," Hobbes says.

Now he's speaking my language. "It's a strong roster. No reason we can't be a top contender for the league title." I'm here for the paycheck, but I'm really here to win.

Troy pushes his chair back from the table, his shoulders

relaxing for the first time since we entered the room. He thinks we're done here. Even Jordan's weasel face loses a few creases, and he stops grinding his teeth.

"There is one part of the contract I'd like to discuss." The words have been agitating in the back of my throat for the past hour while I debated whether to keep quiet.

I can't.

Troy shoots me a look, his eyes widening because he instantly knows where I'm headed with this. He shakes his head ever so slightly, urging me not to say more.

When I mentioned my reservations before the meeting, Troy shut me down fast. "This isn't the time to rock the boat, Donno. Just keep your head down and do what's being asked of you." Normally, I take his advice, but after sitting here kissing ass and doing what everyone wants, I'm dying to lay down some boundaries going forward.

"What's that?" Hobbes asks, looking down at his phone, which vibrates with an incoming text.

"The new VR game. I know FIFA has the rights," I say, referring to the soccer federation that oversees all the clubs and holds the World Cup tournament. In soccer, they rule all.

I look at Troy whose frown tells me I'm going to catch hell as soon as we leave the conference room for bringing this up. I mouth "sorry" because even though I'm a stubborn son of a bitch, I feel contrite about going against his advice.

Hobbes looks up, smiling. "Yes. I'm pretty pumped about it. The company designing the game is top of the field. Every game they design wins every award and gets top marks in player satisfaction. I have no doubt they'll deliver a kick-ass product."

"I'm sure. Anyhow, I know there's a clause in my contract to opt out of participating in the game, not having them build a player profile for me. I'd like to opt out."

I watch Hobbes for a reaction. A tiny tick in his brow tells me he's surprised but the smile remains frozen on his face. "I see. Can I ask why?"

Scrubbing a hand over my two days of scruff, I know I owe him the truth. Hobbes has been nothing but good to me since I drowned myself in bad ink over the past month. "I'm not crazy about having someone dig into my life to create an accurate profile, given my recent . . . overexposure in the media. Maybe after I've played a season and people are focused on my game again, we can revisit."

Troy swallows hard. Jordan's eyes have gone as wide as silver dollars because I haven't mentioned this to him at all. I hear frantic throat clearing from his direction as he figures out how to do damage control while I run wild doing the damage.

Jordan sputters. "Um, I don't know if that's such a good idea. People will wonder and assume you have skeletons in the closet now that you've piqued their interest with the fighting. Plus the owner has invested in the Strikers personally."

Like I give a flying fuck about the ownership structure. "One fight." My voice is clipped. "It's bullshit that throwing a punch at an asshole has followed me for a month. Enough already. Can't people move on?"

Hobbes exhales a sigh. "Listen, Donovan, you're a fantastic player, and I'm really looking forward to a great three years. I don't want to start that on the wrong foot. Can we at least table this discussion and get back to it at a later date? The gamers aren't even in early drafts of the design. There's no reason to make a decision today."

I don't want to be difficult, and I like Hobbes. He shouldn't have to keep the peace between me and my management, and I'm glad he's basically ignoring Jordan. So I nod and smile as I've been doing every damn day since I got into that fight. I put on the pleasant face I've perfected where my cheekbones rise and my eyes calmly communicate that everything's great. "Of course. To be continued."

Maybe the game designers are a lazy bunch, and the game won't be ready for years. I can only hope.

We all shake hands and Hobbes brings me in for a hug. "Hey, can I drag you around and introduce you to some folks? They'll want some selfies and whatnot."

"Sure, sure. No problem." That I can do.

Hobbes says his goodbyes to Troy and Jordan and escorts me down the hall with a pat on the back. I hear Troy's placating voice behind me. "D, if I don't catch up with you later, I'll see you at the banquet."

I wave a hand in his direction, but I don't dare look back at their faces.

The only direction for me now is forward.

CHAPTER 3

atum

"WHY ARE YOU LIKE THIS?" Joan peeks over her green reading glasses to glare at me, her eyes narrowed as though she can answer her question by staring.

Old enough to be my mom, Joan treats me more like a friend than a daughter. Yet when she purses her red lips at me and looks like she's about to give me a lecture, I feel like a kid who brought home a report card full of Ds.

"By *this*, I assume you mean bad at mahj." I point to the mahjong tiles atop my board. My only option with Joan is to divert and distract, which works about half the time. If I can get her talking about how I missed an obvious opportunity to go for a better tile configuration, she might abort whatever lecture she has planned.

"You needed that five dragon, so yes, you're in trouble, but you know exactly what I mean. You have a broken social meter. You should want to go out."

I now regret having told them I need to leave our game early to attend the Strikers banquet. Of course, I factored my weekly game into the tight timetable for researching soccer, blow-drying my hair, and Ubering to the banquet. Priorities.

"My meter is fine. I shouldn't want to go to a boring work function. They're painful." I keep my gaze focused on my tiles and the mahjong card in front of me, hoping to salvage my game.

As usual, we're playing on the balcony of the apartment Joan shares with her husband Felix. It sits two floors above mine in a modern, four-story glass and wood building for which we pay exorbitant rent. Our mahjong fourth, Alice, lives on my floor.

Studying the card in front of me gives me no new ideas for how to make lemonade out of crap, so I discard a tile that I think will throw Joan off.

"Nice try," she says, smugly, leaning back and folding her arms over large breasts that sit like a shelf on her chest.

I love our foursome, even if Joan nags me too much about my nonexistent social life and Alice takes so long on her turns I'm aging in dog years. Felix, I've learned, is mostly in it for the snacks Joan makes—always a cheese plate, often brownies, and sometimes margaritas and chips. I've never won a game on margarita days, and I secretly think Joan knows that and makes them to gain any advantage she can.

Our weekly game started two years earlier when Joan and I ran into each other near the mailboxes, where we were both obsessively checking on whether the annual new mahjong cards had arrived. Once we realized we could get a game together in the building, she recruited Felix and I brought my next-door neighbor, Alice, who'd told me she needed a hobby.

My older sister, Cherry, sometimes fills in when one of our four can't make it because she works in Silicon Valley and I taught her to play. She's the only one of my four sisters I let into our little game circle—only two years apart, we've always been close, and the older ones can be a little bossy.

"Jo, leave Tatum alone. Mind your own business," Felix tells her. At five feet, five inches tall with brown bushy hair and a beard, Felix positions himself as the small but mighty voice of reason in our group, and he uses his eyebrows for emphasis. Right now, they sit high on his forehead as he tsk-tsks his wife.

She looks away from him, shaking her head. "You mind your own business and let me help my friend." She picks up the next tile and discards a three dragon, crooking an eyebrow because she knows she's just sunk any remaining chance I have of winning. "Tatum, hon, you're not going to win this round anyhow, so get your butt downstairs and get dressed. Honestly, I've never seen anyone so resistant to socializing."

"I'm resistant to going to a rubber chicken dinner at a hotel and talking to people I don't know. My boss made it seem like I won a prize but really it's more of a long errand."

"Oh, whatever. It's a chance to get out, dress up, have a cocktail. I can't think of anything wrong with that." Joan takes a tube of lipstick from the pocket of her red sweater and dabs it on her lips. "Not to mention that it's a room full of young, fit soccer players. Who wouldn't want to go?" She fluffs her hair as if she's preparing to go herself.

"Married people, for one," Felix says, dryly.

"You should be flattered that I'd rather hang with you guys," I tell them.

Alice picks up a tile and discards it practically without looking at it. Staying focused on the game, she never makes small talk until we've finished a round. Joan's eyes shoot to Alice's still-empty board and she nods, interpreting Alice's strategy like a savant.

Joan draws her next tile and grins. "Oh, yay. Mahj." She starts laying her winning tiles out so we can see them.

"I almost had you," Alice says, examining the tiles to make sure Joan didn't make a mistake.

Felix displays his. "I was going three, six, nine but I needed some jokers." He always shows us what he hoped to do. Oddly, my weekly game doesn't bring out my competitive streak the way work does. Probably because it's not going to determine my life trajectory.

Alice dumps her tiles into the center pile and starts scrolling on her phone in its pink leather purse wallet. A couple years older than me, Alice plays methodically and wins more often than Joan, which makes Joan all the more gleeful when she prevails.

A moment later, Alice turns the phone so I can see a headline and a team of guys wearing Strikers jerseys. "This is who you're complaining about spending the evening with?"

I glance at it and another uncomfortable surge of nerves erupts in my stomach. "Ugh. People are writing things about this shindig? Great, there'll probably be media there. I probably have to wear a dress." I tap out a text on my phone to Cherry, who has more fashion sense than me and an impressive wardrobe.

"Well, I'd assume so. It was big news when Donovan Taylor signed with the team," Alice says, glancing at Felix for confirmation.

He nods and leans in to read from Alice's phone. "Oh yeah, the press will be there. They're announcing all the new sponsorship deals and naming rights. Bajillions of dollars exchanging hands. People care about this. Just maybe not you."

"Great," I grumble. "I was picturing something akin to our high school sports banquets where we all sat at round tables, ate food trucked in from a local pizza place, and the coaches handed out trophies."

"Sounds like fun. But that's not how they do things in pro sports, I'm afraid," Felix says kindly.

My phone pings with a reply from my sister.

Cherry: Score! Went to the mall on my lunch hour and bought two dresses.

I shake my head. Of course she did. It's lucky that Cherry has a big paycheck and no husband or kids because her shopping addiction is next level.

Me: Awesome. I'll take anything.

Cherry: Slinky black dress coming your way!

Why does she have to sound so excited?

Me: Tranquilizer dart coming yours

Cherry: Haha

I probably should have clued in when Charlie's assistant pressed an engraved invitation into my hand after I left his office. My flair for denial runs second only to my competitiveness.

"My boss did say our company is the new jersey sponsor." I lean in to read the news item that has Felix and Alice so fascinated, and my stomach turns when I notice the time. "Crap, I probably can't play one more game if I want to shower and blow-dry my hair."

"Go. Blow. And if you meet Donovan Taylor, get a selfie." This comment from Felix makes me laugh, and I therefore choke on the water I'm sipping.

I wave a hand dismissively. "There will be no selfies. And why are you so hung up on Donovan Taylor? Who even is that?"

Felix, who I've never heard raise his voice above a calm professorial tone, barks a laugh and practically shouts at me. "You can't be serious. You don't know Donovan Taylor? Come on, everyone knows Donno."

I start shuffling the mahjong tiles so I don't have to meet his disbelieving stare, but I can feel it anyway. My face flushes even though I shouldn't be embarrassed about not knowing something.

"Well clearly not everyone. Do you know who Donno is?" I ask Joan, expecting her to side with my ignorance since she's never mentioned an interest in soccer—or sports. She collects teacups when she travels and works for a New York investment bank.

She nods vehemently. "Yes, and it's even more proof that you need to get out from behind your computer screen. He's like David Beckham—hot, gorgeous, soccer royalty. Maybe you'll meet him. A little jersey chasing wouldn't kill you."

"Like that's what I need. I follow football. I armchair quarterback the heck out of it. Why's it such a big deal if I don't know some soccer dude?" I ask.

Now Alice pipes in, "Because he's a global soccer dude and he's . . . " She fans herself.

My mouth opens but no sound emerges. In the two years I've known her, Alice has not once commented on a man's looks—ever. She talks about her wife, a history teacher at Palo Alto High, she talks about her twin beagles, or she talks about her work at the NAACP. She does not talk about men.

"I feel like I've entered a parallel universe." My face feels hot again. I get up from the square card table and start walking toward the door.

"Hey, no one's criticizing you. Don't rush off." Felix walks over and puts an arm around me. We're the same height, and when I slump against him, his beard tickles the side of my face. "I don't think you have a broken social meter." His voice is soft, kind, and it makes me wonder how he ended up with Joan who never has a thought that doesn't come out of her mouth. I guess opposites do attract.

"No, she's right. I do." I speak quietly and look at the floor, reinforcing Joan's opinion as I hide under her husband's arm. "I just . . . I'm okay one-on-one but I don't know how to work a room, you know? I feel like I'm getting tossed into the shark tank in a seal suit."

Recollections of past social awkwardness flood my mind, with particular emphasis on my brother Finn's engagement party which was filled with economists. In my zeal to get nerdy with some of them, I knocked over a potted fern, spilled wine down the front of my dress, and told a dirty joke about clams.

I don't know why I suddenly involve Felix in my road to self-discovery. I expect my admission to make him relinquish his fatherly instincts, but he pulls me in tighter. "You're discerning about people. Nothing wrong with that. I'm glad I make the cut."

"You do. For sure. Let's hope there's a mahjong-loving marketing exec who I can befriend tonight over a margarita. Then I'm all set."

"There we go. Good attitude. Now, go have some fun." He shuttles me out the front door before I can come up with new excuses for why I can't be the pleasant face of ViviTech for two hours on a weeknight.

CHAPTER 4

onovan

"WELCOME TO SAN FRANCISCO!" Two tall brunettes with long wavy hair, bare arms, and ample breasts each slip a hand around my biceps when I exit the town car that someone high on the soccer food chain sent to pick me up.

"Thanks. That's nice of you," I tell them, tempted to look over my shoulder to see if everyone walking into the hotel gets a similar greeting. I've been in Europe for so long, maybe I'm out of touch with hotel lobby procedures.

But I have a feeling it's just me.

As the women escort me through the hotel lobby to the banquet hall, I glance surreptitiously from one to the other. They could be twins, easily almost six feet in their tall stiletto heels, with plump pink lips and so much mascara their eyelashes look like butterfly wings about to take flight each time they blink.

"And welcome to the team," they say in perfect unison they must have rehearsed.

"Thanks for that as well." They don't look at me, which is just as well because my face has surely fallen slack with surprise. As their heels click and clack on the marble floor, I notice how quickly we're moving and wonder if someone instructed them to get me where I'm going at a fast clip.

There's barely time to take in the opulence of the hotel lobby, with its high ceilings and giant crystal chandeliers, before I'm whisked into the banquet hall, where the flashes from a sea of cameras explode in a lightshow that momentarily blinds me. I'm not sure where to look, so I focus on no one in particular.

A chorus of "Donno!" "Donovan!" "Donno, over here!" only serves to blind me further before the two women let go of my arms and point me toward an anteroom where a gaggle of sports reporters and more photographers have reserved interview time.

I know the drill. I patiently give each of the video cameras a few soundbites about my training schedule, my excitement about living in San Francisco, my enthusiasm for my new team, and our chances at an MLS title. I feel like a certified asshole, spouting from a script written by Jordan.

If I was being honest, I'd say I'm scared shitless of looking like a sellout who ran from the Premier League before losing my starting position to someone younger and faster. But there's no place for honesty here. Or in my mind, for that matter—doubt only sows weakness.

All anyone—my coach, my teammates, the media—wants or needs to see is a skilled star player with the confidence to lead a team to victory. So that's what I'll give them. Only that.

Troy waits patiently on the sidelines, making sure no one asks me for anything that hasn't been preapproved. I left all that negotiating to him, but I know he's worked through how many photos each sponsor gets, how much time I can allocate to each media outlet.

If he makes good on his promise that I won't be asked a single question about the fight back in England, I'll happily pay him his ten percent until the end of time.

After every few interviews, he offers me a fresh glass of water and checks in. "You good? Need a break?"

"Nah, let's crank these out and get 'em over with."

"Good man. Okay."

I smile in photos with the head of the league, the Strikers majority owner, and a few of the team's corporate sponsors who want photos for their social media. For the amount of money the team paid for my contract, I'll do what they ask.

After nearly an hour of interview, photo op, interview, photo op, one little shit decides to slip in a question at the end of what was otherwise a benign, boring interview. "So Donno, I have to ask, what the hell happened outside that bar? You're only known for being a hothead on the field, so it had to have been something worth hitting a guy over."

The room goes silent, and Troy goes into hyperdrive. "That's not an agreed-upon question."

The reporter, whose badge says he's from Sports Alive, some outfit I've never heard of, shrugs Troy off. "It's the only question worth asking, you want my opinion."

Troy gets up in the guy's face. "Yeah, no one asked for your opinion, Drew from Sports Alive," Troy says, squinting at his press pass. "What the hell even is that? A blog or some shit? Interview's over. You're done. Buh bye, Drew." Then he positions himself between the cameraman and me and effectively sinks any hope of additional footage.

It might be funny if the sound of Drew's question didn't set off a fight-or-flight instinct in me that threatens to derail this whole evening. Troy flips the switch back to caretaking agent and offers me a fresh glass of water. I blink hard and take him up on it while I try to compose myself.

Dammit, when will you be able to think about that night without your blood pressure going haywire?

Clearly, not yet.

Finally, the business part of my night wraps up and two new women usher me into the banquet hall where my team's logo hangs on twin banners flanking a dais with a podium. Behind that, a jumbo screen displays a placeholder photo of the Strikers stadium.

I notice a crowded bar set up at each end and thank my escorts for their time. One of them slides a shiny business card into my hand, on the back of which she's scrawled her phone number.

Smiling at her, I thank them both again and make my way to the bar by way of a trash can. There was a time when I couldn't imagine throwing away the phone number of a woman who wanted nothing more than bragging rights for fucking a soccer star. Feels like a lifetime ago, and I'm only thirty-four.

For the moment, no one seems interested in what I'm doing, so I order myself a club soda to sip while I shake hands with anyone who comes my way. It's still preseason, so drinking and eating garbage food isn't technically off-limits, but I'm going easy tonight.

And now I'm finally with my people—players, coaches, sponsors—people who want to talk about soccer. My shoulders relax and my neck unkinks for the first time since I exited the town car.

With preseason training not beginning until next week, I haven't had much time with my new teammates, other than brief introductions, so I plan to remedy that tonight. I've only played with one of them previously, but I've watched hours of game tape and I feel like I already know these guys as players, their quirks, their strengths and weaknesses on the field.

And at the end of the day, it's soccer, a sport I can't remember not playing. Unless I'm on the pitch, I'm watching footage, training, dreaming about the next time. I don't know life any other way.

From what Hobbes explained, tonight is a dog-and-pony show to impress the team's new sponsors who will keep Strikers FC solvent through the coming seasons, when we're expected to turn the club into a force to be reckoned with in the sport.

If they want a meet and greet with the players, they get one. If they want photo ops, they get those too.

I'm not so naïve as to think I can get paid the salary I do without those sponsors feeling very happy about how their money gets spent, so I'll smile in every photo they ask me to take, and I'll play to win the championship—in that goal, we have everything in common.

But tonight, I'll hit the bar for a better drink, sit through a boring dinner, and get the hell out of here.

CHAPTER 5

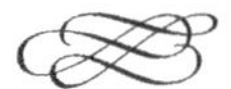

atum

I really do intend to get to the event for the cocktail hour.

The invitation says cocktails start at six-thirty, followed by dinner and a sponsorship presentation at eight. Charlie's requisite mingling needs to happen during the cocktail hour, and I take my duties seriously. Even if I'm dreading them.

In a tiny clutch borrowed from Cherry sits a list of people Charlie would like me to gladhand—including the President of FIFA, the soccer organization which owns the rights to the players and will distribute the VR game we're building, and the President of Operations for the Strikers team because he is the key liaison with the players.

I also have a list of the thirty Strikers team members, as though that does me any good since I don't know what any of them look like. I did do some googling this afternoon, but I focused more on fine points of a game I never cared enough to watch. Looking back, perusing the team roster might have been the better call.

Not wanting Charlie to discount me from the future job I want running the new design team, I didn't admit my negligible knowledge of soccer to anyone in the office. Rule one in Silicon Valley—say yes first, figure out how to do it later.

I can always google the players after tonight and put names to faces and conversations. Meantime, I'll just talk to anyone in the room who looks young and fit, figuring the odds favor him playing pro soccer.

Maybe everyone will even wear nametags. That thought gets me a little bit excited. I'm a visual learner, so seeing a name right below a face is memorization gold.

Fifty minutes ago, when I stood in front of my full-length mirror braless in a tight black cocktail dress that hugged me like it had abandonment issues, I had a plan and a timetable. Ten minutes on makeup, fifteen minutes blow-drying my wavy blondish curtain of hair into a sleek . . . something. Then a thirty-minute drive to the hotel.

That plan only makes sense for a hair and makeup expert, i.e., not me.

I have thick hair. That means extra time getting it fully dry and even more time with a flat iron taming the frizz into something manageable. Then more time with a curling iron and a YouTube video learning how to charm the strands into something that looks effortless but obviously styled.

I only burn my hand twice.

Fine, three times.

The hair ends up taking thirty minutes.

Fine, forty.

It turns out that not wearing mascara to work on most days has decreased my ability to apply it without stabbing my eyeballs. I can't find half the shadows and shades I've used in the past to highlight my eyes and cheeks, but I do the best I can with what I have. I apply a red lipstick shade I can't recall buying and survey my entire look in the mirror before heading out the door in three-inch stilettos.

With my smoky eyes and red lips, I must admit I look better than I expected. Even a little glamorous. And the dress . . . Cherry is one size smaller than me, and this dress would be tight on her. But there's no time to reconsider.

I'm fifty minutes behind schedule.

The Uber app tells me the ride will take nearly an hour in evening traffic. Assuming no accidents, I should pull up to the hotel at a just after seven.

There goes my mingling. And my chance at a cocktail.

I do what anyone would under the circumstances—I get in the car and back-seat drive like my job depends on it.

I EXIT the car at a run—really a wobble, since that's all my stilettos and tight dress will allow.

I feel like a mummified race walker.

Following signs pointing toward the banquet hall, I hike my skirt obscenely high, wrestle my feet out of the strappy shoes and take off at a sprint down a very long carpeted hallway. Outside the banquet room door, I can hear the muffled voice of a man at a microphone as I slip my shoes on and return my dress to public decency.

My forehead already glistens with sweat, and I take a second to fan my face before pulling the heavy door open. Behind a small table, a petite woman wearing a pantsuit greets me with a smile.

"I know, I'm late," I gasp, apologetically stating the obvious.

Her smile never wavers as she picks up a clipboard. "Don't worry. They just started. What's your name?"

I tell her and she directs me to an empty chair at a table near the front. Of course it's a prominent table. Charlie is so chill and quirky that I sometimes forget our company is a Fortune 100 behemoth with a billion-dollar stock valuation. That doesn't translate to an obstructed-view table in back near the kitchen.

So I straighten my spine, ignore the sweat trailing between my boobs under my too-tight sheath, and make my way to the table at the front of the room as though I do it every day in even taller heels.

All I have to do is ignore the several dozen sets of eyes that have fixed on me as I walk the gauntlet between fully occupied tables for eight.

Everyone else is on time? Does no one else have mascara issues?

When I slide into the empty seat, I finally let out the breath I've been holding. I don't dare look at the other occupants of my table. I keep my gaze calmly facing forward as though I've been here all along.

My heart hammers in my chest and I grab the swan-shaped napkin from the plate in front of me and drape it on my lap. Then I slug down half the water in the glass near my plate and ignore the cold drops of condensation that dribble down my hand.

"I think that was my water." The voice comes in a low whisper from the man next to me. I take an extra-long blink, hoping to find myself back home under an oatmeal fleece blanket when I open them.

Nope. Still here, still mortified.

I turn my head to apologize and find myself faced with the sexy smirk of a very attractive man.

"I'm . . . I . . . ?" I stammer, looking at the glass I just put on the table and quickly identifying my own glass closer to my fork.

I pick it up and hand it to him. "Here. Take mine. So sorry," I whisper over the drone of the man at the front of the room who's begun running a short film featuring a flyover view of a soccer stadium.

He doesn't reach for it, so I put it down and push it closer to his plate. Then I notice my handprint left in the condensation on the glass. Ugh. I reach my napkin over to wipe it away.

"Relax. It's just water." He keeps his voice low, but I hear a hint of amusement. I look over again and his face shows the beginning of a smile, his green eyes dancing as he watches my discomfort.

"Sadly," I mutter.

"Here." He reaches for one of the open wine bottles on the table and holds it near the empty glass in front of me. "Red okay? Or I can see if the bar's still open."

"Oh, no. You don't have to do that. Yes, red's lifesaving and great. Thank you." After he finishes filling my glass, he pours his own, stopping about halfway before replacing the bottle on the table.

Gratefully, I grab the glass and start to lift it to my lips but his warm hand on my bare forearm stops me. When I look at him, I see his glass held out to me in a toast. "To boring sports banquets," he says, tipping his glass toward mine.

"Oh. Right. Cheers." I take a sip, then a second. I can still feel the warmth from where his hand grasped my arm and I tell myself to ignore it. Then I exhale, willing the sweat to stop spreading everywhere beneath my dress. I can't exactly mop up boob sweat.

When I put my glass down, I sneak another look in his direction and find him still watching me. "So I guess it's not just me, then. With the dislike for banquets?" I mutter.

He tips his head back, then nods, staring at his wineglass and twisting it in circles by the stem on the table. "You could say that. But we do what we have to, right? It's business."

"Exactly. Business." I keep my voice hushed, matching his. No one at our table seems aware that we're talking instead of watching the drone footage flying us through the team lockers and trophy room of the Strikers' soccer stadium.

For a moment, I focus on the video, thinking about Charlie. He should really be here, basking in the glory of his investment and the announcement of ViviTech's jersey sponsorship. Though I can understand why he'd just as soon pass on tonight —he has better things to do with his time. Perks of being the boss.

"So, traffic?" His deep voice vibrates near my ear, and I feel a surprising chill run down my spine.

"I'm sorry?" My voice sounds shaky.

Damn surprising chill.

"That why you got here late? Did you get stuck in traffic?" I know he's keeping his voice low so I'm the only one who can hear it, but it's having an unintended effect on my body, heat rising in my cheeks and a rippling thrill of pleasure on my neck when his breath hits.

I can't look at him for fear he'll see how he's affecting me, so I sit stiffly looking at the video. "Yeah. Always bad on 280."

"I have no idea what that means. Two-eighty?" he whispers. Fine, I'll look at him. When I do, I see a strong, square jaw, beautiful cheekbones, and strikingly full lips smiling at me like we share a secret.

"It's a freeway. Connects the city with San Jose." I'm nothing if not willing to educate a person on infrastructure.

He leans in and continues whispering near my ear. "Right, I always forget San Francisco's connected at the base. I see all these bridges and think it's an island." He looks up, and his eyes get a faraway look as though he's seeing bridges in a corner of the banquet hall.

"It's a peninsula protruding upward from the land at the bottom." I demonstrate with my hand open like a claw with my thumb sticking up.

He nods. "So kind of like a giant hard-on, pointing up from San Jose?"

I choke on my wine and start coughing, which turns into a

wheeze. Then I slug down the rest of my water. When that doesn't help, he slides his water over and I drink that.

"You okay?" He looks contrite, sobering his expression, but he can't hide the amusement in his eyes.

"No. You just referred to my favorite city as a penis. I don't know what to do with that." My voice comes out high-pitched as I try to contain a peal of surprised laughter, and then I'm a lost cause. Trying to contain it just makes me laugh harder.

A couple of men at our table glance my way but by then my giggling fit has shifted to silent convulsions as I tip my head down behind my palm and pretend nothing's wrong.

I feel a hand—a large, strong, reassuring hand—on my back and he leans toward me and whispers. "I'm sorry. I feel bad about that."

I finally get control of myself and lift my head, aware that my mascara probably trails down my face from the tears. "No, you don't. That is not the face of a sorry person." And now we're staring at each other.

"Yeah, you're right," he admits. "Teasing you is much more fun than watching a drone fly past urinals in the stadium." My eyes grow wide, and I look at the screen in disbelief. Instead, it shows soccer footage on an impossibly verdant field.

I elbow him in the ribs. "You're terrible." I start craning my head to look around the room. "Surely there's another empty seat in here. Maybe someone else's running late because she doesn't know what to do with a curling iron either," I grumble.

He studies me, and I feel the heat creep over my skin again. He reaches a finger toward my hair but doesn't touch it. He mimics the wave with his hand. "Looks like you figured it out."

"Yeah, all hail YouTube."

"Hey, Don. Do you know . . . ?" The man on the other side of him leans in with a question, but I can't hear their conversation over the droning voice of the speaker.

His companion looks my age and has close-cropped blond

hair and a tattoo on one side of his neck. He's good-looking too, but nothing approaching the caliber of the man next to me. I take the moment to size up the one I've been talking to for the past ten minutes.

His suit jacket hangs on the back of his chair, dark gray to match his pants. His white shirt looks crisp and freshly dry-cleaned, and he wears a purple tie patterned with tiny soccer balls. Cute.

His wavy dark hair is swept straight back from his forehead and it's either still damp from a shower or slicked with gel, but it's his face that should come with a warning sign: "Danger Ahead. Sparks thrown from dancing green eyes and sexy smile will cause onlooker's panties to burst into flames."

Until then, the world is not safe.

In the brief time since I hurriedly grabbed my seat, I haven't glanced around the room for the soccer players who must be here someplace. I don't see anyone in team jerseys, but I suppose they don't wear them when they're not playing. For all I know the guy next to me and his tatted friend are players.

I gulp as a sharp pang of nausea hits my gut. Don . . . It's not him . . . Donovan Taylor?

No. Not possible. My brain churns back through reams of quick research I did on the game of soccer, or footie, as the blokes in England call it.

Most of what I learned involved the rules of the game—onside kicks, penalties, possession—plus a lot of minutiae that I found really interesting. I kick myself for not focusing on head-shots of players. The last thing I need is to make our company look bad in front of the new marquee player by showing up late, guzzling his water, and talking about penises.

Wait. Donovan Taylor spent most of his career with the Premier League in England. The guy next to me—Don, not Donovan—isn't British. He doesn't have a shred of an accent.

Just a regular guy named Don. Maybe he's the a mafia don on

the order of "The Godfather," I joke to my dorky self. That would be cool.

My neighbor, The Don, turns back toward me and I continue sizing him up, now that I have a head-on view.

His face is ridiculous, really. No human should look like that and walk around every day, distracting people. His cheekbones and jaw look like a sculptor honed them from a slab of granite, his plump lips part to show pretty white teeth, and twin cheek dimples pop when his grin grows even wider.

It's nice to have this free moment to stare at him unabashedly because in the time we've been whispering to each other, it's been hard to get a good look. Criminal, really, that a conversation should distract me from just . . . gazing.

"Are . . . you okay?" I blink twice at his dreamy, emerald eyes which look concerned about something and that's when I realize I've been gawking at his face without speaking for over a minute.

Yeah, I don't get out much.

"Um, oh. Sorry. Work stress, just thinking about work." It's not exactly a lie. I am thinking about how I still need to buttonhole the head of FIFA and the Strikers guy I missed talking to at the cocktail hour.

He doesn't need to know I was having said thoughts while also thinking about whether his bottom lip is as soft and delicious as it looks.

"So . . . Don? Is that your name?" I ask in a whisper.

He smiles. "People call me that. I'll answer if you call me that. Or you could . . . come up with something you like better. I'm up for suggestions—honeybear, sugarpie, douchebag?"

This guy is too much. I can't decide if he has a giant ego or if he's an awkward person in a model-beautiful package. Regardless, I extend my hand. "Tatum. Nice to meet you."

"Sorry to hear you're stressing. What kind of work do you do?" He tilts his head to the side, seeming interested. Or fascinated by my awkwardness.

"I work in tech. But I don't have algorithms floating through my head, if that's what you're thinking. I'm not writing code on the backs of my eyelids."

I do have algorithms floating through my head.

My nervous laugh annoys me. I hate that I always default to talking about my computer nerdiness in social situations, but even more, I hate that I'm fake laughing to cover up for the fact that I fully own my nerdiness.

I don't feel apologetic about being smart—except when I'm around people who are smoking hot enough to make me nervous. Which never happens. So this is new. And I'm clearly not handling it well.

"This shit is so boring. I wouldn't blame you for writing code," he whispers, sending another zing between my legs. Holy shit, this man can make coding sound sexy.

Before I figure out what to say next, Don refills my empty wineglass and hands it to me. I grasp the stem and take a sip, and another, the wine helping me feel better about Charlie's errand prize I've earned with my algorithm.

If I can get through dinner beside this sexy man and have a few strategic conversations with the people on the list in my purse, I'll leave happy. I just need to report back to Charlie that I represented him and the company well. Then, maybe he'll consider having a conversation about putting me in charge of the VR project I want to run. Game, set, match. Or whatever they say in soccer.

"So . . . is this your jam? Do you banquet hop when you're not working?" He dips his head down again to whisper and again my skin responds with goosebumps.

"Hardly," I admit. "The dress is borrowed from my sister, and so is my good attitude."

"You borrowed your attitude from your sister?"

"She's perkier than me, but honestly, she'd hate it here too."

"Only one sister?"

"Nope, four. And a brother. I'm the youngest."

He looks shocked, eyes going wide. "You're kidding."

"Nope. Finn is the oldest—he's my brother, an economist and awesome guy. Then Isla, who owns bakeries, Sarah, who's a physicist, Becca, a loud-mouth obstetrical nurse, and Cherry, fashionista with the cool dress." I gesture to my too-tight ensemble. "As for the good attitude, it's fading. I gave up a highly competitive night of mahjong to be here and I'm regretting it a little. Though I'm pretty sure these teacups are a Russian design, based on what I've learned from my friend Joan over the years, so that's a bonus. She'll be excited when I tell her." I pick up the teacup closest to my plate and inspect it, nodding with satisfaction when I see Russian lettering on the underside.

Don is silent for so long I put the cup down turn to find him studying me with his head cocked to the side. His eyes flicker in amusement and the smile tugs at his lips. "You're funny."

"I am? How so?"

The shock of recognition causes his brow to furrow, just for a second, before he composes his smile. "You're serious? With the mahjong?"

"Yes."

Running a hand over his chin, he nods like he's not sure what to make of me. "I've heard of it. I think my grandmother plays."

"Cool. It's a great game. Has she offered to teach you?"

"Well, considering she lives in a nursing home in Florida, it hasn't been convenient."

"Ah. Maybe you should visit her. You know, for a lesson. Plus, you know, grandparents love when you visit." Cringing, I acknowledge I am the worst conversationalist in history.

The furrow in his brow returns and he presses his lips together as if he's afraid he'll laugh otherwise. "You're serious. The Chinese tile game."

"Yes. My neighbors and I have a regular meetup. On Thursdays."

"Do you live near a senior center?"

"No, why?"

"I thought mahjong was, you know . . . My grandmother and her friends are ninety..."

I shrug and sip my wine. "You thought wrong."

He studies me, his eyes roaming from my mouth to my eyes and back to my lips. Unconsciously, I lick them, then I wonder why I just did that. He smiles. "Really? How old are the people you play with?"

"They're in their forties."

"Yeah?"

"Fine, fifties. Late fifties. But I'm twenty-nine and I play."

"So you do." He smirks and his eyes don't leave my face. I have no idea what that's about, other than that he seems to enjoy making my lady parts dance a jig in his honor. He's very good at it. His pretty face is almost too much—eventually I need to look away, so I don't damage my retinas. He's a human eclipse.

So I fidget with my wineglass. I refold the napkin on my lap. I glance up to see what I've been missing at the banquet over the past half hour I've spent focused entirely on him.

Each one of about a dozen tables in the room looks similar to ours, filled mostly with men in dress shirts and ties with their suit jackets hanging behind them on their chairs. A few women punctuate the sea of male faces, and they look similar to me, wrapped in cocktail dresses or Hillary Clinton-esque pantsuits.

Tuxedoed waiters roam the room, filling water glasses and beginning to distribute salads, which reminds me I've got a glass and a half of wine in me ,and I need some sustenance.

I notice the people at our own table for the first time. A trio of silver-haired men in suits sit a couple places away from me and I notice that they seem focused on the video. They have their heads together, and they're pointing at the screen and chatting quietly.

Another two men in suits have their chairs swiveled away

from me, so I can't tell much about them other than the fact that they have their eyes glued to the video screen like it holds the answer to all the Dixie cup riddles from the beginning of time.

The only other woman at the table sits directly across from me, so I can't catch her eye through the large arrangement of white orchids. But from what I can see, she looks at least a decade my senior, with pin straight dark hair, expertly-applied makeup, and yellow gemstones in her long drop earrings.

"Do you know who all these people are?" I ask.

"Yeah. Corporate sponsors, agents, managers, athletes, some media, some team management. In other words, mostly people I don't want to talk to."

"Oh. Why not?"

Before he can answer, his attention is whipped to the front of the room, where the video has ended and the man standing at the dais points in our direction. "I'd like to bring him up and welcome him to the team officially. Donno, we're glad to have you here and we're ready for a great season. Ladies and Gentleman, meet Donovan Taylor."

The man next to me stands and walks to the front of the room. It's only when he starts moving away and I get a little perspective that I see that the dangerous face is the least of his fatal assets. He cuts a lean figure in his suit pants but there's no mistaking the tight ass, muscled legs, tapered waist, and carved shoulders of an athlete.

Well, shit.

I am a moron.

Oh, who cares! You just spent a half hour talking to a soccer god. Take the freakin' selfie.

Ahem, not doing that.

I watch Donovan Taylor's easy manner at the microphone as he says his thank yous to his coach, the team, the sponsors. "I'm thrilled to be a part of this club and looking forward to a stellar season. With the roster of talent in this room, we're set up to be a force in the league and I'm honored to play a small role."

As he talks tactical specifics about the game, he morphs from a guy who called San Francisco a giant erection to a sharp-minded athlete and smooth operator whose easy smile can charm an entire banquet hall.

I see the fascinated hush overtake the room as every face turns toward his to take in his words.

And . . . I've done the opposite of spread ViviTech goodwill by asking if his name was Don, not knowing he's the new star of the team, and spewing my ridiculous blather about inappropriate topics at a professional sports banquet.

Um, yeah, you were talking about coding, blow dryers and teacups.

So before he returns to sit next to me, I do what any self-respecting coder with reasonably well blow-dried hair would do.

I get up from the table and bolt.

CHAPTER 6

onovan

When I get back to the table after the impromptu speech Jordan promised I wouldn't have to make, Tatum is gone.

At first, I'm struck by how disappointed I feel at the absence of someone I've talked to for all of a half hour. I don't even know her. I find myself looking over my shoulder for a glimpse of that sleek black dress and the woman who wears it like it's her job.

Maybe she took the opportunity of my boring speech to run to the restroom or make a phone call—or whatever she felt like doing without me sitting next to her, talking her ear off.

I couldn't help it. She fascinates me.

First, she blows into the room with all the subtlety of a category 4 hurricane in that body-hugging, sexy dress, but then she does seemingly everything in her power to tell me she's plain, nerdy, and not really the woman I see in the sexy dress—so much so that I feel pretty confident she's either here on a dare or a bet or some other bit of tomfoolery that explains why she seems just about as reluctant to be here as I am.

I want to know more, and the unfamiliar feeling surprises me. In the months since my pub brawl became all anyone talked about with respect to me, I've shut down, stayed home, and avoided talking to anyone except my inner circle.

But talking to her is like the first yellow sunbeam after eight months of gray English skies. Hell, I sure won't miss those.

People have gotten up from their tables now, circulating and chatting before dessert and the sponsorship presentations. I scan the room to see if she went to talk to someone since she mentioned work and the room contains just about every big soccer name in Northern California.

I don't see her anywhere.

"Hey, the woman who was here, did you see her leave?" I ask Jordy, the Strikers starting right back who's sitting next to me, nursing the one gin and tonic he'll allow himself in the preseason.

"Nah, man. She got up as soon as you started speaking. I know I'm as asshole, but I watched her until she left the room. Shit man, did you see those legs? Is she an athlete?"

"She's . . . a mahjong player."

Jordy screws up his face in utter confusion. "What the fuck's that? Is it like tennis?"

"It's a . . . I don't fucking know. Don't worry about it."

Her glass of wine hasn't been touched since I last refilled it, and I don't see her purse on the table. Waiters walk through the room clearing the entrée plates and I see she hasn't taken a bite from hers. It seems entirely possible that she wandered in here by accident, realized her mistake, and went off to find the coding convention or wherever the hell she's supposed to be.

Jordan comes over and claps a hand on my back. "Nice speech. Perfect tenor. I think from here on out all anyone will focus on is your game."

"I fucking hope so. That's the only reason I'm not out to murder you right now for ambushing me with a speech."

"I know, I know. You can write me out of your will. It wasn't my idea but when the FIFA president asked earlier if you'd do it, I figured it was better not to have you overthink it and work yourself into a tizzy." He demonstrates with jazz hands.

"When have I ever worked myself into a tizzy?"

"You know what I mean. And now it's done, so hit the preseason training hard and enjoy your growing bank account. You've earned this." Another slap on the back and he walks away, headed for one of the other players on his client list.

"You were never in my will," I shout after him.

I really don't give a shit about Jordan and his dumb ploy to get me in front of the mike. It's done. Instead, all my energy goes toward searching for a certain woman in a certain black dress.

It's not just the dress. Or her curves that should make all others wearing that dress pack it in and give up a fight they'll lose.

It's her.

Wide inquisitive eyes, plump lips that she bites when she's thinking, the sharp slant of her nose. She's not willowy and blond or Barbie perfect—she's intellectual, feisty, and really fucking captivating.

She's the first woman I've met in a long time who didn't begin and end with me thinking about a one-night stand. I'm not gonna lie. Jersey chasing is a global phenomenon, and I enjoyed the fruits of my labor on the field. For years.

Now, I enjoy the solitude that comes from leaving the locker room after a game and going straight home. Unfulfilling hookups don't do it for me anymore. I end up feeling depressed at the emptiness after the temporary physical rush.

Not like I'm looking for some happily ever after. I'm not looking for anything except the chance to play soccer. I can't remember a time in my life when I wanted that more than I do right now, just to quiet the voices in my head that make me worry I'm a sellout.

So hookups, Tinder dates, the flattery of women lined up outside the stadium calling my name—I don't need that. Don't want it.

I only want one thing, and it waits for me on a perfectly manicured rectangle of turf.

But this woman . . . I can't deny she interests me. I mean, of course my teammates interest me because I've been playing the sport with guys like them for most of my life. They're basically me.

She's different. Self-effacing, like she has no idea how her eyes sparkle when she talks about something she cares about. And how funny she is when she savages something she doesn't.

I still don't understand what her job is or why the hell she's at the banquet. But I'm grateful. Because let's face it—I'd rather not be here at all.

Playing soccer for the Strikers is a step down for me. The level of competition in the US pales in comparison with the Premier League, but no team there is going to offer a guy in his thirties a contract worth almost thirty mil for three years.

If I stayed in England, I'd just be one injury or false move away from losing my starting spot to a younger player on a hot streak. The fallout from the fight was a stark reminder that my star status is fleeting.

Most guys would take the money and run. Most guys wouldn't question moving to the States for celebrity status and summer camp play on the field.

I'm not them. I wish I could keep playing in Europe, but this is the smarter option. So here I am.

None of it changes the fact that coming home hurts, and it doesn't take a deep dive into my psyche to figure out why. It feels like the second nail in my career coffin after the backlash from the fight. Things are only going in one direction, so I'll take any cheerful distraction to help me avoid thinking about that every day.

And if the paparazzi around here feel like taking a few shots of me talking to a gorgeous woman in a figure-hugging dress, maybe I can get Jordan off my back as well. For all I know, he sent her here and stuck her at the table next to me for that purpose.

If so, I might have to reconsider firing his ass.

I was dreading tonight, I'm not gonna lie. All I could picture was a swath of bloggers, reporters, and photographers trying to get up in my business and talk to me about my life.

"Donno, are you trying to reinvent yourself?" "Donno, do you think your reputation will hurt you on the field? Have you lost your focus?" "Donno, did you sell out?"

I don't want to answer any of those questions, especially the one about selling out.

Don't want to talk about it and I especially don't want to get honest with myself about whether it's true.

I just want to fucking play football. Or "soccer" as I'm forced to call it so no one confuses me for a linebacker. I roll my eyes at the thought.

So, thank you, Tatum, for taking what was shaping up to be an uncomfortable evening and making it . . . fun.

But where the hell did she go?

I'm out of the banquet room a second later, sweeping through the lobby and scanning the groupings of tan and white upholstered couches and low tables in case she came out here to chill. No sign of her, and I'm prowling around like a stalker with no plan for what I'll say when I find her.

I push open the heavy glass doors to the hotel and wave down the head valet parking attendant out front.

"Hey, do you recall bringing a car around in the past few minutes for a woman in a black dress, light brown hair?" I gesture at him, showing the length of her dress and the wave of her hair. He shakes his head.

"It's possible. A lot of women wear black dresses."

Not the way she does.

I loosen my tie and unfasten the top button of my shirt, knowing the sheen of sweat I feel on the back of my neck has nothing to do with the thermostat in the room. All I need is a glass slipper to complete the ridiculous picture of myself as abandoned prince.

Sulking back to the banquet hall by way of the real bar at the hotel, I figure I'll get myself a decent drink. The table wine doesn't excite me.

Two steps into the small hotel bar, I see a swath of black fabric which calls to me and immediately has me picking up my pace. It only takes me a few strides to reach the dark oak bar, where Tatum sits on one of the stools, legs crossed at the ankles.

She doesn't see me, too engrossed in a conversation with the bartender. "I won't tell anyone. Look at me, do I look like I'm selling government secrets? Trust me, there's no one to tell. I have no friends."

I bark a laugh at that, and she turns, clearly surprised to see me. "I find that hard to believe."

She crosses her arms over her chest and gazes at me warily. "Why are you out here?"

Taking a step closer, I counter. "Why are you?"

CHAPTER 7

onovan

"I WAS LOOKING FOR A DRINK. And looking for you." I take a step closer. "You didn't leave behind a glass slipper or anything, so I was worried I'd have to give up."

Inhaling a deep breath, she turns back around and speaks into her lap, but I see she's smiling. "I'm leaving soon."

While she's looking away, the bartender takes the opportunity to switch out her mostly-empty cocktail tumbler for a full one, nodding to me. I hold up a hand to let him know I don't need a drink.

"I'll talk to the manager and try to make it happen," the bartender tells Tatum. "Give me a few minutes." He steps away, leaving an uncomfortably loud silence between us.

"Can't say I blame you for bailing on the banquet." I take a step closer. Two more feet and I'll be able to sit on the barstool next to hers—if she wants me there.

"Oh, no, I'm not. I'm leaving the bar and going back to the

dreaded banquet. But I wanted to buy something first." Tatum still doesn't look at me, and I want to reach for her face and tip it up to mine, but I barely know her and I don't feel like I've earned the right to touch her.

Perching on the barstool, I wait. When she still doesn't look at me, I nudge her with my elbow. "Hey. Tatum."

"Yeah?"

"Okay, I'm beginning to think we've got some kind of *Phantom of the Opera* thing going here. Is there a reason you're hiding your face from me?"

She turns. "No. I'm just mortified because I spent all that time talking to you and had no idea you were 'Donovan Taylor, God's biggest gift to soccer since sliced bread.' Not that soccer has anything to do with bread. You probably avoid carbs, being an athlete or whatnot. And here I was hearing people call you Don and thinking you were Don Drysdale or Don Draper or something." She sounds defeated. "Also, where's your accent? I thought you were from England."

I can't stop myself from grinning at her. "Okay, I need a minute to unpack all that." I push a hand through my hair while I think through everything she just lobbed my way. "First of all, the air quotes. I'm pretty sure I've never been called God's gift to anything, but I ignore most of what people say, so maybe I missed something. Second, I play soccer for a living but that only makes me recognizable to people who watch it, so who the fuck cares if you don't know who I am? Also, I played for fifteen years in the Premier League but I'm from Michigan, not England. You were getting closer with Don Drysdale since he's an athlete, but I watched *Mad Men* and I'm pretty sure Don Draper's fictional. And an asshole. And third, I eat carbs. Love them—bread in all shapes and forms, especially if you're offering to bake it."

She nods slowly and reaches for the drink the bartender left for her. "My sister bakes. Sourdough. She owns a bunch of bakeries." Her demeanor is thawing. She's still giving me the side-eye but at least I can see her face.

"You get a family discount on bread?"

She shrugs. "She usually just gives it to me."

"How it should be." Now I do reach for her chin, guiding it with my finger so she's looking at me. I have the urge to do more, to run my fingers across her jaw and see how her skin feels as I continue down the length of her neck. But she already seems a little wary, and I don't want to spook her by coming off like a handsy creep.

But my chest aches when I withdraw my hand.

Her eyes follow my fingers as I put my hand on the bar next to hers. "How about we start again? Tatum, my name is Donovan Taylor and I'm a soccer player. I'm new in town, and it's very nice to meet you."

Then I pick up my hand and extend it toward hers to shake it. When she places her palm in mine, the warmth of her skin makes me want to tug her closer. But I'm not trying to score. If anything, she so sufficiently intrigues me that I find myself fighting physical instincts in favor of talking to her more. "Nice to meet you," she says, turning the rest of her body to face me. "I guess I should have done some research so I'd recognize the players."

"So just so I'm understanding correctly, you're at the Strikers sponsorship banquet but you don't know who's on the team?"

She takes another sip of her drink and exhales. "I don't know anyone in that room."

Now I'm back to thinking she's an event crasher and I feel a tiny bit apprehensive talking to her in case she works for TMZ or some gossip blog. "Are you . . . supposed to be at the banquet?"

She puts her head in her hands. "Ugh. Yes. Like I said, it's for work." Then she spills it all. Her boss invested in the team, and his company, ViviTech, is our new jersey sponsor. He sent Tatum to spread company goodwill among the soccer executives, so she did a lot of homework on the game of soccer but didn't google headshots because she went down a rabbit hole reading about obscure game rules.

My brain bumps when she mentions ViviTech, the company building the VR game I don't want any part of. But she doesn't seem to be aware of that.

"That sounds . . . stressful." I feel bad for her. These events are god-awful even for a person who cares about soccer.

"You think?" She puts both hands on the bar and shakes her head at her predicament.

"Yeah. I'm not kidding. I thought I had it bad, having to get up and make a speech I hadn't planned ahead of time, but your gig, that sounds a hell of a lot worse."

"Thank you for saying that. It's fine. I'm just not a bright shiny human who loves talking up strange men . . . I mean, men I don't know. The only saving grace, apparently, is that my boss is worse at it. And he's not here, so he'll never know I crashed and burned." Finally, she grants me a small smile, and I feel damn victorious.

"I can see now why you'd rather throw in the towel in favor of a good cocktail."

Her eyes narrow. "What? Oh, you think I came in here to drown my failures? No. I'm not counting myself out yet. But I am trying to convince the bartender to sell me one of the hotel's teacups."

"Okay, you've lost me."

As if on cue, the bartender returns with a small bubble-wrapped bundle and presents it to Tatum, who opens it to examine a teacup painted with gold lines and pink roses. She nods and wraps it back up. "It's okay with your manager?"

The bartender places it in a handled bag and nods. "Just don't go telling all your friends."

"Never," she says soberly, as though the world is filled with people demanding hotel teacups.

I order a vodka soda, and Tatum explains that she wanted to buy the cup for her neighbor's collection. "This is your mahjong neighbor?" I ask, putting the pieces together from our earlier conversation. I'm touched that she saw a teacup and went out of her way to buy it for a friend for no reason.

"One and the same. I feel like you know my entire life story now." She smiles and clinks her glass against mine when the bartender hands it off to me. I'm captivated by her ease and candor. And her smile.

"I kind of doubt that." I've barely scratched the surface with her, but I find myself hanging on every morsel of information I get, eager for more.

We talk some more and leisurely sip our drinks while the bar fills up with a late-night crowd.

I don't want to leave our corner of the bar—it's the closest to contentment I've felt in ages—but the last thing she needs is me preventing her from doing her job. "Okay, I guess we should probably get back in there so you can schmooze for your boss."

Her eyes grow wider, and she inhales a shaky breath. "Introvert alert. I don't schmooze." She does smile, however, and it lights up her face in a way that's contagious. I grin back at her, watching her chew on her bottom lip and feeling the urge to sink my teeth into it. And so many other things.

"What do you do?" I'm not asking about her job anymore, and from the blush crawling over her cheeks, I think she knows it.

"Um . . . " When she realizes I'm staring at the way she's biting her lip, she stops, swallowing hard. "Listen, I just need to get through this event and not get fired. You got any ideas?"

Considering I know most of the people in that room, I can help her. "I have a few. Let's get our tab, and I'll see what I can do."

From there, we walk back into the banquet hall, where the presentations have ended, the bars have reopened at both ends of the room, and people have begun milling around with fresh drinks.

I guide her to Gianni Infantino, the FIFA president, and make introductions. Then I stand back while Tatum regales him with tactical minutiae she crammed into her brain earlier in the day. Within five minutes, she has him laughing and promising to call her boss in the morning. "I hope you'll be heavily involved in the new project," he tells her.

"That's the plan." She shakes his hand, her smile wider than I've seen it so far.

I take the time while she's talking to pose for meet and greet photos with some of the sponsors and shake a lot of hands. Instead of gritting my teeth through every minute of it, my mood is light, and I genuinely don't mind the gauntlet. I start getting swept along in the high spirits everyone seems to feel about having me on the team.

For the first time in memory, no one asks about the pub fight or whether I'm sad to leave England. The focus stays on the future, one where I have a high-profile starting position. The excitement from the people in the room lifts me up.

Jordan catches my eye and nods toward Tatum, and I know what he's thinking, but I'm not convinced his ridiculous dating plan makes any sense. The last thing I need is complications from a woman. My interest in Tatum only goes as far as tonight, or at least that's what I'm telling myself. Whatever it takes to get me through the evening with my sanity intact.

A few minutes later, I reconvene with her and take her to meet Jeff Hobbes, who becomes instantly charmed with her joke about how she'd never seen a photo of me, heard my name was Don, and mistook me for the head of a mob family.

She rattles off a few more names from her list and I ferry her over and make introductions. "By the way, you may think of yourself as an introvert, but you're good at this," I tell her with an odd sense of pride in her abilities, which is crazy since I did absolutely nothing except introduce her.

That earns me a smile, but she doesn't go as far as agreeing with me.

Finally, she tells me she's checked off all the names on her list. "Phew. Okay, glad that's done. Now I can go home. Thanks, new friend. You saved my bacon. Good to meet you tonight." She gives me a playful punch on the arm. "I'll try to get out and see a game, now that my company's paying your clothing bill."

"I'd hope so. Especially since you've memorized stats on how often set plays result in a penalty versus a goal."

"Funny." She starts walking toward the exit of the ballroom and I find myself chasing after her like a puppy. Fortunately, she can't take long strides in that skirt she's wearing, and I catch up quickly.

"Wait, hang on."

She slows only a fraction and looks at me while continuing her racewalk toward the front of the hotel. "Yes?"

"I, um . . . enjoyed talking to you." I feel like a sixteen-year-old bumbling for words and hoping to score in his dad's Buick.

"Oh, me too. I was dreading tonight. I can't thank you enough for your help." She's not picking up my train of thinking at all. Normally, I'd have had a woman slipping her hotel key into my pocket an hour ago, and she's running for the hills.

Watching her wide hazel eyes scanning my face for a clue about why I stopped her, I realize we're not on the same page. This is a work event for her. It's a work event for me too, and I curse Jordan for putting any other idea into my head.

But we're almost at the rotating glass doors.

I have mere seconds before she's gone, so I need to be direct. "Tatum, can I call you sometime?"

She tops walking and squints as though the question is odd. "Why?"

I can't help but laugh. "So I can ask you out."

"I mean, I guess. I just don't get why you'd want to." She tilts her head, studying me as though I must have some ulterior motive besides wanting to see her again. I see that I'm going to have to spell it out.

"Because I'd like to see you again. On a date. Soon. Preferably tomorrow."

"Oh. You would?"

"Yes."

"Oh."

"Oh?"

"That just . . . it wasn't what I expected you to say. Not after I mistook you for Don Cheadle."

I shake my head, a chuckle escaping at her lunacy. "You do know he's Black."

"Yes. And a really good actor. Did you see *Ocean's Eleven*?"

I nod at this woman who defies words.

She grins like we share a secret. "It's one of my favorites. So . . . okay. I guess you can call me if that's what you want to do . . . " Her voice trails off.

She doesn't sound convinced. Or look convinced by the way she's squinting at me. Maybe I can remedy that.

Meeting her gaze, I take a step closer to her and watch as her eyes widen and she cocks her head slightly, as if asking what I plan to do. But she doesn't step away. One hand holds her purse, and she places the other one flat against her chest as if steadying herself.

Slowly, I reach for that hand and peel it away, interlacing our fingers. I can feel her slight tremble as I give her hand a squeeze. Her eyes don't leave mine, but she seems slightly less wary, her features settling into something that looks like nervous acceptance.

She's not smiling, but she's not biting her lip either. She's waiting to see what I'm planning to do.

Oh, and I have a plan.

Taking one step closer, our bodies are so near I can feel the heat of her skin through my shirt. I want more but I'm careful not to spook her. I tip her chin up so our eyes meet again, and I notice for the first time that their light brown is flecked with gold and rimmed with gray, complicated like I can tell she is.

Cupping her cheek, I lower my lips to hers, brushing them softly at first and feeling for her reaction which comes in the form of a tiny sigh. It might as well be a symphony for the way it just obliterated all other sounds and senses in my world.

I shift my angle and take her mouth again and she responds by pressing her lips ever so slightly harder against mine. Then her hand comes up to the back of my head. She was holding her purse a second ago, so she must've dropped it on the ground because her fingers wrap around the nape of my neck, which instantly heats under her touch.

Then she presses softly into me, our lips never breaking contact.

Finally, I do what I've been thinking about for the past hour and take a tiny nibble on her bottom lip, then swipe the tip of my tongue across it to ease the sting from my teeth.

She opens her mouth on a tiny gasp, and our tongues find each other instantly, slowly tangling and exploring in a way that feels like every second and every touch is important.

I planned to give her a good kiss. I know how to do that. I've kissed plenty of women, especially when I developed a fan following of jersey chasers in every city we played in. I know what a good first kiss feels like—the anticipation, the buildup, the beautiful first taste that leads to everything else.

But this kiss is something else.

My lips, my skin, my pounding heart—and yes, my dick—are responding to her like she's lit a fuse that can't be extinguished. It's too late to go back. The only option is to sign on for the full force of explosion or be incinerated to a standing pile of ash.

In under a minute, it's clear I'm a lot more invested here than as a means to wrangle a future date.

All I can think about is that I'm furious at the valet parking guys for not sending her Uber off the Golden Gate Bridge so I can carry her upstairs to my hotel room and never leave.

Her lips taste faintly of gin and her skin hints at an intoxicating combination of jasmine and grapefruit. But it's the way her body melts against mine that has me certain this is nothing ordinary. I have to stop kissing her and lean away, just to make sure I'm not the only one feeling it.

She wobbles, unsteady for the first time since she crashed through the ballroom doors. Both of her hands grip my arms and she leans her forehead against my chest. I'm equally dizzy.

"I . . . I wasn't expecting that," she breathes.

Good.

"Never say Don Knotts isn't full of surprises."

She smirks. "Touché." Then, remembering her discarded purse, I bend down to retrieve it and hand it back to her. Her cheeks are flushed and she stammers. "So, now that we did . . . that, do you still want to go on a date?"

I bark out a laugh. "Um, hell yeah. Even more so."

She shrugs and raises her brows like it's crazy talk. "Okay . . . "

It makes me want to grab her hand where she's placed it back against her chest as though trying to control her heartbeat. I know the feeling. The feel of her skin instantly warms me. "You really don't see yourself, do you?"

"I mostly stay away from mirrors, if that's what you're asking." She grins. That smile, her odd sense of humor, and her guileless honesty have captured me from the moment she wiped her handprint from my waterglass. She *has* me.

"It's not."

"Oh."

"Here we go again."

"I know. Bad habit. So . . . thank you . . . for implying what I think you were."

"I was. I meant it. And you're welcome. I'd like to see you again." I bring her knuckles to my lips and kiss them gently. "Can I please have your number?"

She gestures with a tip of her head for me to hand over my phone. Regretfully, I let go of her hand so I can unlock the phone and place it in her open palm. After typing furiously for a few seconds, she hands the phone back to me. "I put myself in your contacts."

I take her hand and bring it to my lips, then I speak quietly like I don't want to spook a frightened animal. "Good luck with your work, Tatum. It was really nice meeting you."

She stares down at her hand as I release it and her gaze roams over my lips in a look of pleasant surprise. She matches my tone. "Really nice meeting you too." Her smile is sincere.

Then she kicks her shoes off, bends to pick them up, and jogs to the waiting car. Like no woman I've ever met in my life.

After she drives off, I look down at my phone to where she entered her name in my contact list. But instead of her name, she's typed in Cinderella.

CHAPTER 8

atum

By eight in the morning, I've run a few miles, showered, and driven to work.

Normal. Ordinary. Everyday.

Nothing about my routine screams radical transformation from my former self or life-altering series of events that have thrown me onto an alternate plane.

Except that I can't stop thinking about Donovan Taylor. Specifically, Donovan Taylor's raspy low voice whispering in my ear and the sexy musk and lime taste of his lips when he kissed me.

I'm pretty sure that happened.

Chills rush over my skin when I picture the dimples in his cheeks when he smiles. And he was smiling at lot while he introduced me to everyone on my list and waited patiently to help me work the room.

The stress of arriving at the banquet late, talking to the right executives, and yes, kissing God's biggest gift to soccer all took a toll on my emotions.

So much so, that by the time I felt the hum of the Uber driver's Chevrolet cruising down the freeway to Palo Alto, I couldn't distinguish dream from reality as I allowed the lights of passing cars lull me to a state of semi-consciousness. Slumping against the window, I brought my fingers to my lips, begging them to tell me that my brain was a liar, that they did not just go rogue and kiss the hell out of a soccer star at a work event.

But no amount of begging would suffice.

As my mind replayed the events of the evening, I tried to reconcile two warring feelings—that Charlie would fire me once he found out about my lack of professionalism and that I'd never, in thirteen years of canoodling with frogs, been kissed like that.

Twenty minutes later, the Uber driver snapped his fingers at me outside my apartment building to nudge me awake and out of his car, and I zombied upstairs and went to bed.

That's the last thing I remember.

I slept like the dead and woke up with a hangover thanks to the unfortunate combination of red wine, cheap gin, and not enough food.

The power bar I scarfed down after my run and the liter and a half of water I drank have made me feel only semi-human, as I sit in my cubicle and wait to be fired for being wholly unproductive. I'm relying on strong coffee to get me the rest of the way to consciousness.

I'm so screwed. Charlie sent me to the banquet to quarterback his mission with soccer executives. Not to kiss the quarterback.

And yet . . . I can't stop thinking about him.

With the lingering swoon I feel, remembering Donovan's breath on my neck when he whispered about his grandmother's mahjong game, my mind is anywhere but at work. And that's the only place it belongs. The only prayer I have of keeping my job rests on being so highly productive that Charlie has no choice but to see my value, despite my poor decision making.

After one more slug of coffee, I dive into writing lines of code for the VR project he hasn't tasked me with yet in hopes of impressing him.

Oh! This is really cool, but I can make it cooler.

That's all it takes. As soon as I immerse myself in the puzzles of finding better algorithms, I become single-minded in my focus. The professional Tatum has kicked the unprofessional soccer groupie to the curb.

"Hey, how'd you manage last night at the shindig?" Terrance's face practically blinds me with its bright, wide-awake glow. The way his eyes dance as he grins at me, I start to worry I've come to work without shoes on. Or pants.

Or he knows something.

After checking and ascertaining that I'm covered with clothes, I narrow my eyes at him. "Why do you seem so gleeful? What am I missing?" And because my brain still feels half asleep, I take a long swig of coffee, wincing because it's now lukewarm.

He shrugs and sips his own coffee from a mug with a joke about java script and java beans with instructions about coffee pots and fill lines. Coding humor. "I just know how much you hate talking to strangers so I'm here to give you shit about it. And bring you a maple glazed donut."

From behind him, Terrance produces a grease-streaked bag and hands it to me. I bury my face in the bag and sniff, so Terrance won't notice the blush that's crept over my cheeks thinking about a particular stranger. "Thanks for this. And the night wasn't so bad, actually."

"No? Do tell. Did you discover a love for the 'beautiful game'? You know that's what they call soccer, right?"

"I wouldn't go that far. The beauty is still a mystery, but the event was fine. I managed."

And traitor that it is, my phone pings with a text.

Donovan: Hey, Cinderella. It's me. The soccer guy who kissed you at the banquet. Donovan. In case more than one guy kissed you . . . um, hope not. How's your morning?

Of course the phone sits face up on my desk, of course Donovan's name appears on his contact info, and of course Terrance has Superman-level ability to read from a distance.

"He's texting you? Donovan Taylor has your cell number?" His eyes go wide, and he leans in to read the text, but I manage to flip the phone over before he can.

"You know, for a married guy, you sure do seem to have a thing for Donovan Taylor."

He shrugs. "I wouldn't mind having a bromance with him."

I dig into the donut and hum my approval at the maple goodness. "What is it with everybody and this man? I mean I get that he's good-looking and all, and apparently he's handy with a soccer ball, but . . . what am I missing?"

Terrance barks a laugh. "A lot. He's a legend. Holds multiple records for goals in a season, received the Golden Boot, and he's dated about twenty Scandinavian supermodels. He's. A. Legend."

"What's a Golden Boot?"

"An award given to the highest scorer in the league."

"And he won it?"

"At least twice. I'd have to check."

"Oh. Well, that's impressive." And now I'm overwhelmed because the feeling returns of his hand wrapped around my jaw while his lips melted me into submission.

"Yes." Terrance's chuckle snaps me back to reality, where I have to grapple with the disconnect—the guy I talked to last night didn't seem like a soccer player.

And what, in your vast experience, does a soccer player seem like?

"I think I need a soccer primer." Part of my problem lies in the fact that I've seen only small snippets of games on TV, and only then by accident when flipping channels between football games. So I really don't know what I'm missing.

Terrance looks around our open-plan office, grabs a chair from an empty desk, and wheels it over. He flips a leg over the seat and sits on it backwards, folding his arms over the backrest. "You know nothing at all about soccer?"

"I told you, I follow football. Soccer always struck me as a lot of green space and very low scores. Pass."

His upside-down smile conveys pure pity. "Okay, I'm going to give you a lightning round education on the game and why everyone loves 'this man,' as you put it. And then we're going talk about why 'this man' has your phone number." He's air quoting up a storm.

I reach for his hands and still them. "Fine. Lightning round. Then I have to work."

"Okay. You know how kids in America grow up playing baseball and idolizing baseball heroes? Same goes for basketball and your obsession, football?"

"Football. Talk football to me."

"Fine. In the US, we have several different sports to choose from. In most countries, it's just soccer. Kids in England start playing when they can walk, and they all hope to play professionally. That's true in Spain, in Sweden, in Argentina. Soccer is it. And their teams and leagues are phenomenal. Imagine if every kid here grew up playing football. They'd all want to be Peyton Manning. They'd come up through academies, and if they were lucky and super talented, they'd play semi-pro. Then if they were even more talented, pro. But only the elite few would make it to the kinds of teams that make up the Premier League. And even fewer end up in the Champions League. Donno has done both."

"Okay, that's intimidating. Glad I didn't know that last night, or I'd have been forced to drink another six glasses of wine in order to look him in the eye."

He cocks his head at me. "That bad?"

"What?"

"You like him. It's kind of obvious you hit it off if the guy's texting you. So let's talk about that."

"I'd rather hear more about the 'beautiful game.' Talk to me about that." Now I'm air quoting.

"No you don't. I know you learned about the game fundamentals before the banquet and probably got your introductory coaching license because you're *you*, so tell me what I want to know."

"Which is what?" Fearing that I have telltale signs of being kissed written all over my face, I don't look him in the eye.

"I dunno. Is he a good guy? Does he seem like he'd go out and grab a beer with normal people and just . . . I don't know, talk soccer?

Now I look at Terrance, because he's ridiculous. "You seriously want me to set you up on a bro date, don't you?"

He shrugs. "There is one thing you should know if you plan on being friends with the guy, which is that he's a little controversial right now."

"What's that mean?"

"He got into a fight a couple months back and it led to fines and a whole lot of bad things said about him because he wouldn't explain himself."

"A fight on the field? Do they do that? Like hockey?"

"A bar fight. And no, soccer players don't typically brawl on the field. Except Suarez, who sometimes bites people, but that's a whole other thing."

"Wait, what?"

"He sometimes . . . Forget it. Off topic."

"But you're saying the 'golden boy of soccer' has some dirt on him?"

"Yup, and footage went viral and he refused to comment, so it blew it up even more. Speculation that Donno has anger management issues, that the pressure's getting to him, this is the beginning of the end . . . You know, stuff like that."

How did I not know this?

"How did I not know this? I consider myself an educated person. I read. I know . . . things. But somehow, I've missed a global phenomenon. Moving to San Francisco. Surrounded in controversy. Next you're gonna tell me that rice is the most valuable crop in the world."

"Rice *is* the most valuable crop in the world."

"Mind. Blown." I demonstrate with explosive fingers beside my head. "But I actually knew about the rice thing."

"I figured."

"No one knows why he went off on the guy at the bar?"

Terrance shakes his head and takes a packet of M&M's from his pocket, offering me some. I hold out my hand. "Donno never said. Really screwed himself by refusing to talk about it because the story lingered for weeks. That's like a double eternity for gossip rags."

"I didn't know there was a time period longer than a single eternity."

"You're such a stickler for accuracy."

"No, just science. Reality. Stuff like that."

"Whatever, nerd."

"You say that like we don't have the same job. And the same personality."

"Please. My job is to come here and write some lines of code because I've been trained to do it and I like to earn enough money to eat. Your job is to fangirl over technology and invent new ways of coding that will change the universe."

I can't help the small smile that creeps over my face at his description of my potential. "You flatter."

"I do. And you love it."

I do. Even though I haven't done anything remotely groundbreaking in my seven years working in tech, I fantasize that someday I will.

"So, Donno. Can I assume from his text that you might see him again sometime?"

Before I can answer that, I see a text alert from Charlie.

Boss Man: Please come to my office

And of course, Terrance's X-ray eyes pick up on it as well. "Word travels fast. Maybe he knows you talked up the team's hottest player."

My stomach drops. I wonder what else Charlie knows.

I waste no time pushing my chair back and moving toward Charlie's office. "Seriously, Terrance, stop calling him hot or get your man card examined."

He walks a few paces with me and drops into his chair as we pass his desk.

"I meant hot on the field. He's the real deal. The Strikers didn't offer him nine million a year for his beautiful face . . . " I shoot him a look. "And yes, I'll check on that man card."

CHAPTER 9

onovan

Training camp starts at seven sharp, and no one arrives late. After playing in Europe for so long, I'm not sure what to expect. I know the MLS is a little more chill, but I hope I'm not the only one who's here to win.

Those fears fall by the wayside immediately when I arrive to find everyone pumped and ready to have their asses kicked in training.

These guys want a title.

Initially, I'd planned to finish my season in Manchester and head straight to California to find a place to live and spend some informal time meeting the other players.

But after the media frenzy erupted over the fight, Troy and Jordan advised me to lay low in England for an extra month until interest in the story died down. That way, I'd arrive in San Francisco for a clean, fresh start.

The plan made sense, but it meant I'd had to do house hunting via video conference. It also meant my bonding time with the team got pushed back a month.

After Tatum left the banquet, I took the opportunity to get to know the players a little better in a casual setting, even though none of us would have chosen a casual setting involving suits and ties if we had anything to say about it.

After introductions to a few of the teammates I hadn't met yet, talk quickly turned to soccer—game tactics, technique, how it felt to play with some of the world's greatest—Messi, Ronaldo, Rooney. Yeah, I had some stories.

The time I spent getting to know my new teammates over a last round of drinks has made today a lot less awkward. But the time I spent with Tatum puts a grin on my face that has no business at training camp. I can't fight it.

She hasn't texted me back, at least not by the time I head out to the field. I don't spend the interim staring at my phone in anticipation. I only check it six times.

I'm sure she doesn't keep her phone beside her at work. There could be a million reasons why she wouldn't respond right away that have nothing to do with disinterest in seeing me again. At least, that's what I'm thinking when a ball comes sailing at my head.

"Heads up!" Tommy Dyson shouts, standing on his toes and raising a hand in the air.

I lean away and trap the ball with my chest, laying it at my feet where I pop it up and juggle it from my knee to foot, foot to knee.

Then I give it one good dig and pass it back to Dyson, accurate as hell, landing it right at his feet, thirty meters away. "Back at you." Sometimes when I shout, a tiny bit of British accent comes out, something I've picked up from being there for so many years.

It only happens with certain words, and I didn't notice it much when I lived there, but since I've been back, I recognize the way I pronounce certain words and don't want to sound like a pompous wannabe British asshole.

Dyson dribbles the ball closer to me and yells, "You want to run some passes?"

I nod and we move clear of other players and widen the distance between ourselves. Dyson gives me a lob through the air, and I trap it like I did the other one before sending it back to him, hard and straight on the ground.

He kicks another one high and I let it land at my feet, dribbling two steps before hitting him back with my left foot.

"That's a solid left," he shouts, lobbing another high one. I chest trap that one and juggle it from foot to foot before sending it back hard with my right. "Okay, I hate you and fucking love that you're on this team, man," he says.

"Thanks. Luck of genetics," I tell him. It's not false modesty—I have a silver bullet that has nothing to do with training.

I'm ambidextrous, a rarity in soccer that gave me an advantage from the very first days I figured out that both sides are equally strong. Most players spend years trying to even out the way they favor one foot over another, and almost everyone still has a preference.

Not me. I can score from either foot, from either side of the goal.

And because I don't have a preference, it messes with the other players' heads. It's harder to defend against me because I can switch my scoring foot without thinking about it.

We move a bit closer together and keep passing back and forth, keeping the ball on the ground and kicking bullets at each other, feeling the satisfaction in each contact with the ball.

We run drills for the first half hour of practice, cutting in and out of cones on the field, running slalom around a set of posts, getting our knees warmed up for the brutal lateral movements that are no friend to joints. My two knee surgeries can attest to that, and I'm one of the lucky ones with only two.

I trap the ball, pass it off.

Trap, pass.

After a month of laying low, it feels great to be back on the pitch, smelling the mixture of sweat and turf baking in the hot sun. The Strikers' training facility has all the bells and whistles that go along with being a top rate facility, and I fight off the slight wistful feeling I have thinking about my old team.

Our first days of preseason felt very different from this because we've had incredible continuity for the past few years—same coach, same trainers, and the majority of players stuck around. Starting preseason when I haven't built the trust and shorthand with my teammates feels wrong.

In part, it's my fault for moving here later than planned, but I can't reverse history. I'll get to know them all in due time. And I'll watch game footage of their past few seasons each day until I know each player's ticks, strengths, weaknesses.

"Hey, I thought California was supposed to be sunny," I yell to Dyson.

"You complaining already?" he snipes, kicking a bullet to my left foot.

"Not complaining, just surprised." The foggy early morning gives me a measure of comfort because it feels a little like the gloomy weather in Manchester.

"You're in Fog City now, mate." He does his best bad impression of a British accent.

As we continue to pass, I take a glance around. Everyone looks fit and eager, judging by the fact that they're kicking the ball hard in warmups. The field is a sea of Adidas stripes—on all our gray practice jackets with the team logo up and down the legs of the shorts we all wear.

I've worn number eight for my entire career, and I got lucky that no one on the Strikers roster laid claim to it before me. Athletes have their superstitions and one of mine revolves around keeping the number eight on my back.

After a half hour of disorganized warmups, our head coach Clyde Derry takes the field, followed by his trainers and a small film crew that plans to document our first day of training for the team's various fan pages and social media.

Derry doesn't say a word. He doesn't have to. Within seconds, I hear a beeping sound over the facility's loudspeakers and jog with my teammates to the far end of the field.

The beeping stops and we wait. My adrenaline races through my chest and limbs and I inhale a deep breath of the oxygen I'll need to get through the suicide drill. I'm focused, one hundred percent in my element. It makes no difference whether I'm playing for the Premier League in England or in a park league with no one watching but the pigeons—I'm here for the game.

The drill will have us at a full sprint to the top of the box, then back to the baseline, then to the penalty spot and back, then midfield, and so on. All at top speed, all in a race with the other guys on the team.

The beep counts down. Three, two, one . . . and thirty pairs of cleats pound the turf at full speed.

For better or worse, my three years in America has begun.

CHAPTER 10

atum

My heart thumps in my chest as I walk to Charlie's office, wondering why he'd call me in twice in two days. Then I talk myself down. He just wants to know how I did with the executives at the banquet.

Right?

It has nothing to do with the fact that I monopolized the team's star player all night. Nothing to do with how I turned to jelly the second his lips brushed against mine.

Ugh. So. Unprofessional.

As I walk quickly through the office, the memory of Donovan's smile flooding my brain, I weigh the odds that my boss wants my head on a platter. On the plus side, I saved him from having to go. On the negative, I might be worse in a crowd than him.

Charlie stands with his back toward me, forearms arms

pressed against the doorframe when I get to his office. So I knock on the wall next to him. "Hey, Charlie."

He spins around so quickly it looks like he's practicing a dance step. "Tatum. Greetings." He shakes my hand with vigor.

"Morning. How are you?"

"Nice of you to ask. I skipped my yoga session this morning, which was a mistake since I'm already slouching. And I'm unhappy with today's calendar—too many meetings, not enough time for thought. Our pyramid is upside down, sitting on its rotund ass."

I laugh at the image, but I understand his reference. Charlie has a firm theory that we need to work according to an inverted pyramid, with thoughtfulness occupying the widest part, productivity in the middle, and convening for meetings taking the least amount of time. I can't fault his theory. It works.

"Can you cancel some of the meetings?" I ask, watching him spin away from me again and put a hand on his forehead like the sight of his office gives him a headache. Without knowing who he's meeting with, I can't be much help.

He doesn't turn back toward me, but I see his shoulders relax. "Technically, no. I didn't schedule the meetings, so I won't cancel them. But I suppose I can opt against showing up for them."

"Well, that seems like a solution."

He spins back around. "Does it? People might wonder why I'm AWOL. If I can be a no-show, why can't they? But then again, I need to be judicious about my time, which means not spending too much of it worrying about whether or not to attend my meetings." Now he begins to smile, his eyes crinkling at the corners. "I've become my own meta joke."

I smile back at him, and he relaxes a bit more, moving to take a seat behind his large glass-topped desk. "So, tell me, did you enjoy the banquet?" He steeples his hands on his desk and rests his chin on top.

"I did. I met the contacts you suggested, and explained how

our VR technology is a game-changer. Everyone seemed to see the value in physical therapy for players and the gaming aspects."

His expression reveals nothing. "So you enjoyed yourself."

"It was a very nice event. Added bonus, I learned a few things about soccer. Strikers look like a promising team."

"Promising, yes. Before I considered investing, I ran regressions on all the available data—player contracts, injury rates, breakout stats—of all the teams in the MLS this year, the Strikers have the best shot at emerging as an underdog Cinderella story and winning the league, barring unforeseen variables." It might sound like a lesson or a reprimand, but I know Charlie well enough to understand that he's agreeing with me, not trying to tell me I just said something obvious.

"Exactly." I wait for signs that some valet parking attendant outed me to Charlie, and he knows about my shenanigans with his new star player. But from the faraway look in his eyes, I get the impression he's thinking about something else entirely.

Maybe I've told him all he needs to know.

"I started working on a new algo for building player profiles. I know we don't need it yet, but I thought it would be good to have some samples for when we do."

Charlie still doesn't answer. He brings his fingers to his lips and fixes his eyes on the ceiling, going deeper in thought. I wait, crossing and uncrossing my legs and wishing I'd finished my coffee. My thought process still feels muddy.

Would it be bad to run down the hall and get a fresh cup while Charlie sits here working through his thoughts?

"Tatum," he says, finally looking me dead in the eye. "You sat next to Donovan Taylor at the banquet."

My heart starts thudding in my chest. "I did. The seat was empty, so . . . " I trail off before admitting I arrived late.

"Did you find him personable?"

I feel a blush warm the back of my neck and I look at my lap, steeling myself. "He seemed nice. Easy to talk to. Have you met him?"

"No. I avoid encounters with celebrities and the like. I enjoy discussing the game and the tactical implications of carrying certain players on the roster. That's a hoot. Management has indulged me a bit there, and as I said, I've done my research. But meeting with players . . . no, I leave that to others."

"Got it. Makes sense." I furrow my brow and wait him out. Nothing about our meeting makes sense because he hasn't told me why I'm here, but this is his process.

Charlie nods, his eyes roaming to the oversized computer monitor on his desk. I watch his eyes dart around the screen but from my vantage point, I can't tell what he's looking at. "Okay, good. Potentially helpful. We'll see how it goes."

How what goes?

"I . . . okay." I wait, wondering if there's more to this meeting.

Finally, Charlie fixes his gaze on me. "Apologies. I just rearranged my meeting schedule. I feel so much better."

"Oh, great. Need to right that pyramid." The longer I sit here, the more stressed I feel about the pile of work on my desk, but I can't say that to my boss.

Getting his meeting schedule worked out seems to shake Charlie out of his fugue state, and he fixes his gaze on me again. "Okay, where was I?" He doesn't wait for me to answer before snapping his fingers and grinning. "Right. Donovan Taylor. The banquet. As I mentioned yesterday, we're positioned to innovate once again in the gaming space. No one's done a VR game that allows fans to be the athlete and either relive pivotal sports moments or create new ones. I'm really excited about the potential, and I want us to be first to market." His eyes sparkle and he shimmies his shoulders.

I've put in my time at this company, and I've taken one for the team at the banquet. I may not get another chance to put myself up for the job I want. "I'm excited too. In fact, I'd love to lead the team on this if you'll consider me for the job. I mentioned I've been working on some modifications to some algorithms, and I love this product."

I need to prove I'm the obvious pick to lead the division.

He looks surprised. "You do? Aren't you the one who's always trying to get me to develop a VR therapy program for trauma patients?"

My heart starts thumping. I see my chances dwindling because my do-gooder side bugged Charlie one too many times about making a therapeutic VR product. "Oh, that. No, I was just making conversation. The sports game is where I see potential, and as I said, I'd love to—"

He holds up a hand. "I hear what you're saying, and I admire your ambition. I'll consider you, I will . . . " He stares off and I get the feeling there's a but to the conversation.

I don't dare blink as his eyes come to mine.

Charlie's mouth pulls down into a grim line around his words, "But we do have an issue with Donovan Taylor."

My spirits deflate. Shit. One unintentional kiss, one highly unprofessional moment of letting my guard down, and I've tanked my chances at the job I want.

I swallow over a lump in my throat. I could play dumb. How much does he know? "What's the issue?"

Charlie shakes his head, a furrow taking root in his brow. "Apparently Donno's expressed reluctance to be involved in the game. No idea why, and I'm told it's not a definitive no, but . . . until he signs on, I won't rest. He's the star of the team and a big reason why people will play the game. They want to be Donno. A game without him makes no sense."

Interesting. I wonder why he said no.

Charlie snaps me out of my reverie by drumming his fingers on his desk. "Anyhow, my guess is he doesn't see the potential of the game. Understandable, since it's not even in beta. A lot of people who've never played a VR game don't get it. I'd like to plan a walk-through to motivate him and remove any reservations. Since you're a friendly face, I'd like your involvement."

I exhale my relief that not only do I still have a job, but I might even have an advantage if my face is friendly enough. "Sure. Fine. Whatever you need. Just let me know."

"Perfect, Tatum. You're a good team player. I'm surprised you want to lead this product, but I'm not saying no, so . . . we'll see how it goes." He puts on a set of noise canceling headphones, effectively ending our meeting.

Slowly walking through the twisting configuration of modular workspaces where most of my colleagues sit wearing headphones like Charlie, I return to my desk and puzzle over what just transpired.

Did my boss just ask me to convince Donovan to sign on and be a part of the VR project in exchange for a job leading it? Because it sure sounded like it.

I want this. I can do this.

There's only one thing I can't do—kiss him again. Not a problem. I'll start by replying to his text in a professional way and keeping things all-business.

I will not google his pretty face.

Anymore.

CHAPTER 11

onovan

After two weeks of training with the team, I know two things for sure: these guys train harder than I expected, and they want to win a national title.

That means every practice is grueling, with guys showing up early, watching game tape until late, and asking me a billion questions about strategy as though playing against Pogba and Ibrahimović gives me a handicapper's advantage.

Not gonna lie. It does.

I'm so content immersed in the game twenty-four/seven that I almost don't have time to think about anything else. Or anyone else.

Almost.

I can't get Tatum out of my head.

It makes no sense. She makes no sense. We connected, I know we did. If I had any doubts that she liked me, our kiss put them to rest—no one can fake that delicate, breathless, sensual sigh. And now . . . nothing.

Her responses to my text—okay, texts, plural—were brief and humorless, so much so that I wondered if she's given me a bogus number. The last thing I need is to be flirting with some stranger via text, so after a couple tries, I stop.

I've never had trouble getting a woman's number. I know it's just the jersey, but women I've met over the past dozen years have been all too happy to let me know exactly where to find them.

Simply by being different, she's a beguiling riddle I'm desperate to solve.

Now that the team has begun to settle into a training rhythm, I have even more mental space to fill with thoughts of her—the curve of her neck when she dropped her head to laugh at some dumb thing I said, her elated smile when she succeeded at buying a hotel teacup, the firm shape of her calf muscles when she walked in those shoes she swore she hated.

If I have my way, she'll be wearing them again. And hopefully nothing else.

But first I have to get her to talk to me or go out with me —something.

So even though I'm still dead set against a video game that allows the designers to crawl inside my head and use whatever they like to give players the experience of being me, I'm making the trip down to Palo Alto from our training camp because I hope to run into Tatum at ViviTech and find out what happened to Cinderella from the ball.

With my head off in a dream and my dick half hard because of it, I don't even notice thirty minutes zip by while I'm traveling south on an empty freeway. By the time I pull up to the business park where ViviTech's offices are located, it's a little past two.

The club has given me the entire afternoon off from working out with the team to demo this game. During preseason. When we still have a lot of work to do if we want to be competitive. Hobbes is sending a not-so-subtle signal about its importance.

The GPS on my new electric car does all the heavy lifting, and before I know it, I've found the offices and parked. I know it's ridiculous, but I find myself glancing around the lot wondering which car belongs to Tatum. I'm grasping at anything that will reveal more about her. I imagine her in a Prius or a Leaf—something environmentally responsible and not flashy. Maybe she rides a bike.

My heartrate kicks up a notch, and I have to admit that it's not the meeting with a tech billionaire that has me starting to break a sweat. It's the thought of seeing her.

Before walking inside, I take a sweeping look at the world that is Silicon Valley. It doesn't look like much, in that it's not a skyscraper-rich busy downtown. Everything is spread out, the buildings modern glass and metal, no people milling around.

The area screams productivity in a robot vacuum sort of way —everything happening in efficient secrecy while no one's looking.

I push through the glass double doors and check in with a receptionist in the wide open, spotless lobby that sits under an enormous skylight. Sun fills the room with more light than I've seen in a year in England.

Two low gray couches flank a glass-topped coffee table, and I can hear pops from a game of ping-pong somewhere nearby.

"Donno!" a male voice intones and I look up to see a lanky young guy in a black ViviTech hoodie coming toward me with an outstretched hand. "Charlie Walgrove, chief executive weirdo around here."

"Pleasure. Thanks so much for having me."

"Not at all, not at all." As he shepherds me through the office, I notice that I tower over him by at least half a foot and watch as he trudges over the hems of his wide legged jeans as he walks. He's about as unassuming a presence as I could imagine, yet people talk about him being the next Bill Gates. I like that he doesn't give a shit whether his pants fit. It makes him approachable.

While we walk through a sea of cubicles, he continues talking, giving me a tour, I think, but I don't hear a word he says. I'm only focused on checking each desk we pass for a certain woman with flecks of gold in her eyes.

By the time we get to his office, my spirits have dialed down a few notches, and I've faced reality. Maybe she works for a completely different part of the company in an office nowhere near here. And now I'm stuck listening to this guy tell a joke about implanting things in plants.

I laugh hollowly, cursing my stupid libido for convincing me to come for a demo I don't want on a product that doesn't interest me.

"Donovan, hi." Her voice rings like soft music in my ears, and my head flips to see Tatum sitting in Charlie's office with a notebook on her lap.

No more black dress, but I don't care. She rocks the ripped jeans and red, long-sleeved T-shirt like she stepped out of a Gap ad, only better. With her hair twisted and knotted on top of her head and a pair of horn-rimmed glasses framing her hazel eyes, she looks like every man's fantasy of a hot librarian.

My instinct has me reaching for a hug, but I see her flinch and note that she works here, so I extend my hand. The warmth of her skin envelops mine, and I feel calmer than I have in two weeks, while I've worried I'd never see her again. A wink accompanies her smile and I don't want to let go of her hand.

Charlie keeps talking and I nod at appropriate moments, but I can't take my eyes off Tatum who jumps in and explains something here or there.

She's smart, funny. She gets right to the point and breaks things down in a way that makes sense, something Charlie hasn't been able to do. Her effortless intelligence and ease in the room mesmerize me.

A couple other people join us in the office after a while. More talking, more explaining. More nodding from me. I really couldn't care less what they have to say.

Finally, Charlie says the words I've been hoping for since I agreed to this meeting. "I'm going to let Tatum take it from here and show you how the technology works in a gaming setting."

He goes silent after that, and everyone in the room seems to understand their cue to slip out of the room. Tatum indicates with a tip of her head that I should follow her.

I don't hesitate, but I do try not to fixate on the sexy curve of her ass in those jeans as she walks along. But it's hard.

If I wasn't sure two weeks ago, I'm certain now.

I'd follow her anywhere.

CHAPTER 12

atum

CHARLIE DOESN'T MESS around when he wants something, so it shouldn't surprise me that he's already scheduled a walk-through of our barely-developed game with Donovan.

He and I standing in the VR room, which is really just a four-walled space with some quilted bumpers on the walls and a soft, pristine floor. The reason for that becomes obvious when someone tries out a new virtual reality game for the first time. The technology is so real that it messes with balance and perception and people usually bump into walls and fall down.

Safety first.

"This would be a great room for a nap, don't you think?" I blurt out when we enter the VR room, which looks a little like a padded cell.

Donovan raises his eyebrows when I pull the door closed. I wave my hands. "I wasn't suggesting we take a nap. In here. Together. Just that sometimes I fantasize about having a nap pod with temperature-controlled air and pillows everywhere . . . never mind. Seriously, new topic, please."

Welcome to my swamp of awkward. Come on in, the water's ice cold.

Donovan's smile takes the sting out of my embarrassment as he surveys the room. "I like the comfy padded walls, but I don't know about napping on the floor. I'm a satin sheets kind of guy."

My eyes go wide and my breath hitches before I force myself into a shaky calm. "You are not. I call bullshit."

"Fine. You got me. No satin, but I do like extra pillows. I'm with you there." He smiles, and the damn dimples start playing a game of chicken with the butterflies in my stomach. It's hardly a fair fight.

I need to steer us out of the bedroom and back to our awesome VR product. Unfortunately, I can't recall a single thing that makes it awesome.

Arms folded across his chest, Donovan leans against one wall. I take in his soccer-honed physique, noting the swell of his biceps over his chest and the muscled thighs that fill out the legs of his low-slung jeans like they're writing the denim a love letter.

I notice some ink on his forearms that wasn't visible at the banquet under his long-sleeved dress shirt. It's all sexy as hell and I'm not quite sure what to do with myself—once again, I'm in a work environment where I can barely do my job because he's so distracting. All I want to do is get closer and examine his ink.

Some Italian master ought to be sculpting him right now. He could hold his own next to Michelangelo's *David*, easy.

He'd look good naked standing in a museum.

My hands fly to my cheeks to stop the runaway blush. I have no idea what's wrong with me, other than the fact that I've spent a good part of the past two weeks replaying moments from the banquet and embellishing them. Now that the idea of him dropping his pants right here and now has entered my head, I'm witless and staring.

"Tatum . . . ?" Donovan hasn't moved from the wall. He crooks his brow and shoots a grin that convinces me he knows exactly what's on my mind.

I literally shake my head like a cartoon character to snap myself back to reality. "Yes. Sorry. Let's get you into a VR headset and play some football."

He smirks. "Football, eh? Are you giving in and calling my sport by its proper name?" He may have even dropped a slight British lilt into his voice. Because he wasn't sexy enough already.

Moving to the cabinet where we keep the headsets and controllers, I shake my head. "Ah, no. You're playing regular football today. I used it for the prototype because I had more player data."

"Okay, we need to have a conversation about that. There's only one game of football and it's the one I play. None of this 'regular football' shit."

"Is that so, cocky footballer?"

"Cocky?" He looks surprised but not offended.

"Oh, come on. You're so cocky. You must know that."

"I don't think it counts as cocky if I live up to the hype." The cheek dimples are waging war again and I'm losing.

I shake my head. "So cocky."

He pushes away from the wall and starts moving toward me. "I have another issue. You said I'm the one playing. I see two headsets."

"The games come with two, but I'll be observing and making sure the game works. It's still in beta. I don't want you to freak out when you get tackled. I'll observe and coach you through it."

He barks a laugh. "Tackled? I don't think so. I'm pretty sure I can hold my own against a cartoon linebacker. Doubt I'll need a coach."

I can't keep the knowing smile off my face. Oh, this going to be fun. Just like that, he went from gorgeous, intimidating baller to regular guy I plan to crush with the technology I've designed. Cartoon linebacker, my ass.

"Suit yourself, footballer. I'll leave you to it." I hold my hands up and back out of the way.

"Oh no. Two headsets, you're playing. I don't care if I get tackled. I'm not going in alone." Meeting his gaze, I see a flash of uncertainty. Or even . . . nervousness? It charms me that he doesn't want to go in alone.

Then the possible reason dawns on me. "Donovan, have you ever played one of these virtual reality games before?"

He shakes his head. "I've played plenty of video games. Can't be that different."

Now I'm grinning with pride. "Oh, but it is. This will blow your mind. Especially when you're about to make a game-winning catch and I get an interception and tear up the field. The fans will boo you all the way back to Manchester."

"There are fans?"

"Not real fans. None of it's real. But you'll feel like they are, I promise you."

He nods, intrigued. "Okay. Let's go. But you can forget about that interception. I'm a fast runner." His thighs flex beneath the dark denim, and I have to stop myself from staring and wondering how they'd feel wrapped around me.

Focus, Tatum.

"I don't doubt it, but it doesn't matter for the purposes of this game. You'll become whatever player you choose and everything you do will be based on their stats, predispositions, style of motion, and thought patterns when it comes to the game. All the avatars are based on hours and hours of game footage, interviews, and analysis."

He stares at me, impressed. "Wow, I had no idea you had to be so thorough to build a game."

"Maybe we don't have to be, but that's how I'd do it. I think it all matters to the authenticity, which matters to the users."

He rubs his hands together. "Okay, so if I'm picking, I want a fast avatar that can kick some ass."

I can't help smiling. I love that even in a fake football game with no stakes, he wants to win.

Notch one on the list of ways we're similar. Not surprising.

Once I outfit Donovan in the headset and get the controllers into his hands, we do a few run-throughs of him playing alone so he can get used to the equipment before we face off against each other.

On my computer screen, I can see what he sees, which is a wide-open field. And he has the ball.

"Oh baby, here we go. I see nothing but fresh green grass and I'm on the move!" he shouts as his body shifts and dodges the defensive players who get in his path on the screen.

His player is fast, but he's up against a professional defense that has a few tricks up its sleeve. "Whoa, what the hell? Where'd that dude come from?" Donovan swerves and tries to cut right, but the defensive tackle is on him and runs him out of bounds. He's hunched over and protecting a nonexistent ball in his fists.

"Okay," he says, straightening up and tipping his headset up to flash his green eyes at me. "I think I'm ready. Put me in coach. Now it's you and me."

I cock my head to the side. "You sure? I can teach you a little more about how it works before we go head-to-head. I have an advantage because I built the thing."

He waves me away. "Nah, I'm good. I've got sports instinct. I'm ready. Suit up."

I push the file cabinet with the equipment against a wall and move the computer out of the way so we can move around the space. With two people, it can get physical. Once I have my headset and controllers ready, I set us each up with avatars and start the game.

Spoiler alert—I built an awesome prototype, and he has no clue.

We face off. I dodge, he runs, and I chase him out of bounds again. I'm just warming him into the crazier aspects, where he'll feel like he got launched into the stands by a Mack truck of a linebacker with a grudge.

"First and ten. Nice run," I tell him, watching him get into his quarterback stance. Peeking under my goggles, I see a grin on his face. He thinks he's going to score easily. "Watch the defensive formation on the next play."

"What's that mean? I don't know this sport, remember?" His smile is a mile wide, and I haven't heard him disparage 'American football' in a few minutes, so I take that as a good sign.

"It means you should find an open teammate and pass. You'll never get past them on a running play," I tell him, knowing he wants to run and will probably not take my advice.

I have a leg up because I know the tactical strategies of all the players. He doesn't. So when he catches the snap and tries a running play, I hold my ground as defender and shoulder him hard. I mean, not really. We don't make contact at all. That's the beauty of VR.

He goes down on the padded floor with the force of two-hundred sixty pounds of muscle and flesh knocking him backward.

"Holy shit," he says, starting to take off the headset.

"No, no, keep it on. Stay in the game," I urge. He withdraws his hand, but I lift mine and can see from his slack jaw that he can't wrap his brain around what just happened.

"I can't believe you just body slammed me. That's not very neighborly of you." His avatar is looking at me with a scowl that has nothing on the expression that's really on his face, and I try not to laugh.

"I didn't touch you. I'm way over here. You can peek," I tell him, not wanting him to think I actually knocked his legs out from under him.

I watch him peek under the goggles, surprised that I'm

nowhere near him. "Huh. I could've sworn I felt you knock me down."

"I know. That's the crazy cool thing about VR. It messes with your brain to convince it that everything is happening so your fight-or-flight responses engage. I've seen fearless adults in simulations on the roof of a skyscraper wearing a jetpack. All they have to do is step off the building for the jetpack to kick in. And a lot of them can't take the step off the roof because they're terrified they'll fall—it's that real."

"Hmph." He shakes his head, realization dawning that this isn't your daddy's video game.

My player offers a hand to help him up. "Ready for the next play? Second and fifteen."

"Why fifteen?"

"You got sacked, my friend. You lost five yards. Next time, try a passing play." I hope my avatar's grin is as wide as the one I'm wearing, though he probably can't see it under my player's helmet.

I set up another play. This time I'm on offense and he chooses to be a burly linebacker from the Philadelphia Eagles. I go with Aaron Rodgers. He's fast and ruthless and I think he can outwit Donovan's player with his strategy on the field.

"Hike," my Rodgers avatar says, catching the snap. A second later I'm surveying the field and see a possible opening to run and another decent passing opportunity. I decide to try a combo, running first, then making a shorter, better pass.

But I don't anticipate that Donovan's player isn't just a giant truck on the field—he's faster than I remember when I did the programming. So when I take off for the early run, he's on me before I can complete the pass.

And when I say on me, I mean he tackles the crap out of my avatar, and I feel the impact with every bit of my mind and body. I go flying and end up on the padded floor in a heap. A second later, I feel the heavy crush of Donovan land on top of me.

Pulling my headset up, I start to laugh. He pushes his up on his forehead, a shocked look on this face that he actually tackled me. "Oh my God, Tatum, I'm so sorry. I did not mean to shove you down."

"You didn't. But your avatar came at me so hard that my brain felt the tackle, and I lost my balance. You did too, which is why the momentum threw you down." I can't stop laughing at his baffled expression. "I don't even care that I just fumbled. The look on your face is so worth it."

He's getting into the game, I can tell. Hopefully, this demo will sell him on participating, but we're not there yet.

He pulls off the headset to rake a hand through his hair. I can see he's still reasoning through what just happened. Meanwhile, I'm splayed on my back with him pushed up on one elbow, his face about a foot from mine.

He blinks and shakes his head. "Wow, it really felt like I tackled you." He doesn't move away, and I watch his expression change as his gaze roam over my face, starting at my eyes and landing on my lips.

His expression grows cloudy and the tight muscles in his chest flex with the effort to draw breath.

I freeze.

Our lips could touch with the tiniest effort. I stare at his lips so long I think I've memorized their shape. I want to feel them. I want to kiss him.

My heart hammers so fiercely, I'm certain he can hear it. Unconsciously, I lick my lips. His eyes are heating them like a midday sun, depriving them of life. There's only one thing that will satiate them—him. His lips on mine.

But I can't move.

I'm certain my expression looks dreamy as I indulge in him, inhaling the familiar scent that I haven't been able to sweep from my mind in two weeks.

He returns my stare with an equally searching, melting look of desire. Just a few inches closer and we could . . .

He swallows and his eyes drop from my face.

Then I watch every muscle in his beautiful arms flex as he pushes himself up to sitting. He's still close to me but he's made the smart call, the right call. Thankfully, one of us has the presence of mind to do it.

Hello? You. Are. At. Work.

And Charlie is no doubt recording our session.

I scramble to my feet and put some distance between us, moving so quickly that Donovan starts to laugh. "I take it back. I know I bragged about being fast, but you're faster."

"I've been in some races," I say, apropos of nothing. I put my headset back on so I don't have to look him in the eye.

"What?" I hear him say. The words come out of the mouth of his giant linebacker avatar who's still lying in a heap on the ground.

"Triathlons. Short ones, sprint distance. I used to be really into them. Now I do a couple a year when I have time to train. But I'm not a sprinter. I'm too tired by the end to sprint, so I don't know why I brought that up. I guess because you said I was fast."

The linesman sits on the ground nodding at me, and I realize how ridiculous I probably look. Pointing at him, I try to direct him back into the game. "Your ball. You can pick a new QB if you want to try out another player. I'll surprise you with some giant tank on the field. You won't even know what hit you." My voice sounds shaky, but I push through when I see the linesman nod.

"You pick someone good for me. I don't know the players," he says. "The last time I watched football, Harrington was the quarterback."

"Who's that?"

"Joey Harrington? Played for the Lions."

"Um, okay. Don't know my ancient Detroit players. I'll make you Patrick Mahomes. You're welcome."

He shrugs. "Thanks? Don't know him. You could be telling me you're making me Elphaba and I'm going to fly in with evil monkeys and it would make as much sense." Coming out of the mouth of the burly linebacker, it cracks me up.

"You know *Wicked* but you don't know the highest-graded quarterback in the country?"

He shrugs. "Who doesn't know *Wicked*? Again, global phenomenon, unlike your American football business."

"Oh, I'm gonna make myself a three hundred pound defensive tackle, and you won't have virtual teeth afterward, footballer."

"Bring it."

After I reset the play with Donovan on offense, we go again. I want to tackle the heck out of him, but I go a little easier so we don't end up in another tangle on the ground. But I've programmed the game well, so another defender takes down the wide receiver he passed to.

As soon as the down ends, his QB strides over to me. "What the hell kind of defense was that? You let me make the pass instead of intercepting the ball."

"Intercepting the ball? Aha, now who knows nothing about football?"

"I know enough to see you went easy." Patrick Mahomes stands mocking me with his barbell arms crossed in front of his chest. It's quite a sight.

And my inner competitive warrior hates that I just let him get past me. So I take off the kid gloves. "Fine, you want a strong D? You're playing with fire now. Here we go."

We set up the play once more and Mahomes decides to run. My guy doesn't have a prayer of catching him if he gets past, so I use what I know about Mahomes to position myself in the center, with a plan to cut hard right and block him just when he thinks he's clear.

It works.

My player hits Donovan's so hard, he lurches back and I hear him hit the padded floor just as I see Mahomes get the ever loving wind punched out of him by my oaf of a defender. I laugh at how Donovan keeps going down when there's no one actually hitting him.

But the technology wreaks havoc with my brain just as much, and the sensory stimulation is too much to keep me on my feet, and I go down too, knocking helmets with Mahomes as I land on Donovan in a heap.

Before I can rearrange myself, I feel Donovan's arms encircle me and pull me against his body. He's laughing so hard that his chest rumbles under me. It's a seductive sound coming from deep within him. I push up my headset and lean my head away so I can see his face.

Half of his is still hidden behind the oversized goggles but the expression on his face is pure joy. I love that this is his uncensored response to a demo I designed, but even more, I love the way that kind of joy looks on him. I didn't see a shadow of it the night of the banquet, an event that practically revolved around him.

When he loosens his grip on me so he can take off the goggles, I roll off and lay on the floor next to him. I can't stop the fits of laughter at how both of us are so into whupping each other in this game. "You've met your match, Mahomes," I tell him, turning my head to look at him.

His eyes snap to mine, serious and direct. "I can see that. I like it."

I swallow hard. Not sure if he's talking about the game. I kind of hope he's not.

Another long look passes between us, and I feel the weight of his green eyes assessing me. Again, just inches separate us, and my heart thunders in my chest at the thought of how Donovan's lips would taste.

I'd really like a refresher course.

His stare makes my skin tingle, and I the breath leaves me as I momentarily lose the ability to speak. I bite my bottom lip because the intensity of his gaze makes me nervous.

My back craves the heat from his hands, and I regret that I rolled away. I can't exactly climb back on top of him. Not without a football-related reason. And we've been at this a while, so I'm pretty sure he understands by now what our games can do. I can't keep setting up scenarios that will land us on the floor.

Well, I could . . .

But he sits up and twirls the headset around his finger. "So . . . that's how a VR game works. Pretty cool. Fans of American football must love it."

I smile at his insistence on calling it American football, even as the hope balloon in my heart deflates at the lost moment. "The game's not out yet. I just used football for this demo since I know a lot about the game."

He turns to face me more squarely, pointing an accusing finger. If he wasn't smiling, I might think he was angry. "We need to remedy that. There's only one football, and it's the Beautiful Game. I'll get you up to speed on the fine points of the game if I have to take you out on the pitch myself and run drills." He nods to drive his point home.

Throwing up my hands in mock defeat, I tell him, "I've been learning. I swear."

Again, another heavy silence passes between us as our eyes lock. If I had more experience with gorgeous star athletes, maybe I'd have something wittily seductive to say. But sadly, I've got nothing.

Again, I remind myself I'm in the VR lab at work, and despite how attractive Donovan is, he's not here to see me. I have a job to do, and it's finished.

As if proving the point, my phone pings with a text from Charlie. I read it and push myself to standing. "Charlie sends his apologies that he can't chat with you some more. He just got pulled into a meeting, and he wants me to emphasize that he dislikes meetings. I can walk you out."

Donovan hops from the floor to his feet so quickly I'm convinced the move must be some kind of soccer drill he does a hundred times a day. I put the equipment away and usher him out of the VR lab.

If I have any questions about how appropriate it would have been to kiss Donovan, I get a crash course as I escort him back through the office. My colleagues emerge from their workstations like rodents to the siren call of the Pied Piper.

"My man," Paul says, pushing to the front of the crowd and shoving his hand out for Donovan to shake it. The way he acts, you'd think he and Donovan are old friends. "Can't wait for opening day. Gonna be epic."

I want to gag at his weird attempt to seem cool. With his pale slip of a body, his shaggy, unkempt brown hair, his rimless tinted glasses that look like he's wearing sunglasses indoors, Paul is taking a video selfie and jumping around Donovan like he's a wax figure.

Before I can usher Donovan out of the building, more people swarm him, regaling him with their memories of key plays in games going back ten years or more. They push forth scraps of paper from their desks for autographs. They ask for selfies and he genially obliges.

I stand a few paces away marveling at how my mostly quiet, focused fellow computer nerds have turned into fanboys. Of course they have. Most of the visitors to the ViviTech campus are other developers and coders, about as interesting as a doorbell.

Then there's Donovan. Gorgeous. A sports legend. And so out of my league.

CHAPTER 13

onovan

I NEVER THOUGHT I could have that much fun playing fake American football. I fucking hate the sport, but I could play all day with her.

"Here, I'll walk you out," Tatum says after guiding me away from the throng of her coworkers who remind me that some people actually watch soccer.

Just not her.

It amuses me, actually, that she has such blatant disinterest in the sport—but not in all sports. This football thing drives me crazy. I need her to understand the beauty of the game I've devoted my life to, and I intend to be the one to make her see it.

"We'll be in touch," a guy who introduced himself as Pauley calls after us. I debate turning to see if he wants to keep talking, but Tatum herds me along with her elbow.

"Keep walking, I'm saving you," she sings quietly through gritted teeth. When we get farther away, she explains, "He's my worst nightmare. Trust me, if he'd had five more minutes, he'd be inviting himself over for dinner. And getting drunk. And filming it."

"Ah, there's always one. Thanks for the save."

She ushers me quickly toward the door, waving an arm like she's trying to clear a path through smoke to get us to safety.

"Sorry about that," she says when we get outside. "You'd think at their place of work . . . but people have no shame."

I laugh at her discomfort. "It's fine. Not like it hasn't happened before."

She cocks her head in surprise. "Wow, I guess you're used to it. I don't know how. Feels so invasive."

"Like you said, you get used to it."

"Crazy." She shakes her head, walking me to the side path that leads to the parking lot. "Anyhow, it was nice seeing you again. I hope the demo wasn't too annoying. If you have any questions . . . well, I'm sure Charlie would love to tell you more about his plans." She rolls her eyes and takes a step back toward the building, raising her hand to wave.

In another second, she'll be back inside behind all that glass and metal and unless I want to stalk her in the parking lot—um, probably a bad idea—I need to act quickly.

"Wait," I say, not sure what I plan to follow up with. I just know it needs to be good.

She stops moving. "Yeah?" She turns to look at the front door to the building as though she's having a hard time resisting its magnetic pull.

I'm baffled. Is she going to pretend she didn't feel anything back there? I looked in her eyes. I know what I saw.

Two hours of playing, flirting, accidentally touching, and I find it hard to believe she isn't a little bit interested in where it could go. I'm starting to think I've lost my mojo.

"Hey, do you have plans for dinner?"

"Dinner?" She looks at me blankly like she's unfamiliar with the concept.

"Yes. Food, you and me, when you're done working. If it's not for a couple hours, that's cool. I've got errands to run."

I have no errands to run in Palo Alto. I've never been to Palo Alto, so what the fuck kind of errands would I run?

"You do? Here?" She cocks her head and smirks. At least she has a sense of humor.

I splay my hands in defeat. "I have no errands. But I would like to take you to dinner. Come on, as a thank you for showing me all of this." I don't want to make her uncomfortable at work, so I'll couch it in work terms.

"You don't have to thank me, really."

"I know. I just want you to have dinner with me."

Her chin trembles when she swallows, and I want to reach out and run my fingers down the column of her throat where I can see her pulse thumping. I ache to touch her warm skin, and I'm kicking myself for the lost opportunities when I had her alone on a padded floor.

She opens her mouth and hesitates before blurting, "I . . . tonight's my mahjong night."

I fight the urge to wince at getting turned down in favor of a tile game with the elderly. "Doesn't have to be tonight. Just . . . have dinner with me. One date."

She doesn't look convinced by the way she's squinting at me. She takes a deep breath, and I see the wheels cranking in that beautiful brain of hers.

"Fine. One dinner. I'll tell you more about the game. Deal?"

I don't give a shit about the game unless it entails landing her on top of me, but maybe I can work that into our dinner. So I agree. "Deal. I'll text you, and you'll respond with something cute and friendly. Then I'll respond with witty flirtatious banter. And so on."

She grimaces and closes her eyes for a moment, but when

they open, they look focused and intense. "You're determined to be difficult, aren't you?"

I lean in and barely graze her cheek with my lips, whispering in her ear, "Cinderella, if flirting with you counts as difficult, then you bet I am." When I hear the tiniest of sighs, pick up her hand and kiss the back of her knuckles. Then, smiling to myself, I walk away.

CHAPTER 14

atum

"I'm not going to go."

I stand in Joan's doorway, giving her a quick recap of my evening at the banquet, my conversation with Charlie, the virtual reality walk-through, and Donovan's unexpected dinner invitation.

I don't expect her to argue with me. I expect her to tell me I made the right call, given that I'm me and I don't date celebrity soccer players, or anyone else for that matter. She knows me. She accepts me.

But Joan stands in her kitchen, arms folded over her pink tie-dyed T-shirt, glaring at me. This is not a woman who struggles for words, so her silence gives me pause.

"What?" I ask, still holding her newspaper which I brought up from downstairs. I was surprised to see it still sitting in the lobby of our building at eight in the evening, and I assumed Joan would want it before it became really old news.

When Joan makes no move to take it from my hands and continues staring distastefully like I told her I ate a baby, I lean into her apartment and put the paper on her marble-topped entryway table next to a bowl of lemons.

"Here you go."

"Thank you." She shakes her head with a frown like I'm a poster child for lost causes. "But we have a problem."

"We do?"

She nods as I crane my head for a sign of Felix somewhere behind her. Surely, I'm interrupting their date night and she'd rather be with him.

"Most definitely. And Felix is out with his book group, so you and I have plenty of time to talk about why we're saying no to dinner with a hot athlete."

"I'm not sure this qualifies as a 'we' situation. I'm all good with my decision. I didn't tell you so you'd judge me."

Joan wraps her thin fingers around my forearm and pulls me in for a quick hug. Before I realize what's happened, she's walked me into her apartment, closed the door, and ushered me to her kitchen table where I'm told to sit.

Then she busies herself taking items out of the fridge and various cupboards. "I'm not judging, but we should talk about this."

In under two minutes, Joan has displayed brie and crackers on a plate with grapes, placed a small bowl of spiced nuts at the center, and added dried apricots, baby carrots, and pitted green olives in their own ceramic containers. Then she cracks a can of seltzer water for me and pours herself a glass of wine. I don't question any of it.

Except that Joan and I don't discuss my love life, not really. She knows about the bad dating decisions I've made over the years, and I've always assumed we had an understanding—if I feel like talking, I will. Otherwise, we don't.

In this case, I don't.

So I slice off a piece of brie and carefully position it atop a water cracker before biting half of it into my mouth. Joan watches me while I chew. And stall. I don't look her in the eye.

This may end up being a test of wills, and I'm plenty stubborn.

Joan pops a cashew in her mouth and sips her wine. "Okay, look, it's your business. I realize that. I say what I'm about to say out of love." She reaches for my arm and smooths it like she's petting an animal. "I worry about you."

That's it. That's all she says.

After waiting to see if there's more and encountering only Joan's overly dire expression, I burst out laughing.

"What's got you worried, Joan?"

"At your age, you shouldn't be turning down dates. You're not going to meet your soulmate playing mahjong with me."

"Well, I could if you'd invite some new people for a change."

Her pressed lips tell me she's not amused. "Not the point. You need to meet someone." She emphasizes each word by pounding on the table. Crackers fly off the plate.

Fixing the plate, I stare at her. "Why? I'm twenty-nine. I have plenty of time to find a soulmate. Years. I'm the youngest in my family, and no one's married yet. If you want to have a therapy session, I'll bring over my sister Isla. She's almost thirty-six."

I don't bother to mention that Isla has been dating her fiancé Owen for over a year. It hardly helps my point.

Joan shakes her head. "I just don't see why you'd turn down a date, especially one with Donovan Taylor. Most women would sell out their ride-or-die for the chance at one dinner with him, and you're acting like he's not your type."

"He's not."

"I call bullshit. He's everyone's type." Have I mentioned that Joan is way cooler than me and talks like a millennial? Well, it's true.

I inhale a cleansing breath because I really didn't bring Joan's newspaper intending to have this discussion, and now I see the only way out is through. "Fine. I respect what he does as an athlete and he has a pretty face, but that isn't enough to make him my type."

How about the kiss that turned your insides into hot melted chocolate?

"Oh, forgive me. What's required to reach your standards in order to have dinner with a man?" Joan rolls her eyes to emphasize her sarcasm.

"What I'm saying is that a guy like him has most certainly had his pick of women—jersey chasers from all over the world throwing themselves at his feet. So he's going to . . . expect things."

"Oh." Her eyes grow wide and she nods. There's a hell of a lot of understanding in that *oh*.

"Yeah."

"I had no idea. A virgin at twenty-nine." She looks me over from head to toe, her lips pursed as though puzzling through a riddle.

My cheeks heat and I wave my hands around because I've given her the wrong idea. "No, whoa, I didn't say that. I'm not a virgin. Don't worry."

"Okay, so you've had sex. Really great sex?"

"I've had . . . experiences."

"Lady friend, that's not the same thing as great sex, not when you're calling them 'experiences.' Did you have sex in a lab or something? Was it part of a study? I know you're a scientist and all."

"Oh my God, no! I did not have sex in a lab." I don't bother to tell her that I did have sex with my chemistry lab partner in college, but we were in his dorm, not the lab.

Not the point.

Joan grabs a handful of nuts and throws them back into her mouth. She speaks while she chews. "Okay, here's your opportunity. You've got a handsome athletic guy interested in you. Let him show you what he's got. Now's the time to jump on that horse. You're young, you're adorable, your breasts are perky—you must go forth and have the great sex," she says through a delighted smile.

"I will consider it, okay? But can we talk about something else? I'm not really comfortable hearing you go on about great sex when I see Felix almost every day. That's painting a picture I don't need to see."

She waves a hand dismissively. "Oh honey, I'm not talking about him. I'm talking about all the men I knew before him who paved the way."

My gag reflex protests this conversation. "Okay, even more so. Please. Tell me something else. Anything else. Tell me how you always manage to have the perfect ingredients on hand to put together professional-looking appetizers. Tell me where you lived before you moved into this building. I don't care."

Joan laughs and winks at me. "The key is smart shopping. I keep all these little snacks on hand, so I can throw them together without thinking about it."

I spread another slab of brie on a cracker and bite into it, savoring the taste. "I could eat this for dinner every night. You're right, I need to shop better."

"I don't want to think about what might be in that fridge of yours."

I stand up to leave, grabbing my purse from where Joan tossed it aside when she hugged me. "Bread, butter, jelly. Breakfast foods. Most of the rest of the time, I'm at work." I don't bother to tell her about the two shelves of pickles, hummus, and artichoke dip I sometimes spread on bread as a go-to meal in a pinch. It won't help my case.

"You're a sad, sad story."

"I'm a tech employee. It's what we do."

She kicks her tennis shoes off and walks me to the door. "You call that man back and tell him you're more than available. Come on, do it now." She gestures toward my purse.

"I'm not going to do it with you standing over me. I'll do it later. I will."

She wags a finger at me, and I feel certain she must have been an annoying mom. But an effective one. "Promise me."

"Joan, seriously."

"Yes, seriously. Promise me."

"Fine. I promise." I don't cross my fingers behind my back, but I really should.

She kisses me on the cheek, and I hear her crunching on a carrot before I make it to the elevator. I text Donovan and say I'll meet him for dinner. One dinner.

CHAPTER 15

atum

Two days after I bodied Donovan to the floor—virtually—I'm having trouble thinking about much besides our impending dinner. Purely for work purposes. I've agreed to see him but we've yet to set a date.

Each time our paths have crossed in the office, Charlie has gone out of his way to extoll the potential impact of his VR soccer game. He jumps right in, talking about developing the software that will allow everyone and their best friend to inhabit the athletic bodies of their favorite soccer hero and compete in the World Cup.

Unless their favorite is Donovan Taylor.

"We need him, Tatum. His people said he was impressed with your demo. I've encouraged him to follow up with questions. I'm optimistic." Charlies says all this in a single breath while passing by my desk. There's no opportunity for rebuttal, discussion, or debate.

Then he's gone, and I sit like an unwatered plant, withering from the heat produced every time someone mentions Donovan's name.

I blame the Donovan-induced zoo in my brain for why I don't hear Paul sneak up behind me. So I don't know how long he's been there or what he's heard when he intones, "Sounds like someone's taking Charlie's suggestion literally. Way to take one for the team, Finley. I didn't know you had it in you to get laid for a promotion."

I turn and glare at him, tempering my response because I must. Even though Charlie is head of the company, Paul is still my direct supervisor, which means he has the power to fire me if he can convince Charlie I don't have enough skill for the job.

I don't doubt that he'll make up whatever crap he wants to get his way. "I'm sorry, what are you referring to?" I ask, my stony stare conveying more boredom than annoyance.

"Nothing. Just . . . way to be a go-getter. I enjoyed watching your VR demo. It was . . . enlightening." He walks away before I can school the shock in my expression.

Did he really spy on us in the VR lab? Or is he just trying to unnerve me and so I'll admit to something I didn't actually do?

Either way, I vow to keep my head down at work and my personal life—if going to dinner for work purposes counts as a personal life—out of view.

The last thing I need is company gossip about having dinner with Donovan.

"He's an asshole. You really need to report him to HR," Terrance says from behind me. I didn't know he was there.

He gets the king of all eye rolls at that one. "Oh, please. He'll deny he said anything inappropriate, and I'll lose out on all the good projects here." I've worked in tech long enough to know how things work. Only eight percent of software developers are women. We don't set the standard for workplace behavior. Not yet.

Someday, we will, and I intend to do my part in paying it forward for other women. But until that day arrives, I'll pick my battles, and Paul Peters is not worth my time.

Terrance shrugs. "I can't tell you what to do, but you know my opinion. Meantime, maybe work on mindfulness so you don't murder him."

"Duly noted," I grumble with a salute, and Terrance knows I'm dismissing him and the conversation.

But thoughts of Donovan aren't so easily dismissed. In fact, I'm reminded that he texted me earlier and I need to respond.

My hand goes quickly to my coffee cup so I can down the last of it in a preemptive settling of my nerves. Then I grab my phone so I can reread the text.

Donovan: Morning, Cinderella. It's me, Donovan, the guy you tackled in the VR room. How are you?

It amuses me that he persists in reminding me who he is. And the Cinderella thing is kind of cute.

Me: Hi, Donovan. Thanks for clarifying. Could have been embarrassing. I'm fine. How about you?

I don't expect him to answer right away. If nothing else, the one thing everyone kept stressing at the banquet was that preseason training is demanding and grueling. He's probably out running and squatting or whatever soccer players do to warm up.

Donovan's response comes quickly.

Donovan: Tired. Three hours of training will do that. On a break now.

Me: Three hours before noon? Are they trying to kill you?

Donovan: Seems like it.

Me: Well, nice knowing you while it lasted.

I expect another few rounds of banter, so it surprises me when my phone vibrates with a call. Donovan's face fills the screen. I pop on my headset and answer the call, "Hi."

"Hey." The velvet of his low voice warms me from the inside out. I unconsciously look over my shoulder as if anyone in my vicinity would notice my head to toe blush. "This is better. Wanted to hear your voice." I don't remember him having the voice of an easy listening radio announcer, but if he felt like having a second career, there's one waiting for him.

"You don't sound like a man on his deathbed," I tease, immediately dropping my voice to a whisper in case Paul or one of his minions lurks about.

"No? Guess I'm going to afternoon practice, then." He doesn't sound disappointed. "Why are we whispering?" He quiets his own voice, and now it just sounds hot and sexy.

I lean my head back and fan my face with a file folder while my mouth makes things up. "I'm in the library . . . So what, three hours isn't enough? They make you practice in the afternoons as well?"

"Oh, yeah. We're hard core around here." I smile when he continues to match my hushed tones.

"You love it, huh?"

"What, practice? Not always while I'm in the throes of a suicide drill, but killing our keepers with practice PKs is pretty damn fun. And yeah, I love the game." I can hear the smile in his voice. He sounds so easy and comfortable in his skin, and I really wouldn't mind getting to know him better. The way footballers and coders naturally spent time together.

Idly, I google "Donovan Taylor," intending to look at game footage. But the autofill after his name gives me options I hadn't considered: *Donovan Taylor girlfriend, Donovan Taylor fight, Donovan Taylor disciplinary action, Donovan Taylor record, does Donovan Taylor have a wife?*

The last one makes me giggle. It's not lost on me that the most frequent search terms have nothing to do with the game of soccer.

Meanwhile, I'm staring at a picture of his rakish smile and tousled game hair, feeling my heart skip a beat, and I realize he's still talking. "So what do you think? Want to have dinner with me tonight? Someplace we don't have to whisper?"

I shouldn't be googling the man while talking to him on the phone, so I swivel my desk chair away and stare at my lap in order to focus on the conversation. "Wait, dinner? Is that what you just said?" My voice sounds a little high-pitched and hysterical. I hadn't really expected him to ask me out, even though he'd said as much two days ago. I just . . . didn't think he meant it, I guess.

"Um, yeah. Does that work for you? Do you eat dinner, or do you just crash banquets and drink all the alcohol?"

"To be clear, I wasn't crashing. I was supposed to be there, I just didn't belong there. Subtle but important difference."

"Well, I disagree. You made my night infinitely better. But we can argue about that over dinner. You haven't said you're busy, so I'm taking it as a yes. What time do you finish work?"

My brain spins, trying to come up with reasons why I can't possibly have dinner with him tonight. But given Charlie's implication that the job I want rests on Donovan's cooperation, I don't have much choice. Maybe I can convince him to participate if I explain the technology and its potential. Maybe I'm being offered an inside track to a promotion. I need to play the game.

"It depends. Sometimes I leave at seven, go for a run if it's light out, maybe hit the grocery store. Other times I'm here till ten."

He's silent for a second before exhaling like I'm trying his patience. "How about tonight? Are you planning on staying that late tonight?"

"Oh. No. I can be out of here by seven."

He speaks slowly like he doesn't want to spook me. "Perfect. Do you need to go home first, or can I pick you up there?" His voice is like liquid satin I'd like to trail over my bare skin.

And he's asking too many questions that I don't have

prepared answers for, because I don't normally get asked out on dates by hot men I have to ignore in favor of my career prospects.

I look down at my jeans and hoodie. "Um, I guess we could go from here. Unless . . . I'm wearing jeans right now. Can we go to a jeans-appropriate place?"

He laughs. "We can go anywhere you want. I'm new here, remember? So I'll see you at seven in jeans. If you direct me to a taco truck or five-star burger joint, it's all good." I can hear the smile in his voice and it makes me grin like I imagine his soccer groupies do.

I hang up before I lose my nerve and cancel. I have several hours to focus on writing code before I have to worry about seeing him. So I do what any hardworking coder would do—I swing my chair around and go back to googling my date.

The first picture that comes up shows the dimple popping in his cheek alongside his million-dollar smile as he holds up the Premier League trophy. Now I'm an uncontrollable lust bucket of desire from the hot back of my neck down through the ache at my center that's begging me to leave my desk in search of a vibrator, pronto.

From looking at a photo.

One damn photo.

And now I've agreed to have dinner with him.

Good luck getting through that.

IT'S the middle of the afternoon and I'm way behind on my work.

Actually, that's being generous.

I haven't done a stitch of anything productive since I fell down the Donovan Taylor internet rabbit hole.

Wow, people like to write things about him.

They also like to take his picture. I had so many choices of where to begin, but I wanted solid information so I started with his biography.

I read about his years playing youth academy soccer in Michigan before moving to Barcelona his senior year of high school to play with an academy there. Words like *phenomenon, world class, astounding* came up again and again.

So after about an hour of reading articles and watching game highlights, I can't look at anymore. I also can't focus on work. Which is why Terrance finds me staring at the morphing fractal image on my screensaver instead of writing the code I promised to knock out so he could work on the next step.

I've got nothing.

"You daydreaming?" he asks in a quiet voice which still makes me flinch and grab my heart.

"Don't. Do. That. Terrance, seriously, you almost gave me a heart attack." It's not his fault I got lost in thought, but no one should sneak up on a person.

"Sorry. You weren't wearing your headphones so I figured you heard me walk up."

"I didn't, and I'm not done with the code. Sorry."

His eyes widen in shock. I've never not finished something on time. "Oh. Harder than you thought?"

I should lie and tell him I found it tricky, but I can't admit to being stumped by computers. But Instead of promising I'll get him something shortly, confusion, emotion, and maybe a little low blood sugar takes over and I slump over with my head on my desk. "Terrance . . . " My plea sounds pitiful even to me. "Do you have any candy in your desk?"

His eyes shift from surprise to understanding. The only other time he's seen me fold in the face of a coding task was when my last relationship imploded two years ago. Hence the self-imposed ban on dating. It's worked out well for me so far. "Come," he beckons.

I follow him through the cubicle farm to where he retrieves

two Reese's peanut butter cup packages—then three, then an entire bag of mixed candy—and waves me along to the common area, past the brown couches and ping-pong table. We settle at a small worktable against one wall, away from our colleagues and bouncing ping-pong balls.

"Spill. Who's the guy?"

There's no point in beating around the bush. "Donovan Taylor. He asked me out tonight."

Terrance's face erupts in glee, his mouth a wide-open smile, before he takes his cue from me and sobers his expression. "And this is a problem." His voice sounds dire.

"Yes, because it's complicated."

"It's one date, and you said he's a good guy. How complicated can it be?" He rips open a package of peanut butter cups, hands me one, and takes a bite of his.

I gesture in the direction of Charlie's office with a sigh. "Did you know the company wants Donovan Taylor to be part of the new VR project and he's not interested?"

Terrance shrugs. "It happens. In the FIFA game, there are always athletes who decide not to participate for whatever reason. No one can make them, even though FIFA owns the rights to the game."

"Well, Charlie would really like him to change his mind," I tell him, looking Terrance in the eye so he gets my point.

He shakes his head, leaning his forehead on his hand. "So, what, you're gonna sleep with him to get him to change his mind?" The distaste in his expression makes me appreciate him all the more.

When I bite into the peanut butter cup, my world suddenly feels brighter. "Oh, thank you, sugar rush." I savor the taste and finish the entire thing before eyeing Terrance's stash. He pushes the bag toward me, and I select a package of SweeTarts before answering his question.

"No, I'm just going to talk to him. Professionally. I love the game concept, so I'll give him a hard sell and hope my passion is contagious. Then I'll figure out what his reservations are and convince him. I'm being handed an opportunity to have his undivided attention, and I should use this ridiculous dinner he wants to have and just . . . convince him."

Terrance snaps to an upright position. "Oh. Well, that'll work. Sure."

"Really?"

He quirks an eyebrow. "You're adorable. But he's a world-class athlete. He doesn't need the fame and he doesn't need the money. So whatever fancy words you plan to use to convince him, all I can say is good luck to you."

"I'm gonna convince him. I want to run the new division."

"Tate, I'm rooting for you. Just . . . don't get too worked up if it doesn't pan out. You're a coder, not a salesperson." He leaves the bag of candy, pats me on the shoulder, and heads back to his desk.

Three more peanut butter cups in, the sugar has me imagining myself doing superhuman salesperson things. I will recruit Donovan Taylor to headline our new game.

I will.

I hope.

Then I quietly freak out at the table before running home to ditch my hoodie for a black long-sleeved T-shirt and a long gray paisley scarf I can wrap around my neck. I only look about four percent better, so I put on my red lipstick, pull my hair out of its bun, and head back to the office.

That's it. That's all I've got.

CHAPTER 16

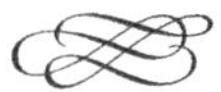

onovan

"So some of it's zeroes and ones like you've probably heard of, but that's only one computer language and that has more to do with encryption, which isn't my area of specialization, though I've thought about it. Thought and rejected it. I'm mostly coding in html, which is the backend of anything you see on the internet. But with the enhanced algorithms we're working on now, we're creating a completely new virtual reality experience, which, as you saw, is next-level groundbreaking and just incredibly cool."

Finally, she takes a breath.

Thank fuck. I've been watching her with what's probably an astounded look on my face for the past twenty minutes.

Man, the woman can talk about computers.

At first, I thought it was nervous energy, but energy implies a finite supply of something I hoped would deplete itself eventually.

Not a chance. She's been spewing information like a rocket ship on crack.

There's a glimmer of the woman I remember from before. She still mesmerizes me with the crazy beautiful way the amber-gold flecks light up her eyes when she's excited. She's still funny, though right now it's only because she can't stop talking and that amuses me.

I'm also picturing the body I know she has under her casual work clothes so I'm a little distracted from what she's saying. I know the culture of Silicon Valley is casual, but I'd bet she dresses down to keep from drawing attention to her figure, and I won't deny it knocked me sideways when I saw her in a dress.

And since I'm only half listening to the documentary on the history of virtual reality, I'm also daydreaming about kissing her ruby lips—if they ever stop moving.

And actually . . . there's an idea . . .

With my elbow on the table, I reach my hand across and stroke my fingers down her cheek, letting them linger beneath her chin. She immediately freezes and her eyes lock with mine, questioning what I'm doing. But she doesn't pull away.

She goes completely silent and still, like a bird landing amid a camouflage of leaves. I watch her features settle as the tension in her face falls away, replaced by the loose vulnerability I've been missing.

For a moment, I don't do anything. Just the feel of her soft skin under my rough hands has all my other senses patiently waiting their turn.

Then my eyes fight to take over, roaming over her face, taking in every feature from her wide eyes to her delicate cheekbones and those plump lips which have parted ever so slightly. I can feel her breath on the underside of my wrist, and it has my pulse ticking up a notch.

I could lean in and gently suck that bottom lip into my mouth—and of course I'd like to—but that's not what this is about.

I don't need to grope her in a college bar to make a point.

But I want her to want me to. The anticipation is everything.

Watching her pupils dilate has my pulse quickening some more at the effect I have on her—not because I get off on doing it, but because I get the sense it takes her by surprise when it happens. And I like her honesty.

She has her hands folded in front of her on the table, prim like a librarian, so I lift one in my other hand. Her eyes stay riveted on me as I bring her hand to my lips and press a kiss to the back of her knuckles.

Then I replace her hand on top of her other one and run a finger across her lush bottom lip before pulling away.

She swallows thickly and blinks at me.

"That . . . " Her eyes look glassy but I can still see the golden flecks. She blinks twice and shakes her head like she's willing herself back to full consciousness. " . . . is the second time you've made me forget my . . . everything."

I can't help it if my smile looks a little smug. "Good. Sometimes it's necessary."

She half smiles but she doesn't look sure, immediately breaking eye contact and staring at the table. She doesn't start in on the tech speak, but some of her ice still needs melting, I can tell.

We're sitting in an L-shaped booth at a back table in the gastropub on University Avenue. The place is full of Stanford kids watching sports highlights on TV screens, so no one gives a shit what we're doing, and I'm facing away from the crowd in case anyone happens to recognize me. There was a time when I'd do the opposite, reveling in the adulation from soccer fans whenever I went someplace. But I'm not twenty-two anymore and looking to get laid every time I go to a bar. And since the fight, I value my privacy more than anything.

I don't want or need an audience, not when I'm trying to get her to relax.

She clears her throat. "So back to the VR game . . . "

Here we go again.

We've been here for a while and have finished about half of our respective pints of IPA. Her cheeseburger and my broiled chicken sandwich have yet to arrive.

When I pulled up outside her office building, she stood waiting in front, twirling a strand of her hair and looking in the opposite direction from where I approached. It gave me a moment to admire her in her hip-hugging dark jeans and fitted shirt which reminded me that I need to ask her more about the triathlons she mentioned. Even sprint distance races are a couple hours of endurance work and are no joke. I appreciate that she's an athlete.

I stopped the car and came around to open her door, and she gave me a quick hug before tucking herself into the seat and spending the short drive pointing out sites outside the window—the Stanford Dish, the National Accelerator Lab. Ordinarily those things might spark my interest, but I got the feeling her tour-guiding came from nerves.

Then it kicked in, her speeding freight train of information, as though she's on a mission to fill me with as much data about virtual reality and the stuff she does at work that I'll . . . oh.

"Anyhow, what our specific game provides better than anyone else's is a heightened reality, where the player is so invested mentally that every sense is firing at once, invoking such an adrenaline rush and intensity of pure physical response that hits all the body's pleasure principles in the most divine way possible, almost like—"

"Really great sex?" I rudely interrupt.

A guttural choking sound emerges from her, and her face goes bright red. It takes her a moment to recover her composure, but she blinks a couple times and ignores the heat I can see warming her body. "Um . . . I was going to say flying."

Meeting her gaze with a heated one of my own, I raise an

eyebrow and speak slowly, quietly, "Well, in my experience, great sex is better than flying."

Quietly, she answers, "Is that so?"

I lean in close. "Tatum . . . "

"Hmm . . . ?" She looks down at the table and clears her throat.

"Is this vomit stream of technology information in hopes of selling me tonight on the VR game your company's designing?"

She blushes and crinkles her eyes in embarrassment. "Um . . . maybe?"

I nod. "Okay. This is my fault. I should have nipped this in the bud. You don't need to sell me on the product. Not tonight. Your demo was incredible, and your mind already impresses me beyond belief. If I was going to put myself in the hands of anyone to conscientiously build an accurate avatar, it would be you."

She smiles, but I hold up a finger because I'm not done. "I give you my word I'll take my time and make an informed decision. And later, if I have questions, I promise I'll come to you. But I don't want you on the clock tonight. I want to get to know you. Can we table the VR discussion and do that? Does that work?"

She answers quietly, "Um, sure. It does. Yes." From her guarded expression, she doesn't look sure.

"Great. Let's enjoy dinner and not worry about work. Sound good?"

I get a nod and a quiet agreement from her, which is a relief, although I feel like I'm about to break a sweat and my brain feels exhausted. But at least now we've gotten the awkwardness about her job mandate out of the way, so we should be able to enjoy ourselves.

Two people. Having dinner. A date.

We talk about her family, and I'm shocked to learn all five of her siblings live in the Bay Area—and they get along and meet for family dinners. We talk about sports, and I do my best to keep the topic away from American football. And we eventually delve into her interest in computers and how much time and energy she's put into landing the job she has.

"You're clearly talented and smart. I imagine you have your pick of opportunities," I say between sips of beer.

"It's sweet that you think that, but it doesn't work that way in this industry."

"What do you mean?"

"I mean, it's completely normal for me to do great work and have someone else at the company take the credit for it. It's just how it is when you're a female in a male-dominated industry."

I'm gaping at her like the words don't make sense. They don't. "I don't get it."

"Okay, well, let's use soccer as analogy. Imagine training with your team to your highest ability, playing in a game and doing everything right—every pass, every instinct is on the money—then you do what you've been hired to do and carry the ball to the top corner and score a beautiful goal. And at the end of the game, your coach congratulates someone else for it and the goal goes into their stats and they get a promotion."

I shake my head, willing what she's telling me not to be true. "I understood it without the analogy, but it makes no sense. The idea of that makes me so angry. If that's what you're dealing with, it's . . . wrong."

"I appreciate the support but it's just kind of how it is. For now. I'll get to where I want to be. I'll just have to work harder and try not to piss anyone off. In my last job, I was the squeaky wheel. I was younger and didn't know the rules, so I advocated hard for myself. I pushed back and you know what? I pissed a lot of people off. It wasn't the way to play the game." She sips her beer as though she's explaining the rules of gin rummy.

"Someone told you that?" I can't keep the distress from cracking my voice.

"Yeah, my boss. Right before he 'downsized' me out of my job. He eliminated my job title, replaced it with a new title and hired someone else—shocker, it was a guy he knew from Stanford."

I don't even know what to say. This is all so foreign to me. "I guess it's hard to compete with someone from Stanford."

"I went to Stanford."

I can't hide the shock from my face. "Jesus. That's horrible. I can't believe your boss did that."

"Oh, and then he broke off our engagement." She sips her beer and looks at me like all of this is normal.

There must be gray plumes of smoke coming out of my ears from the difficulty my brain is having making sense of this story. "Wait, what?"

"Yeah. Warren and I dated at the end of college and started out at the company together. And after a while, it came to a point where we were both up for the same promotion. Being the adoring girlfriend in my first relationship, I said yes to the ring, no to the promotion. I stepped back and let him have the job."

"You're a nice person. But it sounds like you don't work in a nice industry."

She shrugs. "I was just a young, inexperienced soul with big dreams. I figured I had lots of time, so if I gave up my career aspirations for his, there'd be time to get it back later. But instead, it turned the whole apple cart upside down."

"What do you mean?"

She shakes her head as though it still baffles her. "When we first started dating, I thought he saw me as an equal, but I think he just liked having me as arm candy, someone to pump him up and celebrate his big wins. Back then, I used to dress up and wear more makeup because he liked it, and making him happy made me happy. I was so young and dumb. When he saw me take a step back, he lost respect for me. And the worst part was that I lost respect for myself. It took some time to get it back, which is probably why I hang onto it so fiercely now. And why I don't date."

"Evidence to the contrary. You're on a date with me."

She blinks twice and looks away, and I can immediately see her shutting down, raising walls, hiding behind whatever mental objects she erects to keep herself safe. The problem is I don't know her well enough to understand what I did wrong.

I chuckle to lighten the mood. "Tatum . . . "

She intones a deep imitation of my voice. "Donovan . . . "

"What just happened?"

She presses her lips together and leans her cheek on her fist. "Ugh, I'm sorry. I'm stuck in my head."

"Okay, let's talk about that. Can I do something to help you get out of your head? Do we need more alcohol?" I look around for our waiter. Not that I want to ply her with booze until she talks, but . . . well, maybe I do.

"No. I'm good. I'm just . . . ugh! I read the entire internet, and you can't be on a date with me."

"Wow, the entire internet?" She's so freaking adorable it's hard not to smile.

"Most of it, yeah." She doesn't look amused.

This sobers me because it confirms a bigger issue—that between the time she agreed to dinner and now she learned something about me to make her have reservations. Dirt abounds on the internet.

I have to assume that she's heard about the fight and has probably drawn some conclusions—that I'm violent, hot-tempered, dangerous? I don't know.

I have no idea what's going through her head, which means I have no idea how to right the ship.

"Listen, I know a lot of shit's been written about me after I hit a guy back in England—"

She waves that information away. "People like to focus on negative stuff. I assume you had your reasons."

I catch the waiter's eye and tip my head to indicate we'll need two more drinks.

"I did."

"I figured." Nodding, she takes a sip of her beer. She doesn't even ask me to explain. She's the first one. Ever.

"I wish everyone felt that way. It would have been a thirty-second story."

"My older brother Finn was accused of insider trading a couple years ago, and the media scrutiny was ruthless." She says it so matter-of-factly that it sounds like everyone has a brother accused of insider trading.

"Was he . . . did everything work out for him?"

Sipping her beer, she nods again. "He's fine. The reason I bring it up is that I remember how awful it was for him. He's an economics professor and was shortlisted for a Nobel Prize—so I think people wanted to see him fall and fall hard. Schadenfreude."

"I know the term. I think people do want that."

"He practically hid in his house in LA for months until the case was dismissed."

"Wow."

"I know." She waves a hand dismissively. "So I don't care about a bar fight. I mean . . . I do . . . I'm not saying it's great to go around decking people, but people do dumb things, especially around famous people, so I get that things could get out of hand."

"I appreciate that. More than you know. It feels like since it happened, it's all anyone wants to talk about."

"Not me, I just want to talk about VR."

I laugh. "And since we're not doing that either, we'll just be two normal people on a date."

She barks a sort of laugh, and I give her a side-eye because I still don't understand her weird sense of humor. "What? What's funny?"

"Sorry, it's just . . . this isn't a date."

"Why not?"

"Because I'm me and you're . . . " Her voice trails off as she gestures at me, pointing and motioning around my face. "You . . . and your whole . . . package."

"I'm sorry, my package?" I can't help it. I look at my lap.

She immediately turns pink and squeezes her eyes shut. "Not what I meant."

I reach for her hand and wait for her to look at me.

"Talk to me about my whole package. What are you worried about?" I keep my voice quiet, and her pupils dilate again. I'm dying to kiss her, but I really need this explanation.

She shakes her head as though willing herself out of a fog. "You're an international sports phenomenon with tall Swedish girlfriends and golden shoe awards. So . . . I think you've been sold a false bill of goods if you think I'm Donovan Taylor date material."

My brows knit together because I have no idea what that means. "False bill of goods?"

"Yes. I'm not even a soccer fan."

Something's holding her back, but I'm not sure soccer is really the issue. "Are you saying you don't think we're a good match?"

She stares at me aghast like the answer is obvious. "Do you?"

"Um, yeah. Yes. Most definitely. I like you a lot, even more so when you disagree with me. I'm not into ass-kissers."

She puts her elbow on the table and points a finger at me with a scowl. "I've figured out you're the Tom Brady of the soccer world. Only even more so because soccer is global. You can find plenty of tall Swedish women in San Francisco if you try just a little bit. You should be dating Gisele Bündchen."

"Okay, well, given that I'm pretty sure she's taken, not to mention absolutely not my type, I'd prefer to stick with the person in front of me who I find interesting, witty, and stunningly attractive. Is that all right with you?" I can't keep the smile from my face because this conversation is ridiculous.

She has the audacity to look around to see if I'm talking about someone else. With no one in range, her eyes lock on mine. "Seriously. Supermodels aren't your type?"

"Nope."

"Why not?"

"They're too tall." I say, my face a mask of seriousness. Poor thing, she's just taken a sip from her beer, and it sprays from her lips.

"That's not a good enough reason not to date someone!" She's exasperated.

And exasperating.

"I agree. Just like being a supermodel isn't a good enough reason *to* date someone. Trust me, I've dated some of them, so I know." I sit next to her, invisible racquet poised to volley back whatever cockeyed argument she sends my way.

I've never had this much trouble convincing a woman to go out with me. Strangely, I like it.

Tatum pins me with a frustrated stare, but I sense I'm wearing her down. "Okay, I hope you're not trying to date the nerd girl because you think I'm desperate and therefore an easy notch in your belt."

"Nope."

"Are you nearsighted?"

"Not last I checked."

"Well, something's wrong with you!"

"Why, because I find a computer scientist's brain sexier than a supermodel's legs? Because you're both infuriating and stubborn, and I haven't stopped thinking about you since we met? Not a single hour of a single day. Not one."

Tatum presses her hand against her chest, and I'm starting to recognize the gesture as something she does when she's touched or overwhelmed.

I finally get a glimmer of affection in her eyes. She presses her lips together, but I can see the muscles start to pull on her cheeks. Finally, I get the smile I've been wanting, along with the gold flicker in her eyes. She blinks hard like she's trying one last time to figure out if she's dreaming. "When you put it that way, it sounds like a solid choice."

"It is."

Tatum throws up her hands in mock frustration. "I'm running out of ways to argue against this."

"Thank God." I practically throw my glass down and pull her toward me on the bench seat. Before she can utter a word of protest, I capture her lips and kiss her the way I've been wanting to since she hopped in my car.

No hesitation or games. I want her lips on mine and I don't care if she still needs convincing—I'm going to show her exactly how much I like her.

Inside of a second, the hesitation she voiced is gone, replaced by the quiet murmur of acquiescence as her lips sink against mine.

It's not just her lips. Her entire being folds into me like she's butter melting on a hot griddle.

In the same way she doesn't edit herself when she speaks, she doesn't hold back her reactions to me. She goes with wherever her emotions take her, and I'm fascinated and grateful that I don't have to ask what she's feeling.

I know she's into this kiss.

I know it because her hands roam slowly over my shoulders and wrap behind my neck, and the chatter is gone. She's holding me where she wants me and she's not letting go. Now it's her lips that take control as she tilts her head at a different angle to brush against mine until I'm hard and straining against my pants under the table.

Maybe that's how she goes through life. Maybe it's a computer thing, going by feel. I have no idea, but I know enough not to question it when she's running her fingers along my neck and grazing her tongue across my lip.

I've stopped analyzing it by the time she parts her lips so our tongues can connect, so *we* can connect. And that's a wrap on the arguing.

We're in this and she knows it. Every sweep of my tongue answers one of hers. She takes the lead, throwing one leg across my lap so we can get closer. Then she settles in and lets me pull her body in where it fits perfectly like the missing piece of me.

She pulls back, a little breathless, and leans her forehead against mine. "What is it with you and kissing in public? Is that a thing?"

"With you it is. Never was before." I'm not lying. There are exactly zero paparazzi or social media photos of me making out with anyone I've ever dated. And I know this because I never so much as kissed them on the cheek in public.

But this is completely different because I can't stop myself.

She leans into the crook of my neck, and I feel the softness of her tongue running along my skin until she reaches my ear. When she whispers, "I was just asking. Definitely not complaining," I know there's no point in kidding myself. I'm not here because I'm following Jordan's advice about finding a willing female for a photo op.

I'm here because I want to be with her.

Her mouth is sweet despite the bitterness of the beer we're both drinking. When I dip my tongue inside and swirl it against hers, I feel her respond, pushing her hands from my neck into my hair and leaning her head back on the booth behind her.

I know we're in a very public place, but I feel protective of Tatum—I'm sure the last thing she wants or needs is a picture of us on some Stanford kid's Instagram, so I cup her face in my hand and kiss her slowly once more before backing away. Then I take a quick look around the place.

It's dark, and most of the people are crowded around the bar where the TVs are. Not a pair of eyes—or a cellphone—is giving us the time of day.

Tatum snuggles in under my arm and I pull her close, kissing her temple. "This is kinda nice," she says, tipping her head up to kiss my lips once more. "I think I can eat lefty so I don't have to move."

"I like that you're always thinking."

"I can't help it."

Our food arrives a few seconds later and I wonder if our waiter came by earlier and didn't want to interrupt. His knowing glance when he puts the plates down answers my question. "Thanks, man," I tell him.

He tips his head in response. "Enjoy your food."

Yeah, he'll be getting a fat tip.

CHAPTER 17

atum

I'm beginning to understand the global appeal of Donovan Taylor. That is to say, he wields an undeniable forcefield on everything in his orbit like the world's strongest magnet.

That's the only explanation for the fact that when he touches me—just grazes my cheek with the side of his hand—my insides turn to jelly and my brain cells flee the premises.

They actually flee.

They're off gallivanting in the streets, shouting things like "Gone fishing" and "Excuse us while Tatum kisses Donovan Taylor until the end of days."

His fingers ignite tiny bursts of fire as he runs them along my jaw and wraps them into my hair. And I'm unwilling to resist the pull of his lips when they're anywhere close to mine. He's gentle, then forceful, then urgent—his kisses are their own language and I feel like I understand it fluently.

Without thinking or questioning, I respond touch for touch, stroke for stroke.

That's never happened before. But again, maybe that's because I've never been in the presence of his sheer magnetism which has me in its grasp and won't let go.

Without the ability to think, I become a panting, lust-driven lump of willingness whose only purpose is to inhale the bergamot and lime scent of his body wash and memorize the taste of his skin.

Public displays have never been my thing. I reserve my kissing for a nice indoor couch, and sex missionary style in a well-made bed. Wow, does that ever sound boring. Because it is.

I haven't missed dating for the past two years, and maybe that's why.

I miss Donovan when we go more than two minutes without kissing, now that we've started.

It freaks me out that I can't control this. I have no idea what will happen. But I almost don't care.

He kisses me and my bones disappear. Every part of me melts into him until no lines separate us. I want him more with each graze of his lips, loving this feeling, even if it scares me. I'm torn between what my body obviously wants and my need to stay in control, while my desire surges like lava that will bury me alive.

Push, pull.

I want, I need.

I can't, I shouldn't.

But oh, maybe I can.

It's with that thought that I give into what my body craves and deepen our kiss to that dizzy, breathless place where my skin heats and my body presses into his. Donovan's breath hitches and he growls against my neck, "Tatum . . . You are every fantasy I've ever had."

By the time we've eaten and paid the check, it's almost ten and I know we both have to be up early for work. As we weave our way through the grid of streets in Palo Alto toward the Tesla SUV that came with his contract, I have a thought that's never crossed my mind. "I've never considered taking a personal day from work. Ever. I wonder how many people use personal days to spend a whole day making out."

I hear how ridiculous I sound before the words finish leaving my mouth, but Donovan's deep laughter stops me before I can feel self-conscious. "I'm guessing quite a few." His fingers lace through mine as though we walk through the streets every night like this, comfortable in each other's company, stupidly cute.

"Definitely more fun than making doctor appointments." Where is my brain? I need to stop talking.

"I like the way you think. And if you do ever take a personal day, let me know."

I want to take one tomorrow, but I don't say it. I'm still drunk on his kisses and light-headed from the warmth of his palm squeezing mine.

When we reach his car, Donovan walks us around to the passenger side, but the crazy wing door doesn't go up. He turns me so I'm leaning against the car and rests an elbow on either side of my head. He's easily a foot taller than me as I stand flat-footed in orange Chucks.

The height difference means he has to arch his neck down when he tips his forehead against mine. "I don't want to take you back to your office yet."

"No?"

He shakes his head. "No."

His hands move to cup my face and his lips press expertly to mine. All the restraint we showed in the restaurant gets thrown to the wayside. I wrap my arms around his back and pull him flush against me, my mouth seeking his in a frenzied need to feel more of him in more places if it's even possible.

Each time I feel the warm insistence of his lips, I edge further from myself, the straight-laced computer girl who doesn't go for the soccer star. My useless labels disappear and we're just two people, tongues intertwined, falling off a cliff.

It's magical, this tumble down a pillowy staircase that seems to have no end.

Donovan's mouth claims mine like it's a prize, biting down on my bottom lip, then soothing the ache with the tip of his tongue. I hear myself moan at the sensation and I don't have the presence of mind to feel embarrassed. "I love that sound," he growls near my ear. One hand still cups my cheek. With the other, he hoists my leg over his hip and slowly moves while his eyes stay fixed on mine.

"It's all your fault. You're turning me into this moaning, jelly-legged thing. I can't be responsible for what comes out of my mouth," I pant.

I feel his breath on my neck. "I'm glad." He kisses the skin there, his hips continuing to grind into me, hard length right where I need him. I should rein this in before we get carried away. I don't sleep with guys on the first date, and we've gone from zero to a million in a matter of seconds.

My head drops back because I'm losing the battle with my rational mind, which has again decided to gallop off for a nightcap while my body uselessly tries to hold down the fort alone. "Donovan . . . " I'm breathless, but I feel pretty certain I got the word out.

"Cinder . . . " he sighs, trailing kisses across my jaw before he moves his face a few inches away. "I know. It's getting late."

"Yeah." He's right, but I don't feel ready to give him back to whatever life he has after he leaves here, so I reach one hand up to stroke his cheek and he rests his forehead against mine. I can't stifle my lazy moan.

I appreciate that he isn't pushing me to hop in the back of Elon Musk's fancy car invention, which probably converts into a queen-sized bed on demand. He isn't pushing at all.

He's done everything he could to let me know he wants to be

here with me, and I've done everything I could—and let's face it, probably a bit too much—to let him know that means he's not getting a quickie in the back of his car with a supermodel.

And weirdly, knowing he's fine taking things at my slow a pace makes me desperate to take him home and live out every fantasy I've ever allowed myself.

Yes, *allowed*. I'm a realist, so even my fantasies need to have some bearing in reality, some chance—even if minute—of actually happening.

So If I pictured myself throwing quiet, polite missionary sex to the wind and bringing home a fellow coder who whispered sexy things in my ear all night long, bent me over my sofa, and made me scream his name, there was a chance of stumbling upon that capable coder.

Or if I fantasized about a hot athlete making eye contact with me across a crowded bar and shooting a sexy smile my way, that also might fall within the realm of the possible.

The idea that Donovan is both . . . I'm having a hard time keeping my pants on.

I tip my face up toward his and we lock eyes. His deep green burns with intensity and I will him to know what I want. But in case my eye fucking isn't all that, I tell him, "I'm not ready to let you go."

The fire that's been simmering in his gaze ignites into a blaze, and he never looks away as he lifts me up so I can wrap my legs around his waist. His lips crash down onto mine as he pushes me hard against the car.

We're all needy, tangling tongues and desperate moans. Roaming hands and insistent kisses.

His hands languidly move through my hair, untangling the strands and wrapping them around his fingers. Our mouths fuse and I sigh into our kiss, certain I want more. Certain I want him.

"I live about five minutes away," I pant, taking my hand from his face to gesture into the distance.

"That's closer than my place. Let's go." His voice is deep and sexy. I can't resist.

The doors open and I slide into the passenger seat, watching him round the hood and hop in next to me. As soon as he puts the car in gear, he grabs my hand and brings it to his lips. He doesn't let it go for the rest of the ride.

"You can park in back," I tell him. My spot is empty since my car's still at work and I use the app on my phone to open the gate. As soon as he pulls into the garage, our seatbelts fly off and we're out of the car and in each other's arms again as though we're in withdrawal.

With his arm around me, I lead us to the elevator. We wait silently for it to arrive, but as soon as the doors close, Donovan pulls me close. "It feels like a waste of an elevator ride if we don't make out." He smirks.

"Let's not be wasteful." I loop my arms around his neck again and he presses against me. I love the possessive feel of his hands gripping my waist. He knows what he wants and takes it—on the soccer field, he moves with precision, no action wasted, no energy squandered on the wrong decision. It would be the difference between winning and losing.

He moves with equal precision now, moving his hands up my back until they land beneath my jaw and he cups my face, leveling me with a deep kiss that tells me what he wants. My heart hammers in my chest because he's made it clear it's me.

I only live on the second floor, so the elevator dings just moments later. We have to break the kiss in order to move down the hallway, but it's a short walk. He nuzzles my neck while I search for my key.

As soon as we fall through the open door, everything changes. Our hurried, frantic movements slow to a more luxurious pace. After one more long, slow, deep kiss that curls my toes inside my Chuck Taylors, I lead Donovan over to my couch. He plunks his athletic frame into the center cushion and groans. "What kind of couch is this? It's like the couch equivalent of you—impossible to resist."

It's a good couch. All down feathers wrapped around cloud-like inserts. "I think that's how it was described in the catalogue." My wry smile is flirty, and he nips at my jaw before lavishing my skin with his tongue.

Somehow, he makes me feel so desired that it doesn't matter. His deep green eyes lock on me and don't look away, as though I have him in a trance. His sexy gaze has the same effect on me.

"Can I get you something? Beer? Water? Snack?" I gesture toward the kitchen, visible from my living room because this part of my apartment is one big room separated by a butcher block island that doubles as my kitchen table.

He shakes his head and pats the couch next to him. "Come join me on the irresistible couch."

I hold up a finger. "I'm getting us water. You sure you don't want a beer?"

"Nah, I'm in training, trying to stay relatively healthy leading into the season."

I grab two bottles of water from my fridge. When I look up, I catch Donovan staring at my ass. I raise an eyebrow and he winks. "Hey, I'd be insane to look away."

His eyes roam appreciatively over my body as I make my way to the couch, and I'm glad I ditched the baggy hoodie for the figure-hugging long-sleeved shirt. "C'mere," he says, pulling me toward him so that I'm straddling his lap.

"This is my new favorite place to be," I admit, grinding against him and leaning down to brush my lips against his.

He swivels his hips beneath me just the right way, in just the right place. "Then stay right here and show me your moves."

And I freeze.

Because I have no moves. I wasn't kidding about the missionary position sex being my go-to. It's going to be a problem sooner rather than later when Donovan discovers that I'm a sexual bore.

I figure I have a choice—I can make up an excuse and send him home, or I can forget about it for now and enjoy making out with him while it lasts.

Donovan breaks the kiss, but I can't meet his eyes, so I drop my lips to his neck and kiss him slowly, moving toward his ear.

"Tatum . . . " The deep growl encourages me to keep doing what I'm doing. But his hands brush the side of my face and he turns my head to look at him.

"Hey." His voice is quiet, his eyes concerned.

"Hey."

"What just happened?" He adjusts me so I'm sitting a little farther back on his lap and I can't avoid his eyes.

"I thought you liked that?"

"Not what I mean. You went stiff like a corpse. Then you tried to cover it."

"I did?" Caught, I try to look away, but he steers my chin back toward his face. "I didn't mean to."

"Talk to me. What's up?" He adjusts me again so I'm sitting sideways on his lap with his arm around me. I loop a hand behind his neck. No matter what position we're in, we fit together perfectly.

"Ugh. Do I have to? Come on, let's just resume play, continue as we were." I put up my hands like I'm snapping a remote.

"I'm not a video game."

"I know that. I was kidding. I just meant—"

He interrupts my stammering with another heart-torturing kiss. My insides twist and I feel delicious coils of heat unfurling between my legs. I've never been kissed like this and for a moment, I tell myself it's enough. It's more than I could hope for—I should feel pleased and grateful to experience a kiss like this from a gorgeous man. Even though he's going to leave in five minutes.

Giving my tongue a long, sultry suck, Donovan pulls back again. "Now, don't get me wrong. I want to do that with you for a week straight, but even more than that, I want to know you. So tell me why you froze."

I close my eyes and debate with myself once more. I could lie. Feign a stomachache. Or . . . I could lay my cards on the table and give Donovan a chance.

"I'm just . . . I don't do this all the time, bring gorgeous guys back to my apartment and have hot sex all night long."

His steady expression tells me I've stated the obvious. "Okay . . . are you under the impression that I only came here because I'm trying to help you fill your quota?"

He's so damn cute. "No, I mean, I'm probably not what you're expecting in terms of the hot sex. I don't have moves for that. Since I've mostly had, you know, regular sex with somewhat boring guys."

Pressing his lips together, he tries not to laugh. Then he kisses my temple. "Okay, so far tonight you've given me a disclaimer about dating with the supermodel excuse and now I'm getting the hot sex moves warning. Accurate?" He ticks the items off on his fingers like he's making a list.

"Um, yeah. So far, that's about right." I swallow thickly, hating that I sound neurotic.

"Okay, I'm going to say this clearly, but I'm only saying it once. When I was offered a chance to come see the VR demo, I came hoping to see you. When I asked you out, it was because I wanted to have dinner with you. I want to date you—a lot. And I want to have seriously hot sex with you—when you're ready, and I'd love it if that turned out to be now. And the fact that the men who came before me failed their mission only makes me curse them for calling themselves men. But it thrills me because I am gonna make you come so hard and scream my name so loud that it'll shatter every mahjong tile in the building. Is there anything else you feel like you need to lay on the table, just so I'm absolutely clear on all the ways you somehow don't think you're the woman I want to be with? Think hard, Tatum. This is your chance to tell me everything."

So I do. I think about whatever other worries and concerns about dating Donovan Taylor. And I can't think of one. Not a single one. "Nope, I think I'm good."

"Do you have coffee in your kitchen?"

"Um, yeah . . . "

"Excellent. You're going to need it tomorrow because I intend to keep you up all night while you tell me every sexy, hot, dangerous sexual fantasy that can be accomplished by two people and we're going to do them all. You good with that?"

My heart has just dropped out of my chest and my panties have caught fire, so I nod.

"Where's your bedroom?"

Still in lust fog, I point. That's all the encouragement he needs before scooping me up and carrying me to my room.

Donovan lays me on the bed, careful to keep his hand behind my head until he's laid it down gently on the pillow.

No one has ever cared about how hard my head hit the bed.

Right then and there, if I didn't already get the memo from the way he kisses me dizzy, I know my heart will have a hard time fighting off my body's siren song, "Keep him, keep him forever."

Gently, almost reverently, he unwinds my scarf and lifts my top over my head. I watch his eyes roam over my body, aware he's seen bigger breasts—some probably made of silicone—but his gaze conveys only adoration. And hunger. "Beautiful," he whispers, before bending to take one breast into his mouth over my white lacy bra.

I immediately feel my nipples harden and salute him like he's their new commander. And his tongue lavishes them with praise.

The dappled light coming through my bedroom window casts a magical glow over Donovan's face as our eyes lock. The deep green mesmerizes me, and I watch as the color deepens and his eyes cloud with feral intensity. "Cinder," he growls, brushing a kiss against my neck. "I want to take this slow. So slow. But you test every cord of restraint I have."

"I don't need slow," I pant. "Please."

My body thrums with heat and anticipation, and my breathing sounds more like a gasp before his mouth crashes against mine, taking what he wants, giving me what I need.

His lips pillage like they're on a conquest, ravaging anything that isn't a match for their seductive prowess. I'm one hundred percent their captive.

I'm hot under his touch and I know I'm wet and desperate for him. Our tongues wrap around each other, fighting to pull us closer. When he drags his teeth across my bottom lip, I hear an uninhibited moan and realize it was me.

I'm out of control with him, feeling my way, letting my body dictate what it wants for the first time in my life.

I slip my hands under his shirt and lift it up, shocked—utterly shocked—at how the wall of muscle feels under my fingers. No wonder he didn't order a greasy burger. His six-pack abs feel like they're carved from alabaster and his chest . . . I want to lick it. So I do.

He lets out a guttural groan when my lips touch his skin and I'm emboldened, running my hands back down his abs to his waist and undoing the buckle on his belt.

"Hold up, Cinder. I've got plans for you first," his voice rumbles quietly.

In an instant, he's freed me of my jeans, and I feel exposed. But only for a second. Then I see the wonderment in his eyes, like he's been given a gift. I try to reconcile the look with my body—men don't see me this way.

But his appreciative, loving expression convinces me that he does.

Slowly, he peels the last bit of white fabric from my body and gazes at me like I'm everything he wants. "Relax."

Until he says it, I don't realize I've tensed up. I take a measured breath, and when I exhale, the tension slips away. He pulls me forward in his capable hands.

I know I'm soaking wet for him. How could I not be? And he kisses and sucks the tender flesh like I'm his favorite dessert. His tongue works miracles, stroking and circling until I feel a deep throb of intense pleasure that has me fisting my hands in his hair and crying out.

"Donovan, please . . . " I don't know if I'm begging him to stop because the sensations are almost too much or if I'm begging for more. More . . .

Then I'm whimpering and grinding against him, yearning for everything he wants to give me. I'm coming undone in his hands and I've never felt anything like it. The orgasm rolls and pulls me under, then lifts me again.

It's exquisite pleasure like nothing I've felt before until I crest the wave and everything around me explodes.

I'm speechless. Donovan . . . holy shit.

"That was . . . " I barely choke out words, wanting to give him so much more. "I've never . . . not like that. Not ever like that." My words tumble forth, unguarded and honest. Then I worry I've said too much. But his smile, smug and sweet and hungry, tells me he loves hearing it.

"Always like that. Now, always," he says, leaning over to take a condom from his wallet. As soon as I can piece together a coherent thought, my hands are back on his buckle so I can show him exactly how much I appreciate him.

Sliding his jeans down his muscular thighs, I can't stop staring at the marvel that is his body, so perfectly muscular and capable. He leans back and lets me tug down his boxer briefs. Then I gasp.

Clearly, I possess no self-control, no ability to censor my

reaction to his gorgeous body and his thick length. I feel dizzy and greedy at the same time, my eyes hot and wild.

He wastes no time tearing open the packet and rolling it on. I watch him cover his length, enthralled by its beauty. And its size.

He's careful, working my slick entrance with his fingers once more and circling my clit with his thumb until I'm writhing under his gentle hands. Only then does he slide inside me, filling me until I moan with pleasure.

"Donovan . . . " I gasp. Can't say more.

"Cinder, you are everything," he groans. I have no words left. None. All thoughts have departed as well.

I'm all nerve endings and erogenous zones. Donovan is hitting every one.

So when he shifts us so I'm on top, riding him like the uninhibited cowgirl I never believed myself to be, I feel sexy. I see the depth of heated desire in Donovan's eyes that tells me how much he wants me. It's intoxicating.

And when his rolling, luxurious thrusts start to send me over the cliff into a starry landscape searing every part of my body and drowning it with bliss, I grip him and watch his face, which matches the way I feel. And yes, I scream his name.

CHAPTER 18

Tatum

DONOVAN TAYLOR IS a man of his word.

Keeping me up all night—check.

Many, *many* orgasms—check.

Screaming his name—oh my lord, I'm going to have to apologize to Joan for her broken mahjong set.

I've poured us both coffee from my kitchen, and I'm wearing a hoodie, an old pair of Chucks, and whatever pants were nearby as I walk with Donovan to his car. I told Donovan I'd be grateful for the twenty-minute walk to work so I can force myself awake, but he insists on driving me door to door.

With his arm around me, he moves me a couple steps away so the giant wing door can do its thing. He rolls his eyes. "If I'd known it had these doors, I'd have asked for something else. Feels pretentious."

"Oh, please. This is Silicon Valley. Around here these cars

sprout like leaves on trees. And actually, we're in a drought, so there are probably more Teslas than leaves."

Reluctantly, I untangle myself from Donovan and hop in the car. He goes around to his side and kisses me once more when he gets in his seat. "This was a good first date. You think?"

The idea that a passionate night of rolling orgasms qualifies as a first date makes me laugh. "I do think."

"Kind of makes me want to do it again." He speaks quietly as he starts the car, and it silently glides down the road toward my office.

"You are one smooth operator, Donovan Taylor," I tease.

He smiles, keeping his eyes on the road. "I'm told. Anyway, I don't know what it's gonna be like over the next couple weeks until the season starts. I know my teammates are amped to work hard, and Coach has full days planned . . . " Now I understand what he's trying to say.

"I get it. I'm not going to be offended if I don't hear from you. People have big expectations of you. You need to give the team your full effort." I lean my head back against the smooth gray leather headrest and feel fairly certain it does convert into a bed —it's too comfortable to be only a car seat.

He shoots me a side-eye. "Oh, don't think you're gonna use my schedule to chicken out of another date. You'll hear from me. I just don't know what it looks like exactly yet. That's all I'm saying."

"Okay." I try to keep the skepticism out of my voice. Whenever I've started a new job, I've worked days, nights, and weekends to prove myself. Even if Donovan has celebrity status, I don't think it means he can phone it in. Not for nine million dollars a season.

"This isn't my first rodeo. I can run preseason drills in my sleep." He's so cocky. I'm dying to see him play.

"I'm going to get tickets. I'd like to come see a game." I watch the familiar storefronts pass by as we make our way back to Sand Hill Road.

"Like hell you're buying tickets. Tell me when you want to come, and I'll arrange for seats."

"Oh, you don't have to do that." I cringe at the thought of free-loading. "We've been on one date. You don't have to start getting me free seats to games."

We reach a stop sign, and he levels me with the emeralds he has for eyes.

Pulling me in close, he moves the stray strands of hair away from my face and tucks them behind my ear. "Feels like more than one date."

"It does, doesn't it?" Maybe because of the flirting and the texting and the . . . very long and thorough exploration of ways he can make me orgasm.

He reaches over and smooths the lines from my brow. "I know I don't have to get you tickets, but I want to." He throws up a hand. "Tell you what, in return, I'll let you build me a robot to wash my dishes."

"Oh my God, wouldn't that be the best?" I practically yell.

"It would." His voice is quiet but amused. I appreciate that he laughs with me, not at me. "Tomorrow I'll shoot you the schedule, and you can pick a night that works. Deal?"

I can see from the strain in his expression that he wants to do this for me. "Deal. Done. See you then."

He turns away from the road to cast an incredulous look. "That's not the next time you'll see me. Opener's not for a month."

"Fine. Okay."

"You'll see me soon."

"I'll see you soon. Looking forward to it." I sneak a look at him, taking in his strong jaw and dimples that have no doubt sent a thousand lady parts into rapture.

I could like him—really like him—this man who I'm supposed

to convince to take a gamble on our company so Charlie will take a gamble on me.

Other than unsolvable algorithms, nothing intimidates me more.

BY THE TIME my next mahjong night rolls around—this time with Cherry filling in for Alice—I've seen Donovan pretty much every night since our date. His schedule has been accommodating and so has he.

Most of the time we order in or go for late walks around the Stanford campus. In the same way my body melts into his when I feel the warmth of his skin, we've seamlessly melded with each other.

He finishes with his training day and I finish work, we meet somewhere in Palo Alto, we spend the rest of the night together, and he drives back to San Francisco in the morning and starts over.

It's just easy. I'm not used to easy. Even the casual dating I used to do always seemed to come with complications—competing schedules and priorities, even after one date.

But Donovan is doing what he can to make it seamless for me—meeting near where I work and live, refusing when I offer to drive in traffic to San Francisco, making it very clear he wants to date me and my brain. It's a happy threesome, and I'm constantly amazed.

For me, dating is always fraught, which is why I don't do it much. There's always the risk of losing everything, or at least that was the takeaway of my relationship with Warren.

I lost big time. He lost nothing.

From that, I learned it's better not to risk my career path and the things I've worked to accomplish for a relationship.

And here I am, not even a week since our first real date, and I'm feeling my resolve slipping. It's a problem.

Is it?

I'm not sure if it's a problem. Which is why I'm not paying attention to the tiles at all and why Joan is glaring at me. "You just discarded an eight bam. You could have taken Felix's joker."

I look at Felix's board and realize she's right. "Oops, didn't see that."

"Your head's in the clouds."

"I was up late last night," I tell her, praying Cherry won't pipe up and ask why. I've been avoiding telling her about Donovan because she'll tell my other sisters, and they'll insist on getting together to talk about him and I'll die a slow death in their presence.

As it is, I skipped a family dinner with my siblings this week so I could see Donovan on the one night he finished training early. If they find out, they'll tease me mercilessly because to my siblings, I'm still twelve and gawky with frizzy hair and a boy-repelling overbite.

I level Joan with a look. *Drop it.*

She squints at me and tilts her head in a way that says we will be talking about this later.

All of this unspoken conversation happens between the time I miss the eight bam and Joan's next turn to draw a tile. Cherry is busy spreading brie on a cracker and seems oblivious. Felix probably knows what Joan's up to but doesn't care.

My phone pings with a text that's a lot like the ones I've been getting all week long.

Donovan: They're killing me over here.

Me: Don't they know that if you're dead you can't do the Killer Cross?

Donovan: Ha! Someone's been studying the game. I'm impressed.

Not just soccer, *his* game.

I've become a bit of an expert on Donovan Taylor soccer, which fans in England called DT Footie.

Despite my undying allegiance to American football, which will always be my first love, I'll admit that soccer is an incredible game. I've used whatever free time I've had to fortify my soccer knowledge.

Me: I'm fascinated by how you've done it so many times. We need to talk about this.

Donovan: We do?

Me: Yes. This is all angles and trajectories and physics. I'm fascinated.

Donovan: You can't see me, but I'm smiling at you.

Me: That's the drawback of texting. No visual.

Donovan: It's the drawback of not seeing you in person. And I hate it.

Donovan says that preseason training is kicking his ass, so I can't imagine what the coach is asking of the team. His fitness level is off the charts, so if the workouts wear him out like this, they must be brutal. I know he spends days running for hours on end, practicing set plays, analyzing other teams' strategies, and building the unity the team lacked last season. Then they do it again. And again.

The game footage I've seen—regular season games and World Cup matches and Champions League battles—leaves no doubt in my mind why people fall into a dead faint at the mention of Donovan's name.

He's that good.

He's better than good.

He glides like a gazelle with a rhino's temper.

He doesn't kick the ball. His foot connects with it like the hammer on a pistol, sending the bullet straight into the net.

And his signature move—the Killer Cross—seems to defy the laws of physics when it flies from an impossible corner and bends into the goal just out of reach of a trained keeper.

Every. Damn. Time.

Ordinarily, I'd find someone with that much talent intimidating, especially since he does everything in a very public arena. But . . . okay, I do find him intimidating as an athlete. Even more so now that I've seen his talent myself.

But as a man who wants to date me and who's given me the best orgasms of my life, he has my undying support.

Me: Maybe we can remedy that.

Donovan: Are you free this weekend?

Me: I am.

Donovan: Don't make plans. Keep the whole weekend open.

Me: I won't make plans and you can see how you feel.

Donovan: If I'm awake and alive, I'll feel like seeing you. All weekend.

A whole weekend off? I'm not going to squander it on something that's not memorable—so I sacrifice the mahjong game I'm not going to win anyway to some deep thinking about something fun we can do.

Most of my ideas end with us in bed.

That's a given. *Do better.*

With Joan and Cherry in a fierce battle to win the round, I let my mind wander until I've made up the most ridiculous game I can think of. Then I text Donovan to meet me at a grocery store with twenty dollars and an open mind.

Me: You good with that?

Me: You with me?

Me: You alive?

But I don't see any more blinking dots on my phone. I have to assume Donovan has gone back to training. Or my footballer is fast asleep.

CHAPTER 19

onovan

"Tell me the rules of this game again," I say, as though we're playing a real game with real rules. I'm pretty sure Tatum is making them up on the spot, but I couldn't care less. I'll play whatever hell kind of game she wants as long as we're spending time together.

She sighs dramatically. "Really? I've told you twice already."

I shrug. Maybe I just like hearing her voice. "Once more, I promise I'll listen more carefully."

"Fine," she says, wrapping both hands around my forearm and walking me from our parking spot near the Marina Supermarket toward the store. "We each get twenty bucks to buy five things for our picnic. But we have to be creative. If we buy two of the same thing, both get eliminated. So two loaves of French bread—nix—eliminated."

"Sounds like we're about to end up with forty dollars' worth of condiments.

She looks up at me in mock annoyance. "Oh, you just try that, footballer. I promise it won't end well for you. The point of this little exercise is to buy things that will go well together because we're going to split the ten items in two bowls and mix them. So your little ketchup, relish, tartar sauce cuteness is getting mixed with my M&M's and bananas."

I put an arm around her and tug her closer. "That's disgusting."

"I know. So choose wisely." The deep Darth Vader voice she uses to convey the seriousness of our mission makes me laugh.

Tatum leans in toward me and whispers in an old school spy voice, "Don't know if you're aware, but there's a possible selfie stalker at nine o'clock."

I take a look out of the corner of my eye, and the teenager with the cellphone immediately drops it down. I'm barely recognizable in a baseball hat and a week's worth of beard, so it seems unlikely I'll end up on some kid's Instagram, but I vow to stay out of the liquor aisle in the store just to make sure no one catches me looking like a lush.

I lean in. "Coast is clear, Cinderella. I think we're good."

So far, our time together has involved a bit of this, ducking around to make sure I don't do anything worthy of social media gossip. She gets it, and I appreciate her looking out. But I haven't gone so far as to manufacture a photo op to get pictures of us circulating the way Jordan would like.

I don't want to make her uncomfortable after she told me about her ex treating her like arm candy. But to me, she couldn't be more photo-worthy.

Today, she has on a baggy pair of khaki pants that look like a hand-me-down from her brother, a Wonder Woman T-shirt that's so old it feels like a blankie, and as usual, her orange Chuck Taylors.

In a concession to my preference for seeing her hair down, it hangs in wild waves, kicked up by the wind and flowing down her back when she tips her head back and laughs.

We walk into the front of the store and Tatum takes out her phone. "I just decided we should have a time limit."

I laugh. She's hilarious with how seriously she's taking this. "See, I knew you were making up the rules as you went along."

"Oh, I'm totally making them up. This is not an officially sanctioned Olympic event, but if I have my way, someday it will be." She's so deliberate about it, scanning the aisles of the store from where we're standing and pressing her lips together as though global decisions are being made. It's fucking adorable.

"Hey, are you trying to gain some sort of advantage here, deciding which aisles to take?"

"No, but I'm thinking we should start on opposite sides. That way we're less likely to see what the other person's doing and also less likely to duplicate items." She nods. "Okay. You start over there." She points toward the produce.

"I'm starting right here, if you don't mind," I say, pulling her in for the kiss that's been on my mind since she came up with this nonsensical game. Within seconds, I feel the force of her decision-making seep from her on a sigh as she folds into me like melting wax. I'll never get enough of that feeling, the way she responds to me like she has no control over her body.

Cupping her chin, I look into her eyes. She blinks away the glassy acquiescence and tries to focus. "You know, we could just grab a couple sandwiches and a six pack . . . " We're a few minutes from my apartment, and I certainly don't need to risk a ketchup and banana lunch when good takeout places abound and I can kiss her as much as I want there.

She holds up a scolding finger. "We're doing this."

I nod, then nip at her finger which makes the flecks in her eyes dance. "Okay, boss." I kiss her lightly once more, but I don't loosen my grip on her face. I can't. When her cheeks blossom into a smile, I believe, for a moment, that she might feel the same way.

"I'll tell you what." She's tapping on her phone again and a second later mine buzzes in my pocket. "Answer it and we can talk while we're shopping. But don't you dare tell me what you're buying."

I punch the button and talk into my phone. "Can I give you hints?" She laughs at my voice echoing in stereo over her phone and in person.

"Sure, tiny ones." Then she's walking away, headed for the meat department, which I really hope she bypasses in favor of chips or something that will taste good with the strawberries and powdered sugar I'm already planning to buy.

As I watch the tight curve of her ass round the corner past a beef jerky display, I laugh as she gives it a little shake, fully knowing my eyes are plastered there.

I give into the thought that's been bouncing around my head for the past week. Only now it's solidified into something I can't deny. I have it bad for this woman. She makes me happy in a way I didn't think possible. I don't just like spending time with her. I love it.

Fuck.

Because I think I love her.

CHAPTER 20

atum

"CINDER, can you read me? Come in, Cinderella. Over . . . "

He's been doing it for five full minutes. It doesn't matter that the grocery store isn't that big, and I can pretty much hear the deep rumble of his voice from wherever I am in the store. He insists on pretending he's some long-haul trucker out on the interstate—and I'm the sassy girlfriend back home he hasn't seen in a loooong time.

"I read you," I whisper, trying not to let him know exactly where I am. The whole point is for him not to know what I'm buying, and he's not playing fair because I'm pretty certain he's been in the bread aisle and over with the canned goods.

I really hope he doesn't have a beans on toast thing going, but since he's lived in England for so long, I have to face facts. He might fancy black pudding or something absolutely horrid.

"It's lonely on the road, baby. I miss your sweet smile. Over." The grin in his voice warms me.

I can't help grinning at his antics, even though the competitive part of me worries he's not taking this challenge as seriously as he should be. "Sit tight, footballer. I'm keeping the sheets warm for you. Just get home safely."

I hear his bark of a laugh from two aisles over. "Good." He crackles and crumples what I feel certain are pretzel or tortilla chip bags. Then he crumples them closer to the phone for good measure. "Just picking up some items. Secret items. So don't get a chip on your shoulder and think you know what it might be."

"Quit cheating! Just for that, I'm buying potato chips and our doubles will get eliminated."

"You wouldn't dare deprive a man of his fake cheesy corn doodles." He crunches the bags some more.

I'm discovering that under his muscles, chiseled face, and swagger, the global soccer phenomenon is even more of a goofball than I am. And I love it.

"If I find whatever those are, you bet I will." I move stealthily down the cheese aisle hoping he doesn't have mozzarella cheese balls in his basket. I'm hoping to mix them with some cherry tomatoes, but if he's going in the sweet direction, I'm sunk. Everything in my basket is savory, so it should taste somewhat okay in one bowl—tiny cornichon pickles, the tomatoes, and a box of garlic croutons. I took a risk and threw in a bottle of cold white wine, knowing I may have just ruined any chance of this stuff tasting good if I have to mix it in.

Oh well. Life is full of risks.

I debate over the wine once more in favor of some nice, safe roasted almonds. Then I throw caution to the wind and keep the vino. "Okay. One minute warning. You'd best finish up your cheese doodling and head for the register."

A second later, I feel an arm circle around my hip. "I thought you'd never ask." Holding his basket out of view, he walks us to the cash register where we check out in separate lanes, and he shoots me lovelorn glances that make it hard to find my wits and pay.

"OKAY, MOMENT OF TRUTH." I hold up my groceries in the reusable cloth bag I remembered to tuck into my purse. Donovan twirls his haul in a flimsy plastic bag, which I eye suspiciously. "That looks awfully light. Did you get all five things?"

He peeks inside the bag and pretends to count. "Phew. Thought I lost count there for a second . . . " His smirk does nothing to dull the beauty pageant of dimples. Does the guy never have a day when he doesn't look glorious? Even in his game tape after a grueling ninety minutes of play, he's still the sexiest man I've ever seen. It's sinful.

I hold my bag out to him, ready to size up what we've got. "You want to look first or should we do it together?"

"Isn't there some sort of a rule that dictates the exact timing and order of operations here? I wouldn't want to violate the sacred code of grocery games." I kind of like that he doesn't think I'm a nutcase but also won't shy away from giving me a hard time about my competitive personality.

Never one to forego a chance to make more crazy gaming rules, I give it some thought. "Now I'm thinking we should wait until we get to our picnic spot and dump everything out together."

"And by picnic spot, you mean my living room rug, right?" He twirls the bag on his finger.

He has a point. We didn't bring a blanket for the grass or the two bowls we'll need, so sitting out at a park doesn't make much sense. "Sure. Let's do that."

He reaches for the bag in my hand. "Here, I'll carry that." I raise one eyebrow suspiciously. "I'm just being gentlemanly. I swear, I won't peek in the bag. You can trust me."

I fork over the bag, which he grabs with the hand holding his own bag so he can lace our fingers together with the other. "I do. I trust you." The words leave my mouth and before I have time to think them through. But I realize I really mean them. I do feel like I can trust him. I also feel something else that I'm careful not to say out loud—he's burrowed into a deep space within my heart and I want to keep him there.

He leans over and plants a soft kiss on my temple. And I try to push away the thought that I'm in way over my head.

CHAPTER 21

atum

DONOVAN'S white plush living room rug is littered with the contents of our two bags, but I can't even bring myself to look. Because . . . omg, the view.

"Donovan, what the hell? Why didn't you tell me you bought the entire San Francisco skyline?" I'm not kidding. His apartment covers half of the top floor of a Pacific Heights high-rise with jaw-dropping views of the sparkling San Francisco Bay, including two bridges.

He laughs. "First of all, I had almost no input when it came to finding this place since I stayed in England a month longer than planned. It was all email exchanges with a real estate agent and my accountant. And second, I've barely been here in the daylight to appreciate it, so it's almost as new to me as it is to you."

I'd like to turn around and point an accusing finger at him for not shamelessly bragging about this view, but I can't tear my eyes away from what I see. So I talk to him while continuing to salivate on the floor-to-ceiling glass. "This is . . . I don't know what this is. I didn't know places like this existed. You have all the views of everything."

Since I refuse to move or turn, he comes to me, gently wrapping his arms around me and pulling me against his hard chest. I'm not so entranced by water and bridges that my body doesn't respond immediately to the feel of his strong arms and the warmth of his skin.

"You are all the views I want."

I can't keep the smile from my face. My tenuous hold on the last bit of resistance I had to this man begins to slip. I'm rolling down a steep hill, falling harder, faster . . .

When he dips his head down to nuzzle my neck, my head drops back and my eyes close. "You are the only thing that could possibly distract me from this view," I moan.

"That might be the nicest thing anyone's ever said to me. And it's giving me all kinds of ideas." He drops a kiss on my neck, then trails kisses to the sensitive skin beneath my ear.

The view disappears. With my eyes closed, there's only him and the way he makes me feel every time his fingers touch my skin. I want to meld with him, let him seep into my skin, and give myself over to the two of us being a single being instead of two.

I've never wanted that before. Even when I thought I wanted a marriage, I never saw it as giving up a part of myself for the sake of being something even better together. Warren and I were always two distinct entities sitting side by side, single serving salads in twin containers.

As close as we were at our best, a giant chasm gaped between us. I never wanted him closer because I didn't fully believe we were better as a combined entity. There was risk that came with melding with another person and he never made me feel like taking that risk. I convinced myself that was normal.

Now, with every kiss and stroke of his hand, Donovan digs in deeper to a place where I'm not sure I could separate him from myself even if I wanted to.

It's hard to get used to. But so good.

Gently, Donovan spins me to face him and our lips meet, communicating everything that needs to be said where words would be deficient. No kiss feels deep enough, and as lovingly as our tongues mesh and explore, I want more.

"Hey, I have an idea . . . I have a deck on the roof. Views are spectacular, and we can have our picnic up there, but you have to promise to finish our challenge and not just go all moony eyed over the view. I want to make sure you eat."

I give my head a shake as though it will return me to my senses. All it takes is one sweep of his lips and I forget everything I was about to do. "Oh, our game. I completely lost track."

The pads of his fingers run over my cheeks until his hands tangle in my hair and he sighs. "I know, me too. But I'm dying to see what you have in that bag."

I raise an eyebrow. "A culinary disaster awaits."

We grab a couple of red plastic bowls, and I concede a tiny bit and allow us to bring some forks and glasses, just in case we decide to abandon the whole ridiculous concoction and eat the mozzarella cheese and drink the wine.

Then I follow Donovan through the rest of the three-thousand square foot apartment, noticing the pale gray couches flanked by glass end tables and set up around a large brown rectangle of wood. The giant flatscreen TV takes up most of one wall, but the adjacent walls are all glass, a million rooftops and bay views splayed out to infinity.

He follows my gaze and explains, "I didn't pick any of it, so if you hate it, it's not my fault. If you love it . . . eh, I don't think you love it."

"I like it. It just doesn't seem like you really live here." As soon as the words are out, I worry I might have offended him. I gesture to the perfectly fluffed charcoal and deep purple pillows arranged in a line and the magazines spread on the table. "Or maybe you just have a really great cleaning service."

He nods. "Yeah, I didn't furnish it, and I definitely don't clean it or stack the pillows." He throws up his hands and scans the room as though he's seeing it for the first time. "But pillows are nice, I guess. Eventually, maybe I'll swap some of it out. Or I'll ignore it."

He's such a guy. "I'd be all over those pillows, finding cute fabric and having my sister Becca sew me new covers."

He looks surprised. "So there's actually something you can't do yourself? You don't sew?"

"Funny. No, Becca has the sewing machine and the desire to use it. I just click on pretty things online and hope I can afford them."

He laughs. We pass by a less formal room, kind of a den with equally large windows leading to a deck and farther down the hall, several doors probably lead to bedrooms and bathrooms, but we head for a staircase by the large open kitchen.

I peek my head in as we pass by and try to hold in the whimper of longing I feel for the gorgeous breakfast room under a skylight and the stainless steel top of the line appliances that would bring five star chefs to their knees. "Just keep walking," I mutter to myself.

Can't afford to waste time on the kitchen when there's a roof deck.

When we get to the top of the stairs, I can't help pressing a hand against my chest because I'm pretty sure we're at cloud height. The small den at the top has two couches, a fireplace, and glass sliders that make it an indoor-outdoor space. Donovan clicks something on his phone and they glide open. I don't think I imagine it when the doors say, "ta da."

And we have a three-hundred-sixty-degree view. "This . . . oh, wow." That's it. That's all I can come up with because we're standing on the top of the world.

We drop our shopping bags on the couch and move onto the

deck which wraps around the den with lounge chairs and a fire pit on one corner, a small hot tub hidden from the prying eyes of neighbors with a row of ash trees, and a full bar and barbecue as the deck winds back to our starting point.

"Forget the apartment downstairs, you should invest in a good down jacket and live up here. It's like a perfect treehouse."

"I'm glad you approve," he says quietly. I see it in his eyes—a slight bit of embarrassment at the lavish surroundings. He's not a flashy guy and this place . . . it's all flash.

"As an investment, I think you've made a wise choice, footballer," I say, my voice serious and approving. He pulls me in and kisses the top of my head.

But then I'm off on a tear, checking out every inch of the place.

The building is a dozen stories high, but the hill it sits on is high enough to put us above most of the rooftops in the immediate area. The Golden Gate Bridge spans out over the water to the left and the Bay Bridge looks a tiny bit smaller on the right. The yellow afternoon sun glints on the calm current in the water, creating tiny diamond flecks off in the distance.

Donovan stands behind me while I perch on the edge of the deck and stare. I feel one muscular arm wrap over my chest as he holds me close against his strong body. His other hand twirls through the strands of my hair, catching the ones occasionally taken by the wind and tucking them back. "This is what sold me. I was sitting in my flat in rainy Chester and looking at pictures of this." He gestures with a sweep of his arm.

"I'd pack my bags, no questions asked."

He chuckles. "Yeah, it was a little more complicated than that." His voice gets quieter, more contemplative.

I turn in his arms to face him, a view I'll never get tired of. "We haven't really talked about that part—why you took this job. It's a huge life change. Can you tell me about it? Do you want to?"

He doesn't meet my gaze and I can't really blame him, given

the gorgeousness behind me. But I don't think he's distracted by the view. Maybe he doesn't want to discuss deeper life decisions. and I'm going to have to decide if I'm okay with that.

Eyes returning to mine, he nods and dips his head to brush a soft kiss over my lips. "I do. Let's talk after we finish your game." His eyes dance with curiosity and his dimples wage war on my heart yet again. "I'm dying to know what's in that bag."

I watch him for a moment, unable to decide if this is a diversionary tactic because he never does intend to open up to me. Or I can take him at his word and see what he decides to do.

Either way, I'm in this now. I just don't know for how long. It depends on him, how real he's willing to get with me.

I know it's what I need if we're going to be more than a fling. I need to trust that he's worth risking my heart, so I need him to trust me enough to show me more than his pro footballer exterior.

Shaking off the heaviness in my thoughts, I rush over to my burlap shopper. "I'm telling you right now, I'm going to unleash holy terror if you bought SpaghettiOs or anything that we have to mix with this," I say, pulling the wine from the bag.

Condensation has made the label soggy, but the bottle still feels cold. Donovan sits on one of the couches and extracts the first item from his small bag, presenting it to me.

I take in the square pink box of sugar cubes and tilt my face toward him, questioningly. He kisses me and slips a hand into my hair at my temple.

It takes me a moment to remember what we were doing because my brain instantly scrambles when he touches me. When I pull myself out of the lust trance, I study his face, which is stoic. "Okay, interesting. I'm dying to know why you chose these, and I'm also a little frightened about what else is in that bag."

He gestures to my bag. "You first. What've you got? Or is it all wine?"

"I was tempted, but no. Mostly because I didn't want to carry five bottles around in this bag." With a magician's flourish, I reveal a cardboard box of reddish-pink tiny heirloom tomatoes. "Here's your first real hint about the direction I went. Savory, but these babies could sort of straddle the line if they needed to go with watermelon or something."

He hefts his small bag. "Does it look like I have a watermelon in here?"

I shrug. "You could be hiding it." I smirk and gesture to the bulge in his pants which strains a little harder at the fabric each time he touches me. I can't deny that I love it.

"Okay, in the interest of that, let's move this along." He takes out a gorgeous bin of strawberries.

I grab the first red bowl and the two glasses. "Okay, now we've got the makings of something. Kind of a twist on a bellini —strawberry, sugar cube, wine?"

"I like where this is heading."

I show him the mozzarella balls. He's got chocolate. "We're well matched here. Little salad, drinks, dessert . . . " Then he shakes his bag. It rattles. He shakes it again and I assume it's a box of cookies, continuing with the dessert theme.

But he takes out a box of garlic croutons.

Shocked, I take out my box of garlic croutons. "I'm confused. How do crunchy garlicky things go with your dessert thing?"

Shrugging, he tears open the box. "They don't. I just like them."

"Wait, you can't eat them. We have to eliminate them. Eliminate!" I yell as he tosses a handful in his mouth. Trying in vain to grab the box from his hands, I end up splayed on his lap and he pulls me closer and drops a couple croutons into my mouth.

"I like these too," I say around the croutons. "How weird that we both bought croutons."

"Not weird. We're connected on a deep level," he says with a wink. I know he's joking around, but I want to be connected on a deep level.

"Hey." I know my suddenly serious tone takes him by surprise because his expression sobers.

"You okay?"

"Yeah. Game's finished. I think we both won, so will you talk to me? I want to know you better."

He shifts me slightly so the top half of me fits more squarely across his lap and bends until his lips find mine. Every time we kiss, I'm swept into his vortex of senses—his woodsy bergamot cologne, the sweet taste of his lips that I'm convinced he soaks in sugar overnight, the thrilling tingle of his hands on my skin.

But I don't want to be distracted from my mission, so I pull away. "That seemed like a bait and switch."

"It wasn't. I will talk to you. But first I want to do more of this." This time he's more insistent, pulling me tight against him and ravaging my lips with his.

I drift away from worrying about deeper levels. We're communicating in a way that needs no words. Maybe it's enough for now.

"Mmmm . . . chemists should study you," I tell him lazily when he pulls back an inch for a breath.

I feel the vibration from his chuckle throughout my body. "Why's that?" He rubs his nose along my jaw, and I sigh contentedly, saying nothing.

He's forced to pull away if he wants an answer. I can't tell him squat if he continues touching me. "Come again? Chemists?" he asks, amusement in his eyes.

"You make me so hot when you kiss me, I bet you could power half the city if you made out with a wind turbine."

"Ridiculous."

"Maybe. Or I'm onto something world-changing."

Eventually, we scrap the mixing bowls, pour the wine into glasses, and snack on the various foods. We're out there for hours and mostly we're kissing until my face feels deliciously raw from the scratch of his scruff and my mind feels blissfully free of heavy thoughts.

The sun gives up on us and slips behind a building. In the dusky light, I've pretty much given up on thinking Donovan wants to open himself up any more than he has so far. Then he surprises me and leads me to the hot tub.

"Okay," he says. "Let's talk."

CHAPTER 22

onovan

THE JETS CHURN the hundred-degree water, but we only have our feet in. Sitting side by side, I feel a little nervous about agreeing to talk about myself. I'm not big on sharing, especially now that seemingly the whole world has opinions about my temper.

"So . . . given that you work around computers all day . . . and given the fact that you're a human with a pulse, I have to assume you know about the issues I had before I moved here," I begin.

"The fight that you wouldn't talk about?" she asks, her confused expression telling me it was not at the top of her mind.

"Yeah. We can talk about it. We should. It's okay."

She shrugs. "Sure but only if you feel like telling me. Or you could talk about your family—do your parents still live in Michigan?" She wraps her arms around her knees and pulls them into her chest.

"They do. Happily married. Big group of friends. My dad

works for an auto plant and my mom's a teacher. I have one sister —Julia—who lives in England."

"Oh. Two expats, huh?"

"Something like that."

"Okay, so tell me about this big move back to the States. Has it been culture shock?" She plays with the tassels on one of the striped pillows I brought over to sit on.

I don't want to talk about the move either. Or my reasons for coming. I don't want her to see me as a sell-out. Better that she think I'm a soccer player who's better than bread.

So I turn the conversation back to the fight. It's already partly public knowledge, so I won't have to bare my soul. "I do feel like telling you about the fight," I say, watching her face for her reaction.

She tilts her head toward me, seeming happy to hear anything I want to share. "Okay, I'm listening."

"The guy was my sister's ex-fiancé. She lived in England for most of my professional career, trained as a physical therapist, and worked with me and some other guys on the team."

"But she didn't follow you back here?" she asks, tipping her head to the side so she can look up at me.

It hurts to talk about this part, and I feel my spine unconsciously stiffen. "She . . . didn't want to follow me. She moved there for me, initially. Or, at least, moved there because I was there and we were always close. She wanted to support my career and make sure I had family around. My parents are rooted in Michigan. I wouldn't expect them to leave. But Julia did. She got a job with the first team I was on and stuck by me."

"That's kind of amazing. And she's your only sibling?"

"Yeah. Part of why we're so close."

Tatum pulls her feet out of the hot tub and wraps her arms around her knees, still listening intently. Then her brow wrinkles. "So why'd you pound her fiancé?"

"He was abusive." There's no way to sugarcoat it. I scowl even thinking about him.

Her eyes go wide and she reaches for my hand. "Oh no. I'm so sorry. Is she okay?"

I grasp her warm fingers tighter, letting her presence be a comfort to the memories I hate. "She is now. But it was a mess. She hid it from me for a long time—months of letting him wreck her emotionally and hit her until she couldn't hide the bruises under makeup anymore—then when I finally found out, it broke me. She'd been putting up with pain and a downward spiral of self-worth and she he had her believing she deserved it. I felt so guilty because the only reason she was even in England was me."

She grips my hand harder. "You can't put that on yourself. You didn't make an asshole abuse her."

"I guess. Long story short, I convinced her to leave him, she got a restraining order, and found a therapy group. It's been months of rehab and a lot of life changes, but she's doing okay, and she's happy living there still. It worries me having her so far away, but she convinced me it's what she wants." I shake my head at the night that still haunts me. "But that son of a bitch decides to show up at the team bar after a game. Knows I'll be there, knows I despise him."

"Oh crap. She wasn't there with you, was she?"

"No, thank god. But he wanted me to talk to Julia, convince her to get back with him. Kept telling me he loved her and he'd changed. I wasn't prepared to hear word one from that guy and I told him to walk away. He should have. But he didn't. Kept following me around, badgering me. Finally, end of the night, I'm leaving the bar and there he is, drunk and in my face, telling me what a bitch she is. Saying she pushed him over the edge, that it's her fault he lost his temper. Her fault he hit her."

I take a sharp inhale as emotion clouds my vision, and my chest heaves at the memory of him saying the words. I'd like to punch something. As if sensing it, Tatum lays her hand against my temple. That simple sign of compassion takes the fight from me.

"I dunno, for so long I'd been holding it in, the rage I felt against this asshole. And I guess . . . something just snapped. He wouldn't leave, wouldn't stop blaming her, and I knocked the shit out of him."

She's rubbing my back, her eyes squeezed tight against the awfulness of my admission. At least that's what I think she's feeling. "I'd have wanted to kill him. Men who abuse women don't deserve to walk this earth."

Not what I was expecting her to say. I glance at her, wondering if she is—and hoping against hope that she isn't—speaking from experience. As though she follows my train of thought, he shakes her head. "I just feel unequivocal about this. I'm really sorry for your sister."

"Thanks, yeah, I feel sorry too. As it was . . . well, you know the rest of what happened. Fines, bad press, the whole deal."

"And you didn't want your sister's issues made public, so you said nothing," she correctly concludes.

Nodding, I take her hand and absently rub a finger over the contours. "At one point, she told me she'd go to the press to take the stink off me, but I talked her down. I couldn't do that to her after everything she'd already been through with him. I'm an adult. I can handle a little bad press. I just had no idea how long it would follow me around."

I'm aware of the stiffness in my voice that sounds as though I haven't formed words in a year. Strange how talking about something that's been off-limits for so long makes my jaw feel rusty.

"Your sister's lucky she has you. It's awful. And I'm a peaceful person, but I'm glad you beat the crap out of him. So let's get that clear. You did the right thing. He deserved far worse. And I understand your reasons for keeping quiet about it. You impress me with your valiance."

Her words make my heart swell with affection and appreciation that she takes me for what I am. I kiss her temple and lean my forehead against the side of her head. "Thank you. But it's not about me. It was never about me. That was the point."

"I know. It just sucks that people are so desperate for a story that they turned you into some kind of savage with anger management issues for protecting your family. But people are idiots. We know this."

I can't help but chuckle at the matter-of-fact way she views the world. "Sadly, yes. And I guess that's a large part of the reason I don't want to be part of a video game. A year ago, I'd have said yes, no problem, but now . . . I feel like people already own every part of me—my face, my image, my game footage. Every move on the field is analyzed and dissected, and that's fine. I accept that. It's the game and it's my job. But you're asking me to give the last bit of myself I still have power over. I don't need people to *be* me, feel like they're inside my head, playing my game. I need to preserve something of myself or I'll have nothing left."

She tries to shield me from the disappointment on her face, but I see it anyway.

I watch her digest the information which I know impacts her job, which she takes seriously. She's ambitious and I respect the hell out of it, but I can't make this sacrifice, even for her.

Eventually, she nods. "I get it. That's absolutely your right, and you need to take care of you." I watch the indecision in her expression give way to resolution, and she raises her eyes and they lock with mine. "Don't do the game. Don't do it. I'll go in on Monday and tell Charlie it's not going to happen."

I hate being the one to tell her no. But I have to. I just hope she doesn't see it as giving up because I want her to think better of me. "Thank you."

"I . . . " Her eyes close and she nods. "It's the right decision." She doesn't elaborate, and I get the feeling there's a conversation in her head I'm not part of, but when I see her swallow hard, I know she doesn't want to talk about it anymore.

Suddenly, I feel very talked out. Incapable of anything but nonverbal communication. So I turn her so she's facing me and I can pull her into my arms. Our bodies fit together as though they're missing pieces of each other, and I instantly need her in every fucking way.

Then our lips are gliding against each other, our tongues meeting and speaking their own perfect language. All other conversations are finished.

To her credit, Tatum only needed one set of assurances that I find her sexier than any woman I've ever met. Since then, she's been open to anything and everything, and her list of fantasies is longer than mine.I have every intention of working our way through all of them. If not tonight, very soon.

So it comes as no surprise that the moment I walk us closer to the hot tub, she whips her shirt over her head and drops her rolled up khakis in mere seconds. She stands in front of me wearing only a black lace bra and matching panties and I about lose my mind.

"Hold on. You've been wearing that underneath these grungy clothes all day long and I'm only now getting to see them?" If I was having trouble adjusting my pants before, she just made it impossible.

Tatum shrugs. "I didn't know you were all about the lingerie, footballer."

"Cinder, every guy is all about the lingerie. And you are not playing fair." I move closer intending to lick, kiss, and downright worship every bit of skin that's now available to me.

And I do, starting with her shoulder which tastes as sweet as the strawberries we've been feeding each other in between sips of wine. If any of the guys on my team saw me, they'd give me shit for being pussy whipped, and they'd be a hundred percent right.

She fucking owns my heart.

Her hands undo my buckle and the buttons of my jeans so I finally get some sweet relief from the denim prison that's been torturing my dick for an hour. Stepping out of them, I continue the path I'm weaving down her body with my tongue, feeling grateful when she pushes my T-shirt up over my head. I need her skin against mine. "Now the playing field's a little more even," she says on a sigh.

"Always competing," I tease, slipping her bra straps from her shoulders and palming her perfect teardrop breasts in my hands. Her nipples pucker and harden under my touch and I take one of them in my mouth, rolling it with my tongue until she sighs. I'll never get tired of hearing those quiet acquiescent breaths. They fill every crevice in my soul and make me understand what it means to feel whole.

I sense her go limp in my arms and I take the opportunity to lift her up. Her legs wrap around my waist and I revel at the sensation of her hot skin against me.

Dragging one of the cushions from a lounge chair, I toss it down on the deck and lay Tatum on top of it. Her hair splays around her and I watch her part the beautiful pink of her lips in anticipation.

It's a slow dance when I tease the wisps of black fabric from her body and take a moment to gaze at her naked form. Her hands roam over my chest and down my abs, her eyes following. When she looks up, there's hunger in her eyes I haven't seen before. They're darker, the gold flecks glowing like a lit match.

"I need you inside me," she pants. "Please."

I'm quick with the condom but slow with everything else, easing into her until I feel her heat wrap me in ecstasy. We're past the point of wild fucking to get off. This is something else entirely, and I want to explore all of it, even if her power over me terrifies me a little bit.

She moves and moans beneath my body and I feel her core contracting with every thrust, but the mad frenzy of weeks ago has been replaced with languid tenderness that's so much sexier because it's her responding to me without thinking. And because

I made the choice to open up a bit—even though I only shared a fragment of myself, it's more than I've done with anyone else.

"Donovan . . . " Her whisper turns into a moan near my ear.

I knew I was a goner before but there's no question now that as I hear my name on her lips, I'm completely, uncontrollably in love.

I want her orgasm more than I want my own. My need to worship her body feels like I'm chasing a high from a potent drug, and she has me completely enthralled with every small gasp and shudder and uncontrolled sigh she makes.

I want more of this. More of her. More.

Her legs quiver beneath the light stroke of my hand and her sighs give over to a quiet moan that I feel in my veins. "Come, baby. Let go." My voice gives her the last bit of calm I have to offer because now it's all nonverbal groans and whimpers of agreement. We're both in freefall.

The world around me narrows to one point of focus, and I circle my hips harder against her, thrusting deeper and faster until I feel her start to come undone. I feel it in the clench of her muscles and in her heart pounding against my chest. She gasps and moans and I hold out as long as I can to allow her orgasm to build. And build.

Any world I knew before is decimated by the explosion of us together. I can't live any other way.

As we crest the peak and crash into each other, I marvel at the sensation of desiring a person so fully. And I want her. Not just for tonight. Not just for sex.

I want her for everything.

CHAPTER 23

onovan

Everyone's reenergized after a lunch of lean carbs and a few hours away from the hot noon sun. "I'm aching to get out there against the Falcons," Danny Weston's deep voice rasps out next to me. He's our center midfielder and the guy who runs more miles per game than anyone on the team, hands down.

"Just a couple more weeks and you can have at them," I say, calculating the number of days left before our season opener —eleven.

He rub his hands together in anticipation. "I don't just want at them. I want to destroy them."

"I'm with you, man." He came to the team two years ago when the Strikers were coming off a hot streak, hoping to take them to their first league championship. But due to unforeseen injuries and a player who left the game after a doping scandal, the Strikers finished near the bottom of the table both years.

This year, with an improved roster and a new coach, the

team's chances look as good as they've ever been. "Destroy. Nothing less," he says, punching a fist into his hand and exhaling a long breath.

Weston must have a resting heart rate of around ten beats a minute. In the off season, he trains at high altitude to increase his lung capacity to superhuman levels. I have nothing but respect for him.

"Their defense still looks solid but they're still weak up top," I say. They lost a key forward last year and haven't found anyone with the skill they need to dominate. "Right team to play on opening day. Our odds look good."

"What I'm thinking," Weston says, stretching a calf muscle that's been giving him trouble all week. I cast him a side-eye when I see him grimace. "It's just tight." He doesn't want anyone to worry he's injured. I just hope he's not.

"So how's it going so far? You adjusting to the Left Coast?" Weston jokes.

"Yeah, lotta tree huggers out here, but I'm making it work."

"Real talk, though. You good? It's a big change and I know the media's been all over your ass." I can see from his serious expression he's trying to connect and be a friend. But what good's it going to do anyone to have me getting into personal stuff or sharing my fears about my future? I'm here to be a leader. I know my role.

"Thanks. Yeah, it's all good. Happy to be here, focused on the season."

He shrugs, done pressing me. "Okay, man."

About half the team has already filed out to the practice pitch, and the stragglers are either taking a few more minutes with ice on their muscles or they're stalling, anticipating a grueling afternoon session of pain. The intensity has ratcheted up a notch every single day.

I have to say, I'm impressed. Coach Derry has one of the best coaching reputations on either side of the Atlantic. I did my research before considering changing teams. When I heard he'd signed on to coach the Strikers, it sealed the deal for me.

"You coming?" Weston finishes stretching and slams his locker shut.

"In a minute. I need to send a text."

He leaves and I grab my phone, seeing a new text from Jordan reminding me it would be "great" to be seen in public in the company of a woman. Intuitively, I understand his point. If I want people to stop obsessing about one story, I need to give them something else.

I could just tell Tatum why I need her in a few well-placed photos and be done with it. She's reasonable. She'll understand why it's necessary.

Will she?

If she hadn't explicitly said she didn't want to feel like someone's arm candy, I probably wouldn't think twice. But she did say it.

Granted, she was talking about her ex-fiancé who, by all accounts, sounded like a first rate douche, but still. The last thing I want is for her to feel like she sacrificed her career for mine. She's already dropped the idea of pushing me to be in the VR game and I know she made that concession knowing it might impact her ability to lead the project she wants. Now I'm about to ask her to dress up for glam shots to help my career.

I don't want to do it. I fire off a text to Jordan.

Me: Forget about the paparazzi stunt. Let's find another way to get the media hounds sniffing—preferably involving the game of soccer.

Jordan responds so quickly I'm convinced he sits around staring at his phone.

Jordan: It's already done. Paps will be out Friday at The Tailor's Son. Be there.

Me: Can't you call them off?

Jordan: Maybe, but I won't. What's the issue?"

Me: I don't want to put a nice person through that.

I haven't told Jordan I've been seeing Tatum. He'd jump all over it, and it's none of his damn business. Better to be vague.

Jordan: You're not putting her through anything. You're taking her to a nice dinner, then I assume you're bringing her home and fucking her good. With a couple photos in the middle. Relax.

He's such an asshole. I'm offended on Tatum's behalf, but Jordan's not even worth the effort of setting him straight.

I put the phone down and scrub a hand over my face. I miss the days when I didn't need a publicist to tell me what to do to salvage my public image. But it's nearly two weeks until the season opener and people are still fixated on whether I've snapped. Tabloids are still printing shit about how my aggressiveness on the field is a sign I'm unstable and questioning my mental fitness for the game. I need to do something.

Maybe he's right. I'm making an issue of something that happens every day to people in the spotlight. Tatum and I have talked about that, and she's sympathetic. She doesn't have to know Jordan is manufacturing a photo op. It'll just make her uncomfortable, worrying she has to dress a certain way or look like Victoria Beckham or something. I don't want her to feel self-conscious. She's gorgeous when she's being herself.

If I don't make it an issue, maybe it won't be an issue. I'll wave the photogs off the first chance I get and whisk her away before anyone has a chance to get in her face. Then it will be done.

You're overthinking this.

"Hey, Jordy, would it freak your wife out if you left a restaurant and a photographer from some gossip site snapped some pictures?"

He finishes lacing up his shoes and shrugs. "Why, you know something I don't?"

"Not at all. I haven't been in the States that long, so I'm not sure what to expect from local media and bloggers."

"Eh, you're asking the wrong guy. I'm just Jordy Steiner, left back. No one gives a shit where I eat dinner with my wife. You're Donno. I can't pretend to know what it's like to be you."

I huff out a laugh, shaking my head. "Yeah, can't complain, I guess."

I shouldn't complain. I need to man up, go to dinner, and hope Jordan is the genius I pay him to be. I send Tatum a text.

Me: Are you free Friday for dinner?

Cinderella: Hmm. Let me check with my social planner and my publicist.

She loves giving me shit about having a publicist. If she ever meets Jordan she'll roll those pretty hazel eyes at his uselessness, I have no doubt.

Meanwhile, I stand frozen in the locker room white-knuckling my phone and ignoring my teammates who slam various locker doors and bark insults at each other as part of how we get adrenaline flowing before a scrimmage.

"Hey, man, everything okay?" Jordy asks, concern in his face.

I immediately wipe any trace of irritability from my face and smile at him.

"Yup. All good."

"You coming?" He cranes a neck toward my phone, which I move out of his line of sight. No need to give anyone ammunition to rib me about my social life, at least not until I have a real conversation with Tatum about where this is going.

I hope it's going all the way, everywhere, forever.

"Yeah, in a sec," I say, waving them on without me.

Tatum doesn't text me back for a full five minutes. And like a lovestruck idiot, I spend those five minutes staring at my phone, scrolling through our previous texts with a dopey grin on my face. What the hell has this woman done to me? I used to be immune to emotions. Now I'm reading into old text exchanges for scraps of evidence she feels even half of what I do. I'm losing it.

My heart races in my chest when I see the jumping dots indicating she's typing.

Cinderella: I have to rearrange my dinner with the Pope, but I'll make it work. What time, footballer?

Me: Eight. I'll double down on dessert if you wear that black dress from the banquet.

Cinderella: Gave it back to Cherry. But I'll come up with something dessert-worthy.

Me: To be clear, I'm still very fond of your hoodies.

Cinderella: To be clear, I'm very fond of . . . chocolate desserts.

Me: Please wear a dress and I'll feed you chocolate in the bathtub.

Cinderella: **Tatum has left the building to buy a dress

The smile that pulls at my lips reminds me that nothing will make me happier than taking her to dinner and gawking at her all night in whatever dress she deems fit to wear.

I can't wait until I get this hideous orchestrated media stunt out of the way so I can get past the residual blowback from the fight and move forward.

It bothers me that I've allowed Jordan to dictate how and when I can share our relationship with the public, but I know I need to play by the rules, even if I don't like them.

Part of paying for past sins, I guess.

Dumping my phone into my workout bag and slamming the locker door shut, I resolve to get my damn head on straight. When I reach the pitch, only fifty percent of my brain space is still preoccupied with Tatum. By the time I hit the field and get a ball under my feet, I have one hundred percent of my head in the game. Where it belongs.

CHAPTER 24

atum

I DON'T END up buying a dress.

After texting Donovan that I will, I start thinking about how many hours I've already spent away from my job because I've made plans to see him. On a couple occasions, I've left two or three hours earlier than I normally would so we could have dinner.

Then, after dinner, we've stayed up most of the night, and I've enjoyed every last orgasmic moment of it. But if I'm honest, my work suffers a little bit the next day. That can't happen.

As it is, I spent the morning avoiding Charlie, trying to buy a little more time before telling him Donovan won't be a part of the VR game. It's entirely possible that I'm in denial and holding out hope that Donovan might come around. The idea of failing in the mission Charlie set before me stings a little, even if I support Donovan's reasons for opting out.

For now, I let it all go, exhaling a breath I didn't know I was holding and feeling my shoulders relax. Not that I'm any less worried, but breathing feels good.

I continue focusing on breathing and not thinking for the rest of the drive to Finn's house for an overdue family dinner with my siblings. Normally, I'd listen to an audiobook, but this time, I'm grateful for the silence and the chance to hear myself breathe instead of think.

Breathing—only breathing—turns out to be harder than I realize.

That's why I'm near ecstatic when I pull up to Finn's house in the Berkeley Hills and see Becca and Cherry walking the hill from where they parked. "Hey," I shout. Slamming the car door shut, I jog to catch them before they get to the front walkway. "Do you know how hard it is to breathe and not think?" I ask before hugging Becca and Cherry.

"Sounds awful to me," Becca says, untwisting the blond-streaked knot of hair on top of her head and letting it tumble. "Why would you do that to yourself?"

"It's a Buddhist mindfulness thing. I'm told I need to be more mindful," I admit, knowing I'm opening myself to more questions.

Becca chuckles. "You were vegan at one point, now you're a Buddhist?"

"She didn't say she was a Buddhist," Cherry reprimands. "You're not a Buddhist, are you? It's okay if you are," she whispers to me.

"Nope, not a Buddhist. Just trying to avoid overthinking." I know my sisters will pepper me with questions about Donovan—it's their way—and I'm determined to give them only the necessary details before diverting the conversation and deflecting it to something else. Otherwise, they'll pry, badger, and otherwise annoy the crap out of me. We're like a small sorority, and this is our hazing ritual.

Keeping information from them is futile, especially since I

had to spill my plans to Cherry when I asked her for another dress. And she told everyone else. In some ways, it's easier to have Cherry be the town crier and fill everyone else in. It cuts down on at least a few of the questions.

"Ah, now we get to the heart of it," Becca says, hoisting a box from Rockridge Market onto her palm, ready to present it to Finn when he opens the door.

The front door flies open a second later. "Greetings, sister-lings. Come, Annie's barbecuing peaches."

We follow him, shooting glances among each other, unsure which of us should ask first. "What's that you say?" Cherry asks. "Peaches are a fruit, you know."

"And have you had them warm off the grill with a scoop of ice cream?" Finn asks.

"'Fraid not," Cherry says.

"Well then, you're in for a treat. My wife has better peaches than anyone."

"Okay, first, ew. And second, she's not your wife for another five months. Don't get ahead of yourself, cowboy."

"Just practicing calling her that. I like to prepare," he says, reminding me of why he and I have a special weird bond.

Finn takes the box from Becca and herds us through the house to the back deck, which he's just spent the past several months renovating.

"Oh, wow. It's a masterpiece," I tell him when we step outside. Finn grins, proud his vision has come to fruition.

The redwood deck juts out from the family room in a way that makes it appear to soar toward the horizon. It's large, beautifully refinished, and boasts a sunken hot tub, an outdoor kitchen, and a rectangular table that seats twelve.

As promised, Annie stands at the grill in a novelty apron with a mustachioed man that says, "Mr. Good Lookin' is Cookin'."

"Lemme guess, this apron belongs to you, Finn?" I tilt my

head at him because I can't picture him buying—no less wearing—this apron.

"He won't wear it," Annie says, leaning in to kiss each of us while keeping her hands busy flipping peaches on the grill. "It was a gift. You should wear a gift, Finn," she scolds.

He throws up his hands and goes to the wet bar to pour us all wine. When he comes back with filled glasses on a tray and a bowl of M&M's, I take a seat at the long table and decide I will stay for as long as I can successfully avoid thinking, which just might be hours with this view.

It turns out Annie is also barbecuing baskets full of vegetables, along with skewers of chicken and some sort of marinated cheese on their gigantic grill, so Finn goes over to help flip things and splash around the marinade.

Isla and Sarah, the two oldest, come through the door before I've taken a sip and plop down at the table across from me. "What'd we miss?" Isla asks.

My quizzical look compels Becca to answer, "You were about to share all about your soccer boyfriend. We want the deets! I was behaving myself until these two got here, but now, it's on, sister."

Cherry plops into a chair with so much gusto half her wine spills. Paying no mind to the waste or to cleanup, she reaches over and refills her glass, offering the bottle to Isla. Finn meets my eyes and tosses me a towel. Neither one of us abides messiness.

"Okay, now I'm ready to relax and hear about all the extraordinary monkey sex with the English football star," Cherry says.

Nothing about this shocks me. My sisters have no boundaries, and since I'm the youngest, most of the time they act like they own me. Like I'm a cute pet they can play with.

I do my best to disabuse them of that idea, but it's a struggle.

"First of all, he's from Michigan—he just played in England up until now. And second, I'll tell you about him, but what happens in the bedroom is none of your business." I feel strongly about this, not that it's ever stopped my sisters from oversharing.

"Tell 'em, Tater Tot," Finn says. He's the only one who thinks our sisters are as ridiculous as I do. I have a feeling Annie falls into that camp too, but since she's still new to the family, she generally keeps her thoughts to herself.

"Such a puritan. Don't worry, we'll get it out of you. Isla, hand me the wine, will you?" Becca holds out her hand, too lazy to get up and walk the three feet to where the bottle sits open on the table.

The saving grace of being the youngest is that most of the time my siblings were too preoccupied with their own lives to worry much about mine. But at the mere mention of a man, all that changes. Especially when the man is Donovan Taylor. Apparently.

"How have you even heard of him? I don't remember any of you being huge soccer fans." Certainly, I can't be the only person in America who'd never heard of Donovan before he moved here.

"I'm pretty sure everyone's heard of him," Becca says. "Unless they live under a rock."

"I hadn't heard of him," I admit.

"It's a very small rock," Becca quips.

"It's not so much the game of soccer as pop culture. He's the GOAT," Cherry says.

"Please never say that. You're not young or hip enough," Becca tells her.

"Yes, asking about my sex life is bad enough, but please don't compare my boyfriend to a farm animal." Time to deflect and divert.

Cherry laughs and explains that she's referring to Donovan as the greatest of all time, which does admittedly sound better than an ornery animal who eats cans.

"So when do we get to meet him?" Sarah asks. She's the most

level-headed of the bunch, which means I know she's expecting my answer.

Deflect and divert!

"Never."

"Oh, come on, enough with the family curse nonsense," Annie says. "I've heard you talk about it, but every one of you has ended up happy, so I'm pretty sure there's nothing to it."

It's time for me to refill my glass, and I grimace at her. "Oh, no. I'm the reason the curse exists in the first place. It was before you and Finn met, but I know I told you about Jared."

Jared had been my boyfriend after Warren and all had been going well—right up until the night I brought him to meet my sisters and they ripped him apart. We broke up immediately afterward.

"I still say we did you a favor," Becca says, one clog dangling off the toes of her foot. She's still wearing her nursing scrubs, though she's pulled a hoodie on over her top. "Jared didn't respect you."

She was right. It may be the reason that we all still feel the need to get approval from the siblinghood before signing on officially with any new boyfriend. "I'll bring him to meet you eventually. I promise."

"I like it!" Finn says, wiping sweat from his forehead with his arm. "That means he's a keeper?"

I intend to nod vehemently. I don't intend to let out a loud sigh.

But that's what happens.

"Whoa. What's up?" he asks, stepping away from the barbecue to face me and folding his arms across his chest. "I heard that sigh from way over here."

Until I sighed—or maybe until I mindfully drove here—I didn't think anything was up. But facing the firing squad that is my family makes me honest. "I like him so much. It's not anything about him, but . . . I feel like I'm losing my edge."

Finn laughs. His face actually cracks the widest smile I've seen in a long time and his eyes crinkle at the corners. "How so?"

"I wasn't aware you had an edge. You're so nice to everyone. Unlike Becs and me," Cherry says.

"Hey," Becca says.

"Oh, come on." Cherry smirks. Becca hangs her head in concession.

"My edge at work." I throw up my hands and tell him all about what a scofflaw I've been, leaving early several times and feeling distracted from my job when I find myself thinking about Donovan.

"Okay, I get that," Isla says.

"I do too," Sarah adds, meeting my worried smile with her own.

"Thank you, fellow workaholics. I feel like I'm sacrificing time for my dating life and I know it's going to come back to bite me." I explain how I already failed at getting Donovan to participate in the VR game—just caved like a mound of wet sand because I like kissing the guy and even worse, I understand his reasons for not wanting to play. "I'm a person who gives into reason instead of putting career advancement above everything. Who knows what I'm capable of now?" My voice might sound a little hysterical. I scoop a handful of M&M's and shove them in my mouth.

Sarah sobers her expression and nods solemnly. "I understand."

"You do?" I ask with my mouth full of chocolate. Sarah never judges. Finn silently places a platter of peaches on the table next to a pint of vanilla ice cream and backs away. Barely focused, I heap some on a plate and sprinkle M&M's on top. Who cares that I haven't eaten dinner yet?

"Yes." She pats my hand and looks out at the tree view. "Your one significant relationship ended badly. You made a big sacrifice for Warren and it bit you in the ass. Of course you're gun shy. And Jared was just a loser." All my siblings look at me thoughtfully but not judgmentally, and all I can think is thank goodness I have people in my life who know my history and don't judge.

"But you need to give Donovan—and yourself—the benefit of the doubt and believe you can do better this time. Believe he's a better guy," Becca adds.

I digest her words and try to wrap my brain around this new concept. I'm rusty at believing.

"She's right. I'd hate to see you give up on love because of something that happened years ago with someone who didn't deserve you," Isla says.

"I only intended to give up on heartbreak," I admit. "I guess giving up on love came with it."

Isla nods. "I think it's great that you have someone in your life who makes you want something more than only a career. Try not to see everything as a sacrifice, and try not to see it as the beginning of the end. But don't lose sight of yourself either. That's the trick. Compromise when you can and stand your ground when you need to. I promise, you can make this work."

Compromise. It's a foreign concept.

I need to try that on for size.

"How do I not know these things?" I hear the agony in my own voice.

Sarah puts an arm around me, always my protector since our dad died when I was still in middle school. "You didn't have Dad to tell you this stuff. And he would have. The rest of us fell down on the job if we didn't help you along the way. But we're here now." Sarah's never admitted to any shortcomings as a sibling. None of them have. But I can see the guilt on their faces.

"Guys, it wasn't your job. But thank you."

There's some uncomfortable muttering and refilling of wineglasses.

"Hey, Cher, I may need to borrow another dress from you," I tell her, starting to outline a new plan in my head for how I can be with Donovan and not have it be the downfall of all my hard-fought success at work. Compromise.

I can go to dinner with Donovan on Friday night—it will satisfy my body and soul in a way that working late on a Friday night never could.

But I will not take time from my workday to shop for a dress. Not when my sister Cherry has a closetful of dresses and works right nearby. Thus will begin my effort to find work-life balance.

"Who's hungry?" Annie asks, bringing over another huge platter of food. Finn refills her wine and proposes a toast.

"To compromise, in all things except love," he says, leaning over to kiss his fiancée. They really are too damned cute. And it kind of makes me want to be just like them.

CHAPTER 25

atum

IT'S A GOOD DRESS, I'm not going to lie.

Someday, when I'm standing atop my career mountain and I do have time to shop for dresses, I will hire Cherry to be my personal stylist and spend my money on fashion instead of rent. Really, I will.

Until then, I can stand in front of my bathroom mirror and admire this dress.

First of all, it's red. Being a redhead—the only one in the family—Cherry has more red dresses than the average person. They look amazing with her complexion and hair.

At first, I was skeptical that I could pull off the bold color, but Cherry insisted. "Just try it on, you won't know until you try it on." I tried it on. Then my eyes nearly fell out of my head.

The dress transformed running muscles into curves, keyboard-proficient hands into grace, hoodie hair into intentional waves. We all need this dress.

Looking at it in my mirror at home, I'm still kind of astounded.

The mid-calf red fabric hugs my hips and gives my smallish breasts some kind of va-va-voom power that boosts them at least two cup sizes. Its plunging neckline leaves little to the imagination, but I want Donovan to understand that I take directions seriously. When he asks for a dress, I deliver a *dress*.

It takes me less time than usual to tame my frizz into waves with the blow-dryer and curling iron. And I manage to put on mascara and eyeliner without stabbing my eye. I'm getting better at this. With red lips and tall black heels, I'm just about ready to head out the door when I hear Donovan's knock.

Rifling through my purse to make sure I have my keys, I fling open the door without looking up.

"Wow." Donovan's one word reaction has heat racing across my cheeks before I have a chance to take him in. But when I do, I nearly lose my breath.

The man wears a suit like the future of the modern world depends on it. But I hope it doesn't, because all I can think of is how badly I'd like to rip the suit from his body thread by meticulous thread.

It's a navy suit that wraps his legs in a possessive hug while conveying casual model vibes with his upper half. No tie, white shirt, open at the collar. I can't stop staring, and I'm pretty sure someone turned up the heat in my apartment to over a hundred.

He's shaved, to the extent he does, which means his thicker beard is now a two-day sexy scruff. As if there was any way he could look sexier. His eyes gleam that sparkling green that forest lakes are made of, and they haven't left my body in the two minutes I've spent gawking at him.

He leans toward my cheek but instead of kissing it, his lips brush my neck, leaving a chill so rich and deep that my eyes flutter closed. "Cinderella . . . " he growls near my ear. "Holy fuck."

My lungs gasp unintentionally, and my heart begins a rampage in my chest.

I can barely swallow, barely breathe. The whisper of his breath on my neck sends ripples straight to my core and all I want to do is rub against him like a feral cat.

"I have to apologize," he says quietly when he backs away enough to bathe me in the light of his deep green eyes.

"Why? What's wrong?" I'm half expecting him to tell me he has to do something with the team tonight and we can't have dinner. But he's wearing a suit. And God, can he wear a suit.

He shakes his head, taking my hand and leading me into my apartment instead of out the door. When we get near my couch, he stops walking and sighs, his eyes slowly roaming over my body. "That dress . . . I'm afraid if I have to stare at you across the table all through dinner looking so goddamn gorgeous, I'll never make it out alive."

My mouth drops open. "Oh. I thought there was something really wrong."

"There is. C'mere," he commands, pulling me against him so I can feel how very hard he already is. His voice is a sexy rasp in my ear. "Fuck dinner. I want you as an appetizer. Now."

With my skin on fire and his lips blazing a white-hot trail, all I can do is nod my agreement and lose myself in the rapture of him.

I don't need dinner.

And mission accomplished with the dress.

"Yes. Good. Okay." How many different ways can I tell him how agreeable I am to his plans?

Expertly, without messing up a bit of my makeup, he has me so hot and bothered within seconds that I'm close to screaming his name. His lips trail along my jaw, his tongue following the plunging neckline of the dress, while I hold on to him for dear life, because otherwise I'll slide onto the floor and die in a heap of erotic bliss.

He flips me around so I'm bent over the couch and stands behind me, slowly lifting my dress like a seductive striptease, only I'm the one getting turned on.

He's so effortlessly sexy, and I love that I can induce a reaction that brings him to his knees. And he's on his knees with my dress now lifted over my hips, and he grabs onto my thong underwear with his teeth, pulling it down my legs and off.

"Cinderella, you know I find your brilliance and your wit sexier than anything, but damn, you in this dress is the cherry on top of the most decadent sundae I've ever wanted to eat."

Then, he does.

His tongue, his lips, his hands . . . He drinks me in like I'm a delicacy and unleashes a rolling orgasm that builds and builds until my entire apartment looks like the night sky full of stars and my entire body is ringing like a bell.

I'm pretty sure that's my voice I hear moaning his name, but I'm only half conscious, still lifted on the high of how he makes me feel. I fold like a limp noodle over my couch as he sweeps my hair off the back of my neck and his lips dance across the skin. But it's his reassuring hands on my bare arms and the warmth of his touch that confirm how much I want him in ways that have nothing to do with sex.

"That was the appetizer," his voice rumbles before he kisses the skin near my ear. His scruff tickles and makes my body ache at the same time. Holding me close as my breathing returns to normal, Donovan nuzzles my neck and whispers, "Let's go have dinner. Then come back here, and I'll have you again for dessert."

He slowly, carefully slips the thong back over my feet and slides it up my legs, then I feel the swish of fabric as he releases my dress. When he turns me around to face him, his eyes appraise me seriously. "Don't think I messed you up too much. Do you need a minute or anything?"

I shake my head. I'm not willing to spend even a second away from him. I slip my hand in his, interlacing our fingers. "Let's go."

UNSURPRISINGLY, The Tailor's Son is packed. The Italian eatery keeps popping up on lists of San Francisco's hottest restaurants, and I can understand why. Every bite of food is off the charts delicious.

Ever in training mode, Donovan manages to find the plainest piece of broiled fish on the menu, along with some vegetable sides, but I go straight for the pasta and don't look back. "I will have zero regrets about these carbs," I tell him. "You sure you don't want a bite?" I hold up a square of ravioli and watch him look down at his plate of fish and back up at the sauce-laden pasta.

"I absolutely want a bite," he says, wrapping his hand lightly around mine while I guide the fork to his mouth. "Mmm, that's good."

"Right? Surely, you don't have to live like a monk all the time."

"Oh, I don't. But when I don't know the restaurant well, I tend to order conservatively. Sometimes they slip in half a stick of butter in one dish, and that kills me the next day on the field."

I'm surprised he doesn't know this place since he picked it. "How'd you decide on this spot for dinner?"

"Oh, it was recommended to me."

Out of the corner of my eye, I notice a few cellphones pointed in our direction, surreptitiously, of course. People pretend to be typing a text, but no one texts with a phone aimed across the room. "I hate to break it to you, but people are probably taking your picture. You may end up on some Instagram feeds or something."

I'm surprised, actually, that Donovan didn't request a change when the host brought us to the small table for two in the center of the restaurant. Not only is it not in the back, where we've sat every time we've eaten out, but pretty much everyone here has a side view of him. Maybe he's hiding in plain sight or something.

He looks around, his expression uneasy, but then he refocuses on me and smiles. "You're the only person in the room I see. It's fine. I doubt these people care about what I'm doing."

"It kind of seems like they care a lot. I'm glad you're relaxing a bit about social media and all that."

He exhales and looks back at his fish. "Trying."

Donovan's a little quieter than usual, but I chalk that up to his slight discomfort about being in such a public place. I too am aware of how public this date feels. I'm not thrilled about the idea of people at work seeing photos of me out with Donovan, but I try to convince myself no selfie stalker cares who I am. Any cellphones will be aimed at Donovan. I force myself to relax.

The exclamation point on our dinner comes when the chef visits our table with a special fruit tart which he promises is packed with antioxidants to help with athletic recovery. Donovan eats a few bites of the fruit, and I devour most of the sweet cream and buttery crust.

In the back of my mind—okay, it's front and center—I'm only thinking about the dessert that was promised to me earlier. So when Donovan asks if I'm ready to head out, I can only swallow thickly and nod.

"Take me home, footballer."

"Let's go." His voice is gravelly and deep, and I'm not sure I'll make it all the way home without needing to jump him. But I agree to try.

As we leave the restaurant, Donovan drapes an arm around my shoulders and pulls me close. The second we step outside the restaurant, he turns my face toward his with two fingers and kisses me sweetly.

A second later, I'm nearly blinded by flashbulbs from several cameras all snapping photos at once.

A chorus of "Donno!" "Donno, is that your girlfriend? Who are you with?" "Donno!" erupts from the paparazzi who must have been tipped off that Donovan was inside. My heart starts pounding along with a fight-or-flight instinct I didn't know I had. The onslaught is relentless, and I feel Donovan's large hand tighten around mine.

He leans to whisper in my ear, "Just smile. I'll get us out of here."

I do as I'm told, glad I'm at least wearing a nice dress as the bulbs continue to flash in my face. Smiling uncomfortably, I let Donovan usher us away from the throng, but not before we've basically posed for them and given them exactly what they want.

"Okay, enough," Donovan commands, holding up a hand and blocking us from view as he escorts me around the corner and away. The hubbub dies down behind us, but one ballsy photographer jogs along with us, snapping additional photos. "I said enough," Donovan says, more forcefully this time, pulling me in protectively.

The man backs off, but we keep walking quickly until we're a good block away from the restaurant. "I'm so sorry," he says. "I didn't expect that to happen."

"It's fine. It comes with the territory, I guess. Did that happen a lot in England?"

He rubs a hand through his hair and seems to search the distance for an answer. "Not like that, no. But I told you, I never kissed anyone I've dated in public."

"Maybe that's a good policy for here."

"Maybe so." He closes his eyes and inhales. "Look, I don't know where those photos will end up—hopefully on some blog nobody reads—but in case one of those guys works for *People* magazine or something and they do end up all over the place . . . I just want you to know, there's no one in the world I'd rather be caught kissing in public than you."

It's a sweet sentiment, but I'm still unnerved. I tell myself to chill. This is not a big deal.

"I get it. You play on a global stage. You belong to the world—you have tons of fans and they're going to want your picture. It's okay." I'm not sure it's really okay with me yet, but I'm trying to make it okay by saying the words.

Donovan reaches a hand toward me and cups my chin in his palm. "There's only one fan I care about. And I'd give up the rest of them to belong to you."

My heart rate had finally begun to drop now that we'd lost sight of the photographers, but his words have it hammering in my chest again.

And once again, I feel the pull of emotion. I'm not crazy about having my picture on a fan site, but he makes me not care about any of it.

When I look up at him, trying to find the right words to explain that, I'm surprised at the sudden intensity of his gaze. He's not looking at the dress or my body. Our eyes lock in a vise grip, and I feel the weight of what his are telling me. Then he says it out loud. "I love you, Cinder. I know this is still new, and maybe—"

I lay a finger against his lips to stop him. "Wait. Don't take away from what you just said by qualifying it."

His eyes close again and his face looks momentarily pained. But when he opens his eyes, there's certainty. And joy. "I'm in love with you. That's the takeaway."

My smile spreads so wide it hurts my cheeks. And I feel it too, the irrefutable truth that I've been denying in my head.

I love him. I. Love. Him.

And yet . . . I feel so tentative admitting it to myself that I'm not sure I'm ready to tell him. I don't want him to think it's a knee-jerk reaction to what he just said.

"Donovan, you make me so happy. And I hope you can feel it, and I hope you know it, but—" Now he presses the tip of his finger to my lips, just as I did a moment ago.

"You don't have to say anything. Not until you're ready. I just needed you to know. I love you." Hearing him say the words sends a thrill of warmth blossoming in my chest and sends a glorious chill over my skin.

I stand on my toes to reach his lips, but he bends down and envelops me in his arms, kissing me softly. Then so deeply it curls my toes.

He only pulls back enough to whisper in my ear, "I'm ready for dessert."

CHAPTER 26

onovan

"Okay, sounds good," I tell Jordan when he calls me at nine in the morning after his paparazzi ambush. I say it mostly to get him off the phone because the man could go on for days with his self-congratulatory yammering.

"Great, will be in touch, chief." His high-pitched voice grates on my nerves at this hour of the morning, but given how happy he is that I got the kind of media attention he wanted, I rest content in the idea that I might not hear from him for a couple days.

I hang up and slip back into my bedroom where Tatum sleeps peacefully in my bed, her hair tangled from all the ways I had my hands in it last night and her lips puffy from being kissed for hours.

I love the way she looks, and I'm not excited about waking her to let her know about the photos of us kissing on the *People* magazine website and hashtags like "Donno's girlfriend" trending across all social media.

Watching her sleep calms me, and I slip back between the sheets, wrap an arm around her, and pull her against my chest. Her even breathing feels like a mantra telling me to do the same —inhale, exhale, focus on the present.

But I can't. I feel like I'm living two lives at the moment, one for public consumption and one for myself. Back in England, I was never so acutely aware of the difference between the two. Maybe because there was no difference. Everything I did was in service of the game, and I accepted it.

That was before her.

Before she occupied all of my thoughts when I'm not on the pitch. Before she made a sacrifice in her career goals out of respect for me.

I should tell Tatum that the scene outside the restaurant was a planned publicity stunt to help my image. She'll understand why I didn't want her to worry about it all through dinner.

Then why didn't you tell her last night?

My fear that she won't understand—or worse, feel like I'm rubbing the importance of my career in her face—kept me up for most of the night. I don't want her to feel like a pretty prop.

But you used her for exactly that.

Tatum stirs in my arms and her hand comes to rest on where mine have encircled her. She rolls to the side and I see the sleepy contentment in her face. "Hi," she says, a lazy smile pulling at her cheeks and casting a glow over her face.

"G'morning." I kiss her lightly, my eyes drifting shut when she sighs. "I made coffee."

"Mmm, smart man." She pats my arm and rolls the rest of the way to face me. My vision blurs as I take in her features at close range. I don't even realize I'm furrowing my brow until she reaches up and smooths the lines with her finger. "What's wrong? That's a lot of forehead wrinkling for first thing in the morning."

I slide away a bit so I can see her face clearly, overwhelmed by the wisdom in her gorgeous eyes and how much I want to devour her lips. But first things first. "The pictures from last night are everywhere. I'm sorry."

She takes a long blink, then makes an effort at a smile. "Well, we kind of knew that would happen, right? I mean, that was the point."

For a second, I think she means it was the point of arranging the photo op. "Yeah, I mean, sure. But people have the attention span of a flea. Before the end of today, they'll have moved on and no one will care."

"So where are they, exactly? And do they have captions?"

I take out my phone and we scroll through the ones Jordan gathered for me. Most of them say a version of the same thing, "Donno hits the town with a new girlfriend," "Donno a lover, not a fighter." I know the second one was fed to the media expressly by Jordan.

"So I'm your girlfriend now?" she asks with a wry smile.

"You are. According to *People* magazine and all the gossip blogs worth reading."

"Well, then it must be true."

I kiss her forehead and roll off the bed. "You're a good sport. I appreciate it. I appreciate you." I bend and kiss her more deeply. "And to show my appreciation, I'm bringing you coffee in bed."

She nods and takes my phone, scrolling through the pictures more slowly. "We make a cute couple."

"We do." I smile to myself as I go to the kitchen and grab two mugs and add cream to both before pouring in the coffee. For the first time since Jordan called me at the crack of dawn, I feel sort of okay. Maybe I overreacted. Tatum seems okay with the photos, Jordan's off my case, and now I can fully focus on soccer, the reason I'm here.

But when I get back to the bedroom, I find Tatum glaring at my phone, consternation in her face. I immediately mourn the loss of her carefree morning expression.

Handing over her cup of coffee, I sit next to where she's curled up on the bed, one hand supporting her cheek like it carries the weight of the world. I rub a hand on her back. "You okay?"

Forehead creased in thought, she doesn't look at me. "What are people at my job going to think? That instead of doing my job, I seduced you for my personal enjoyment?"

I swallow hard. "If they think that, they're assholes."

"I work with a lot of assholes."

She sits up and sips the coffee. She's silent after that and I can't tell what she's thinking.

"You know the truth. Does it matter what other people think?" I ask.

Her eyes have a faraway look. "You tell me. Is that why you didn't talk to the press after you hit your sister's ex? Because you didn't care?"

"Pretty much." So why do I feel like such a hypocrite?

She holds up the photo of us kissing and points to the headline, "Donno's new flame." "I'll just have to work a little harder, make them see past this."

An anguished frown spreads across my face. "Tatum, I'm so sorry."

Nodding, she rests her head against my chest, and I wrap an arm around her. "I know. It's not your fault."

But it is. I need to tell her.

I will.

"Tatum . . . " I don't have all the words yet, but I'll make them up as I go. I have to lay it all out there. "I—"

She waves a hand and cuts me off. "You know what? It's fine. I'm a big girl, I can handle this. If people at work want to know who I'm dating, well, now they know. It has no bearing on how well I do my job. So yeah, I really don't care what they think."

"Yeah? Really?"

Sipping her coffee, Tatum leans more fully against me and my body hums at the feel of her melting into me. "Really. And besides, there's that big preseason Strikers thing at the stadium next weekend. People I work with are going to see us together then, so what's the difference if they see a little tongue action in the media before that?"

"Hey, I was a perfect gentleman. There was no tongue action," I argue, loving this woman more every day for her thoughtfulness and enormous heart. "But there will be now." I grab her coffee and slide it onto the nightstand before tackling her on the bed.

She yelps and pulls me in closer. I never want to let her go.

CHAPTER 27

atum

People at work are more interested in who I'm dating than I expected.

Mostly, people are excited to point out someone they know in the social media parade of pictures that have multiplied like bunnies in springtime.

By noon, everyone has returned to the more important mission of getting actual work done. Paul is the only one who continues to comment throughout the day. "Who knew you had a body like that under all those hoodies?" he says, going out of his way to pass by my desk on his way to the coffee room.

I pop my noise canceling headphones on in response.

"I don't know why you don't wear dresses like that to work," he says on another pass by my desk, blowing up one of the social media pics on his phone and showing me his view of my cleavage.

Terrance shoots me a look from across the room, and I roll my eyes. Paul isn't worth the fight.

The only one I'm worried about is Charlie, and as expected, he texts me before the end of the day.

Boss Man: Please come to my office

Me: Coming

Charlie waits in his doorway, hand extended and ready to shake mine. He never stands and waits for me. I can't decide if there's meaning behind it.

"Nice to see you, Tatum," he says, expressionless.

"You too."

I follow him into his office, where he sits behind his desk and squints at his computer screen while I perch on the edge of a chair.

"I'd like to get an update from you since you've had a chance to spend some time with Donovan Taylor. Can you gauge his interest in participating in the game?"

I stare at him, trying to parse his still-blank expression. He's looking at his computer while he waits for my response. It appears that he's going to make no mention of the photos of me with Donovan, if he's even seen them. Though I assume he has.

Still, I'm a professional and I don't need to draw attention to my personal life. He's asking me if Donovan will participate and I intend to give him an honest answer.

"I don't think he's going to come around. He's impressed with the technology, but right now, it's a no. He's not interested in participating." I don't give him more specifics. It's not my place to specify Donovan's reasons.

Charlie nods. "I see." He blinks a couple times and presses his lips together. I feel like I've disappointed him. It hurts to have to tell him I've failed at the mission he set before me. "Well, you did your best, I'm sure."

I swallow hard. Did I do my best? I could have pushed Donovan harder, but after seeing the pain in his eyes when he talked about his sister and lack of privacy that leaves him feeling like there's almost nothing left of himself, how could I? I can't ask him to give that up so I can lobby for a promotion.

"I really did," I tell Charlie, wanting to say more, but I can't form a sentence from the jumble of thoughts in my brain.

"Okay, then." He's not looking at me anymore, and I know that means I'm being dismissed from our impromptu meeting. But I can't just leave this heaping turd pile behind without trying once more to reassure Charlie I'm fit to lead the project.

I stand up, but instead of turning for the door, I speak directly to Charlie over his desk. "His participation aside, I still see the absolute value and potential of the game, and I really can contribute a lot to the creative process. So I hope you'll still consider me to lead it up."

Charlie meets my gaze and nods. Then his eyes return to his screen, and I know we're finished with the conversation.

As I turn to go back to my desk, I give myself a mental pat on the back for being ambitious and asking for what I've earned, all the while blinking back the sting of failure.

CHAPTER 28

atum

IT'S BEEN a few days now since the photos were posted of Donovan and me, and as predicted, it's been a nonissue with my coworkers, with the exception of Paul, who continues to make comments on the kind of dress he thinks I should wear to work.

Sadly, since we'll both be at the Strikers event later on, I'll have to endure the unfortunate collision of my body in a dress with Paul in the same place at the same time. I will endure.

Donovan and I agree to meet at the event since it's at the stadium which sits about halfway between his place and mine, and I barely have time after work to get showered, dressed, and over to the event.

And in typical fashion when I need to deal with hair and makeup, I'm running late.

My only hope is that I don't have to walk another gauntlet of seated guests.

I guess I lack imagination. Somehow after going to the

Strikers sponsorship banquet last month, I assumed this event would mirror the stodgy dinner. And after the requisite announcements and handshaking, Donovan and I would be free to leave.

Not. At. All.

First of all, the Strikers VIP lounge feels more like a raucous cocktail party full of drunk important people. I can't imagine who all these folks are, but I imagine they're corporate sponsors and people who work for those companies that merited an invitation just like the people in our office. They all want a piece of the glory that is the Strikers team before a season everyone hopes they'll win.

I feel like I've walked into the nicest sports bar in the history of the world. Flatscreen TVs showing team highlights beam down from the walls, retro light fixtures bathe everyone in a flattering warm glow, and the dark hide leather on the booths and chairs give the place an upscale steakhouse vibe.

A large circular bar sits in the center of the room, and the line is three-deep to get drinks. I don't see Donovan anywhere, but that's probably because at least three hundred well-dressed people have arrived before me, and a parade of women in cocktail dresses and men in suits files in after me. I had no idea this event would be so huge.

Terrance shoots me a smile from across the room, where he has his arm around his wife, and it looks like most of the Vivi-Tech group is already here, but I decide to grab myself a drink at the bar before going over to them

After raiding Cherry's closet twice now, I finally broke down and went shopping for a dress, which I'm wearing tonight. At the risk of betraying my hoodie collection, I have to admit I love it.

It's a navy-blue sleeveless sheath with one bare shoulder and a skirt that hits just above the knee. The high nude pumps put me over five feet eight, and when I surveyed the full effect in the tall mirror in my bathroom, I felt good.

My hair is cooperating and falls in soft waves. And as usual, I went for the red lips.

As I jockey to get the attention of one of the bartenders through the throng of people, I feel a hand on my arm. Hoping Donovan has managed to find me in this crowd, I turn, but it's not him.

"We haven't met before. I'm Jordan," slurs a small-eyed turd of a man who smells like alcohol and leers a little. He doesn't remove his hand from my arm, so I extend mine for him to shake it.

"Nice to meet you. I'm Tatum."

The bartender nods at me, and I ask him for a vodka and soda.

Jordan removes his hand from my arm and gives me an overly strong handshake. I turn away from him and thank the bartender for the drink, half hoping that when I turn around Jordan will be gone. He's probably moved on to meet and greet someone else in the room.

But no, he lingers, and I feel his eyes roaming over my body from head to toe and back again.

This is why I don't wear dresses.

I take a step away, thinking I'll head back to the bar and refill my drink, but Jordan puts a paw on my arm. again "Hey, don't go. We haven't had a chance to chat."

"Okay . . . " I don't want to be rude to him. Maybe he's a teammate or someone high up on the Strikers food chain. The last thing I need right now is to lose more points with Charlie for not being a team player.

"This must be exciting for you," he says.

I'm not sure what he's getting at, so I smile. "For everyone. Team's looking like they'll have a great season."

"Not what I meant." His smile makes him look like a rodent.

"Oh. What did you mean?" *Who is this guy?*

His eyes sweep over my exposed skin, and I wish I'd brought a parka. He shakes his head. "Nothing."

I feel the weight of eyes on me, and I turn to see Paul watching me carefully. I'm not even sure why, since it's clear I've failed to convince Donovan to agree to participate in the game. That soaring line on my career trajectory is grounded for the time being.

Nevertheless, Paul watches me like he's waiting for something, lurking a few paces away. It might creep me out, except that's just Paul.

Meanwhile, the slurring man in front of me has started talking again, so I force my gaze back to his round bespectacled face and focus on the nouns and verbs rolling out of his mouth. "Anyhow, I 'preciate it."

"Sorry, what?" I smile, feeling bad that I missed what he said.

"Thanks for agreeing to the photo op so I could work my magic."

"Oh, is there a photo thing tonight?" *Did I agree to be in a picture?*

My confusion must show on my face because he explains. "Not tonight. Last week, at the restaurant? That was you, right? Or did I just stick my foot in my mouth?" His disingenuous laugh sounds like a cackle.

"Oh, that. Yes." I still don't know why he's thanking me.

"Think it was successful. Donovan's the hottest bachelor in town. People are eating it up."

"Okay, well I guess it's lucky that photographer happened to get a decent shot, then."

Craning my head to look past him, I try to spot Donovan. From the continual flash of bulbs in one corner of the bar, I have to assume he's there with his teammates, and I debate wading back into paparazzi hell to get away from this small drunk man.

"Well, it wasn't luck. It's called planning. Image maintenance. That's my job, it's what I do, and I'm good at it."

"Oh, okay. Well, congrats." I start to take a step away, but he stops me. Not done preening.

"Thank you. I know it sounds like I'm tooting my own horn, but I was right. Having pics of him with a woman got him trending again. Gossip sites are posting glam shots. People talking about Donno's sex appeal, women wanting to fuck him. We flipped the script. Got people to finally stop fixating on that goddamned fight and start talking about him as the sexiest man in sports."

The pieces start falling into place, and a sick feeling builds in my stomach. "He knew there would be photographers outside the restaurant." It's a statement because the more I think about it—he asked me to wear a dress, he didn't sit facing the wall, and he opted to use the front door of the restaurant—the more I know Jordan is telling the truth.

Donovan made me part of a photo op to flex his manhood and help his image. His game. That's his world. He couldn't admit it to me outright, so maybe he hoped I wouldn't notice.

"Excuse me," I say to Jordan, not waiting for a response. I need some air, and I need time to sort through all the signs I missed over the past month that Donovan needs me in his life as a female fixture, nothing more.

The bar crowd has thinned out now that people have moved through the room to watch some of the highlight footage on the flatscreens and take small plates of sliders, spicy chicken wings, and fries. I grab one more vodka soda and search the crowd for Donovan.

Bingo. Far corner, surrounded by people in suits and a few players I recognize from watching game footage. I know this is not the time or place to get into it with him, but I can't help it.

My face burns hot with betrayal, and I just need a tiny confirmation of what I hope is true—that Jordan was blowing smoke, trying to congratulate himself for doing good publicity management, and Donovan knew nothing about what he'd planned.

That thought rolls through my brain on a loop the closer I get to Donovan, willing my version of the story to be true. Frantically fearful it isn't.

When I'm a few paces away, Donovan turns and catches sight of me. His green eyes sparkle with affection, and he smiles so widely his dimples practically jump off his face.

It's painful how much I love this man. Not just for the way his gorgeous exterior sears the blood in my veins like a branding iron. But for the man I'm still getting to know, the man I hope I will let me in. The man I fear has not and never will.

He holds an arm out to me, beckoning me closer and folding me into him when I'm near enough to touch. My body does its usual boneless melt against him, but my brain is on fire. I know it's the wrong time, but . . .

"Did you know the paparazzi would be at the restaurant the other night?" I ask him as he leans to brush a soft kiss against my lips.

He immediately stiffens—I feel it in his arm around my waist. Pulling his face back a couple inches, his eyes study me. "What?"

"Did you know? When you told me you love me in a dress, was it because you wanted me to look good in your publicity pictures, for your image?"

"That's not what . . . " He closes his eyes, knowing better than to lie to me. At least he respects me that much, but not more. "Yes, I knew. But—"

"It's your career. The game. It's everything. Yeah, I get it."

"No, it's not like that—"

I don't wait to hear more. Staring into his eyes so he's forced to see the hurt in mine, I leave my drink on the nearest tray and pull out of Donovan's grip, moving away. I need to get out of the room before all the available oxygen is depleted, at least that's how it feels as I struggle to breathe. The sickening lump in my throat makes it impossible to swallow, and all I can focus on is the door leading out of the room.

Before I can get there, Paul steps in my path, his eyes hateful but also bleary from the alcohol. I guess I'm the only one who didn't get the memo that the Strikers party is a drunk fest.

Paul lurches to the side when I push past him and keep going. But he follows me, calling my name. When I ignore him, he gets louder.

"Finley!" Paul says, his voice whiny and irritating. I don't want to make a scene, so I turn to meet his smug expression. He'll never miss one more chance to order me around in front of other people. But I'm not interested in being a team player right now.

My gaze again shifts to Donovan. I can't take my eyes off the shocked resignation on his face. I need to see it, to commit it to memory, in order to make it easier to remind myself he's not the man I thought he was. "Paul, give me a minute."

"Why, so you can go fuck in a closet until he signs onto the VR game?"

I close my eyes against the hurt of his words. "That's not what this is," I say through gritted teeth.

"Excuse me?" The deep, menacing sound of Donovan's voice is nothing compared to the look of disgust on his face. "What the fuck did you just say to my girlfriend?"

"Oh, she's your girlfriend now? That's rich. She must really be great in bed," Paul says, the ugly in him seeping out with every word he says. He has the gall to look bored.

Donovan inhales a deep breath, his fists clenching by his sides.

I lean in, keeping my voice calm. "Ignore him. He's a little shit. Not worth it."

Paul is a good six inches shorter than Donovan, but he tries to get in his face, puffing out his feeble chest. The man is insane.

"I said fucking her way into a promotion isn't gonna get her respect at work."

"Shut the fuck up." Donovan's voice is menacing, his eyes tearing into Paul. I watch his hands, aware that he absolutely can't lift a finger against Paul, with the way the England fight followed him for so long.

Paul is drunk and out of his mind, but people have gathered around and he's enjoying putting on a show, basking in his fifteen seconds of fame. "Did you just touch me? Don't fucking touch me."

"He didn't touch you," I say, glaring at him. "Paul, stop it."

He ignores me, his eyes fixed on Donovan and a sad little smile pulling at the corner of his mouth. Paul gives Donovan a shove, but the man's a wall of muscle and doesn't move. Paul has to know that if he gets into a real shoving match, he'll lose.

His antics have grabbed people's attention and I notice a couple cellphones pointed in their direction. "Paul! You're embarrassing yourself. Let. It. Go," I tell him, trying to meet Donovan's gaze, but he won't take his eyes off of Paul.

I loop my arm through his and speak softly, "Hey, just walk away." I know I can't make him move if he doesn't want to, so I heave a sigh of relief when Donovan starts to move. He steps stiffly, as though he's not sure he wants to follow me, but he does.

From behind me, Paul spits out a final insult, "Slut."

Donovan spins on his heel and takes two long strides to tower over Paul. In a split second, he could break his face. I see the loss of control. I understand his need to be more than a bystander to an injustice, but this isn't his fight. It can't be.

"No!" I lunge at Donovan and grab onto him as he's starting to cock his arm. I can't let him do it. Not now. Not over me. He looks down at me and I see the fury burning in his eyes, and in seconds it turns to pleading. He wants to deck this guy so badly.

"I know. He's an asshole. Just . . . walk away. Please." I have his arm in a death grip and can't take my eyes from his face which is fucking anguished, searching mine for clues for what to do. His eyes bear the sadness he feels looking at me, knowing he's betrayed my trust.

I shake my head. "Leave it alone. Please," I plead. He swallows hard and his chest heaves. But he tries to control his emotions and the craziness starts to settle out of his expression.

"Fucking stay away from her." His voice is ice. He glares at Paul, who finally seems to realize he's going to get the crap beaten out of him, if not by Donovan then by one of his teammates.

A few of them huddle around him and the heat in the room dissipates.

The shock of Paul's remarks sting, but a much deeper hurt takes root in my chest and makes it hard to breathe. Donovan lied to me. And worse, he put his career first without even talking to me about how it would impact me or the way people at work might see me.

As soon as I can feel my mind clear enough to make the next decision, I know I need to get out of this room. I need to leave and think through what Jordan just told me and reconcile it with Paul's words.

Nausea bubbles up into my throat, and I feel like I might throw up. I can't do anything else to add to the mortification I already feel under the eyes of each person in this room who witnessed what just went down.

My lungs throb, desperate for air. And I need to run as far from here as I can get.

I move quickly, walking away from Donovan and the scene at the bar as quickly as I can in the se too-high heels. Heels I wore for him. Screw it. I bend down and slip the straps off the backs of my shoes and pick them up so I can jog at a faster pace. The more distance I can create between us, the better.

But he's on my heels, following me out to the parking lot, past gawking teammates, sponsors, and, unfortunately, my boss.

Charlie stands with his mouth agape, watching one of his best coders have a meltdown. He says nothing, but I see the surprise on his face.

It's not enough I failed to do what he asked. Now I'm embarrassing him at his event. "Sorry," I mouth as I pass him. He shakes his head, but I can't even care about it right now.

"Tatum, wait. Let's go someplace and talk," Donovan calls. I can't form words, so I keep walking, but it only takes a second for his large stride to bring him next to me.

I stop abruptly and face him. "Now? Now, you want to talk? You intentionally avoided telling me your little photo op was planned. Why would I even believe anything you decide to tell me now?"

"Because I swear I'll be honest."

"It's too late for that. You don't get to tell multiple versions of the same story. I know the way this one ends." I meet his eyes and see regret, but I push past the pain. "Please don't follow me. Please, Donovan." I don't even recognize the sound of my own voice. It's choked and strained.

But I start walking again, moving through the bowels of the stadium toward the parking lot. I don't think he's following me, but I can't look back.

Damn this narrow skirt for hindering my speedy getaway. He catches up to me in seconds, reaching for my arm. I swat him away and wrap my arms over my chest protectively.

"Tatum, wait. Don't go," he pleads and the pain in his voice twists the knife in my back even more. I love him so much that I can't bear to hurt him, even though he just gutted me.

"I have to. Just . . . please. Let me leave."

"Not without a conversation. I don't know what Jordan told you, but you saw him, he's drunk and everything's about working an angle with him. That's not how it was."

I whip around and face him. "No? So you didn't know photographers would be there that night? You didn't tell me to dress nicely so I'd look better in the pictures, make you look better? You didn't plan it to save your image—kiss me outside the restaurant where you knew there'd be cameras and then said you loved me as some sort of apology?"

He looks like I just knocked the wind out of him.

His face falls and I see the truth, even though a tiny part of me did hope he'd tell me I was wrong, that it was all Jordan, that he didn't know either. But it's clear in his expression that he knew. He just hoped I wouldn't find out.

"I have to go," I say, already walking away. I have to. I can't stay near him. If I breathe his intoxicating scent and allow myself to get lost in the depths of his eyes, I'll cave. I need to walk away.

"Then I'm coming with you. I need to explain."

"You're not listening to me. I don't want to hear your explanation. I get it. This is why you're here, to be a marquee soccer player, with all that entails. I don't begrudge you that. I just . . . can't be a part of it."

"Where does that leave me?"

"You need to go back in there. It's your team. It's why you're here—for soccer. This is your night."

As I say the words, a tiny pleading voice in the recesses of my brain is begging me not to say them. Begging Donovan to disagree and tell me I have it wrong. He loves me and that is bigger and more important than his job.

Tell me you don't believe the romance novel in your head.

I'm smarter than that. Donovan is his job. It's all he knows.

Even though it's been eight years, the replay of walking away from my ex rings eerily familiar. No, I didn't feel about him the way I do about Donovan. I doubt I'll ever feel the way I do about anyone again. Minor details.

"You'd get a promotion if I agreed to be part of the game?" he asks me, his expression stony.

I freeze.

I've never told him that part. It stopped mattering weeks ago. But I know how it probably looks. I nod, and a pit forms in my throat when I try to swallow, tears welling without permission. I hate it. "I wanted to run the division."

"That's not what I asked you." His voice is strained, his gaze unyielding. He can't possibly believe what Paul is saying.

I can't even form the words over the lump in my throat, and I'm desperate not to let him see me cry.

I swallow hard and force myself into composure. "There was talk that if I could convince you to be part of the game . . . it would prove something to my boss and I'd get the job. But once I understood your reasons . . . that part . . . it didn't matter to me anymore. I respect why you don't want to do it, and I told Charlie it's not going to happen. I care more about you than my career. Because I'm an idiot and I don't learn from my mistakes."

He reaches a hand for me but I back away. If he touches me, I know I'll cave. His heat will get under my skin, and I'll lose a piece of myself again. And right now, I fear that I only have a little piece left.

"Let me explain," he says, his hands up.

I shake my head as the tears well up because I can't hear what he has to say. I can't let myself be influenced by how much I love him.

It will break me.

"I can't" I manage to choke out. "You know me . . . I trusted you. You could've just . . . said."

The sob I've been pushing down comes up like a croak, and I put both hands over my eyes. I need to block him from my sight as much as I don't want him to see me falling apart.

He could have said something. He didn't.

I don't need to hear anything from him now.

So I turn and start walking away. Aching with sudden fatigue, I don't have it in me to run, and for a moment I worry he'll come after me and belabor this. But I guess he really does know me because I don't hear footsteps following me.

He doesn't belabor it.

Because he knows as well as I do that there's nothing left to say.

CHAPTER 29

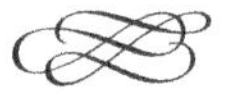

atum

After a weekend in pajamas with two bags of mini Snickers and a whole lot of Netflix, I'm in even worse shape than I was on Friday night. It's some sort of chocolate hangover accompanied by dark circles under my puffy eyes and exhaustion even though I barely got out of bed.

So on Monday, I take my first ever personal day.

I use it to clean my apartment. Then I grocery shop. Then I clean it again.

Then I drive to Oakland, recruit Becca to go for a lake swim, get Isla to go on a hill run, and even convince Finn to meet me for a bike ride. Who says I need an official race day to finish a triathlon before most normal people have climbed out of bed?

When I've run out of tasks and it's still before noon, I fall like a lump on my sofa with a frozen pizza I've undercooked and watch reruns of the *Great British Bakeoff*. My eyes are bleary from lack of sleep and various muscle groups ache due to the misfortune of being attached to me.

Three episodes in, I'm salivating over biscuits and jelly roll cakes when I hear a knock at my door. Deciding not to get up, I turn up the volume on *Bakeoff* and stay where I am.

The knocking gets louder, and I hear my cellphone ping with a text.

Joan: Open your door before I drop my cheese plate

Sighing to myself, I hoist my sweatpants-clad body from the couch and go to the door. "Is there really a cheese plate?" I ask, opening the door a crack and peeking through.

"And wine!" a voice practically yells behind Joan.

I pull the door open and gape at Cherry, whose red jeans, heeled sandals, and blousy white shirt make her look like a peasant fashionista. "Why aren't you at work?" I ask.

"Why aren't you?" she counters, holding up two bottles of wine and pushing past Joan to enter the apartment.

"Personal day. And come on in." I grimace, unsure how I feel about doing my wallowing with other people. Cherry and I already spoke over the weekend, and I gave her a recap of what went down at the Strikers party, so I know she's not here for details. "I assume Cherry told you about my depressing life," I say, ushering Joan in as well.

Joan does look like she's in danger of dropping the oversized cheese board which overflows with cheeses, crackers, bread, all kinds of fruit and condiments, and oddly, a bowl of garlic croutons. The sight of them unleashes a new wave of sadness I hadn't thought existed after two days of my heart aching like I'd experienced a death. Maybe I had—the death of hope.

By the time I close the door and turn to face my uninvited guests, Joan has set the cheese board on the plank top of my coffee table and Cherry has made herself at home in my kitchen, bustling through cabinets and drawers.

She emerges victorious with a corkscrew and glasses,

gesturing with her shoulder for me to sit. The two of them are like a gale force I'm powerless to face down alone.

"I feel like I'm going to get a lecture, and before you say a word, just stop. Okay? I'm fine and I just needed a day off from work. That's what personal days are for, no big deal," I say pointedly, shooting a death glare at Cherry.

She cackles and twists the corkscrew. "Whatever, Tater Tot. You've never taken a personal day in your life, so don't pretend this is normal. That's why we're here—to entertain you so you stop wallowing."

"Great. And you recruited poor Joan to skip work and participate in your nonsense?"

Joan waves me off and leans so far back in my plush recliner she has to talk over her body. "I don't work Mondays, remember? Traded 'em for Saturdays."

"Oh. Right." *Why am I arguing with them? They're not leaving.*

Cherry pours generous glasses full of sauvignon blanc and hands me one. Taking a sip of hers, she says, "Oh, this is a good day-drinking wine. Refreshing."

I put my glass on the table without taking a sip and sink back into the couch with an arm over my eyes. "I'm not in the mood to be refreshed."

Cherry ignores me. And by ignores, I mean she spends the next half hour talking about anything and everything except how I'm feeling and how I shouldn't be wallowing in misery. Deflection turns out to be a decent strategy. I try my hardest to focus on her stories and not let my mind wander back to myself.

"I think I ate salads every day last week, and not because the place near our office is any good. I just kept getting there so late that everyone else already ate all the good sandwiches," she says before going into a soliloquy about the merits of various lunch foods.

The normal Tatum would jump at the foodie geekdom and supply my own useless knowledge about snacks. But she's lost somewhere, numb to interesting conversation, definitely not interesting herself.

To Cherry's credit, she barrels onward, filling the dead airspace with blather, and I'm grateful.

Joan jumps in when she can, agreeing about some lunch foods, adding delightful details about watermelon radishes and how they get their color. Then she talks about the kind of dog she'd have if we were allowed to have pets with fur in our building. "A beagle. Definitely. And I'd name it Snoopy, even though I know Snoopy was more than your average beagle."

"Hang on, what's with the no-furry-pets rule?" Cherry asks between sips of wine. She's already finished half a glass and I notice Joan is keeping up. The way these two are going, I could probably slip into my bedroom in a few minutes and they wouldn't notice.

"I don't know, it's weird," Joan agrees. "But that's what it says on my lease. So I guess salamanders and fish are fine. Hamsters, not so much."

Cherry shakes her head and squints, trying to make sense of the rule. "What kind of rule is this? Hamsters are so much less troublesome than say, snakes, but those are fine?"

I shrug, but it gives me something to think about, so I'm sort of grateful.

Still on a roll, Cherry continues. "You know, the more I think about it, the more I really want to bring a date to Finn's wedding. I mean, it doesn't have to be someone I'm dating, but just . . . someone."

"Really? I always thought weddings were the perfect place to meet someone. It's where I met Felix, did you know?" Joan says, scooping a few crackers onto a plate and slicing off a hunk of brie.

I look at her, surprised. "That's how you met? How did I not know that?"

Joan shrugs. "Well, he and I both know how we met, so it's not something we bring into conversation a lot."

"Whose wedding was it?" I ask, interested in her story. Surprisingly, it doesn't make me sad or wistful. It somehow gives me hope, maybe because so many of my siblings are engaged, and there will surely be weddings one of these days. Other than Finn, they're all lazy about planning them, but soon enough I'm sure they'll get onboard.

Joan leans back in the recliner and folds her arms over her chest, drumming her fingers against the sides of her breasts. "It was his cousin Allen, who married my college friend Laura. We were seated at different tables, but I was a bridesmaid and he asked me to dance a few times that night, and that was it. I liked him enough to date him, and then I loved him enough to marry him."

I can't help but smile. "That's a sweet story. And I like that it wasn't some instalove thing where you saw him across a crowded room and just knew." Wow, I've already become a cynic. Or maybe I always was one.

"He says he knew, but I needed to see him on a few good dates first, make sure he had something to say. And I needed to get him into bed."

"Way to go, Joan," Cherry squeals, raising her hand for a high five.

Joan's sweet reminiscence only reminds me of how far away I am from ever telling a story like that. Depressing. I solve that problem by drinking my wine and fixating on counting how many different varieties of foods Joan has displayed there.

I still don't have an appetite but the longer I look at the cheese board, the more I wish I did. "Joan, if you ever leave the bank, you could be a caterer. These boards are a work of art."

"Thank you, honey. I have a big Pinterest following, and I've gotten some requests through my Instagram. When I have time, I do them for parties."

"And how did I not know *that*?" Cherry asks. "I want to follow you on Pinterest and hire you for parties."

Joan fishes a business card out of the pocket of her black zippered sweatshirt and hands it to Cherry, who examines both sides. "Has all my contact info and my website," Joan explains.

Cherry then continues not talking about Donovan. She goes into a long story about the discussion she had at the wine shop. "He backs up every recommendation with a guarantee, told me if I don't like this one to bring back the empty bottle. But if I drink both of them, the deal's off. So it's now or never, ladies. If we don't like this, I'm not opening the other one," she says.

"Oh yes you are. Even if you hate it, you're not returning wine. No way," I tell her, knowing the only reason she'd go back to the store is if the owner might make good date material for Finn's wedding. "What's he look like?"

"Who?" She plays dumb, focusing on pouring more wine into our glasses to distract from the blush creeping over her cheeks. My sisters all share my Irish genes which make it impossible to hide a blush.

"The wine guy," Joan says, twirling her hair and licking her lips as though he's standing in front of us. She grabs another handful of crackers. I finally break down and grab a plate, loading it with cheese, olives, and whatever else will fit.

"He is. Blond guy with a beard, probably a few years older than me . . . nice mouth. That's what I noticed. Very kissable."

Even though she's doing her level best to distract me from myself, the talk of kissing brings me right back to thinking about Donovan again, how I'll never kiss his gorgeous pillowy lips and how I wish I still didn't want to.

Cherry's phone buzzes and she looks at the screen, grimaces, and types a quick reply without explanation. She works for a tech firm like me, but she's been unhappy there for a while, so she's been quietly job-hunting. "How's the job search going?" I ask her. I spread some brie and fig jam on a cracker and take a bite. "Wow, so good. Maybe I am hungry for something other than Snickers."

"Is that all you've been eating, you poor girl?" Joan tsks, pushing the cheese platter closer to me as though I could fit anything else on my plate.

Cherry's phone buzzes again and she glances at the screen. This time, she can't contain the annoyance in her face. "Dammit. People don't listen." She holds up a finger. "Do not discuss important things without me," she warns, walking to my tiny balcony and dialing her phone.

"You can either have cheap or you can have good. I didn't think we were in the business to cheap out on the important stuff . . . " her voice trails off as she slides the door closed. I watch her pacing the three steps that cover the entirety of the balcony before she has to turn around. Even without hearing her, I can tell she's yelling by the gesturing of her hands and the way she throws her head back in frustration. She lives up to her image as the fiery redhead in the family and never pulls punches.

I sit watching her and don't immediately notice Joan getting out of the lounger and coming to sit next to me until she's practically in my lap.

Turning in surprise, I blink at her. "Hey, Joan."

"We're gonna talk for real now," she says, a slight menace to her voice. Why does everyone feel the need to sound menacing around me? If she wanted to be a serial murderer, I have no doubt she'd be great at it. No one would suspect her and it's clear she has a thirst for blood. With Cherry out of the way, she goes in for the kill. "You're trying your damnedest to get over him and I don't understand why."

"Because it's over and I need to move on."

"Why's it over? Because he made a bad judgment call? That's not a good enough reason. You want to be with him, you help him understand why he can never hurt you like that again."

"I can't, Joan. I've opened myself up to him. I let him know how much regret I had after putting Warren's career ahead of my own. And here I am, like an idiot, doing it again and he flat out lies about how one-sided this all is. Why should I stick around for more of the same when I can cut my losses?"

"Cut your losses," she mocks. "Because this isn't a business transaction. This is love, and when you love a person, you stick around until the person dies or you can't do it anymore without dying yourself. And you're not a quitter. You're a competitor. You go into something to win. So why with this man are you quitting so soon?"

"I can't win this game."

"You can't expect people to be perfect."

"I don't. But I expect them to be honest."

"Can you think of a reason why he felt like he couldn't be?"

"I guess I don't mean that much to him."

"Really? Sounds like he was willing to risk his career to stand up for you against that asshole you work with," Joan says, her eyes warm and wise.

But she wasn't there. I shake my head and tell her the truth. "No. He had a hot-headed moment. He was flying on a cloud, getting celebrated as the team's great new hope, being Donno. And he wanted to look like the tough guy." I close my eyes at the memory. "I can't believe he almost hit a guy just to look like a hero."

"You sure about that? Is that who he is?"

The tenuous hold I've had on my emotions all this time shreds before I can answer her question. My heart aches in my chest and I have to put a hand there for fear the bones will disintegrate and leave a gaping hole.

"Donovan isn't a regular boyfriend. He's 'Donno,' and his career comes first. That's the problem. Been the problem all along."

"Okay, so let him solve his problem."

"He can't. Or he doesn't want to. Either way, I'm done. I can make sacrifices for someone I love, but not for someone who lies."

"Nor should you," Joan says softly. "That's not what I'm suggesting."

"So what, then?" I ask, as the tears well up and roll down my cheeks.

Joan pulls me into her chest which feels like the world's most comfortable pillow. "People are human. We make mistakes. If you run for the hills every time some guy screws up, you'll spend a long lonely life on a mountaintop."

"Maybe that's a good spot for me."

"It's not. But we're talking about forevers here. Stakes are high and men aren't as evolved. You've got to give him time to catch up."

"How?"

"You give him space to be the man he wants to be. Be a little patient, a lot kind, and let him figure himself out. If he can't do that, then we'll talk some more."

I nod, holding on to Joan like she's the life raft in my stupid romantic storm. Right now, she is.

CHAPTER 30

onovan

I CAN'T PLAY for shit.

Shocker.

My focus and concentration don't exist right now—all I can think about is Tatum and how things went south so quickly. It's been two days, but it feels like twenty. My head feels like it's stuffed with cotton, tight and impossible to think straight.

I've spent most of that time working out so hard that when I fall into my bed at night, I sleep without dreaming. I have to push myself so hard that I'm close to a physical breaking point, then I run another two miles at a pace that makes me taste blood at the back of my throat and feel the sting of sweat in my eyes. Then I run one more.

I've shoved four workouts into one, adding on weight in the training room even after the trainers tell me to stop. "I can press one more." "I can handle one more plate, another fifty pounds."

My legs scream to disagree, but the pain tears at a wound I want to rip out completely—regret, regret, regret.

If I had it to do again . . . But I don't.

It's done. Over. Even if I don't want to accept it.

I keep replaying events in my head and questioning what I was thinking. At the time, it made perfect sense to invite her to dinner and nonchalantly have a photographer snap some photos. In no way did I think through how it might appear to her if she learned it was staged.

Why didn't I fucking think it through?

Because you weren't listening to her. She trusted you, and you made her biggest fear come true.

I see that clearly now, but there's only so much I can say in a voicemail or text. I need to see her and explain what I was thinking—or how I failed to think—and salvage the best thing in my life other than soccer. No, scratch that. She's the best thing in my life, period.

She won't return my calls, which I understand, so I've resorted to texting so at least I can get my point across. I've apologized, asked if we can meet and talk, apologized again, laid my heart on the ground fully expecting her to stomp on it. I deserve it.

But the texts have gone unanswered—except for one, to which she politely replied, "Please stop texting me."

We're on a break after the morning training session, and most of the guys are in the training facility with the physical therapists, getting massages and working out any muscle kinks before they mushroom into chronic injuries.

I decide to run a few more suicides on the field. I don't need the beep to tell me when to go. The sweat drips in my eyes, but I like the sting.

I'm halfway up the field and panting like I might cough half a lung onto the field when I hear an angry shout, "Taylor!"

Coach Derry stands near the field entrance with his arms

folded over his chest, his red logo polo tucked into his Adidas training pants. He waves me over and I jog his way, feeling a new ache in my Achilles tendon that almost has me limping.

I can't let him see that. He'll have my head. As it is, he looks like he'd like to murder me and eat my remains. "What the hell are you doing, Taylor?" he asks when I get close enough to hear him.

Wiping the sweat from my brow, I work to control my breathing. We don't know each other that well personally, but I understand his coaching style—no nonsense, get the job done. I respect him and he's shown me nothing different.

So if I have a good reason for running extra suicides, he's not going to question it.

But my reason is shit.

"Hey, Coach. Wanted to get a little more conditioning in before I break for lunch." The tendon cries out in pain and I try not to wince. I've been overtraining and I can't risk an injury. The last thing I need is for him to see I'm pushing myself to the point of unnecessary pain.

"We had a giant morning of drills. That wasn't enough for you?" He squints into the sun, his scowl questioning.

My lungs cooperate and I'm able to calm my breathing somewhat. "Never enough." I give him a grin, hoping to nip the conversation in the bud.

"That's the fucking stupidest thing I've ever heard out of a professional footballer's mouth. This isn't high school. You overtrain and your body's useless on the field. Proper rest is part of training, and I know you don't need me to tell you that because you're killing yourself on purpose."

I open my mouth planning to say . . . something. The words don't come. He's right. I'm acting like an asshole and I'm screwing the team, not just myself.

"I don't know what went down at the reception the other night. I only heard stuff second hand, but everything affects your game. You need to get right in the head, sort your shit. Right now. I won't have you on the pitch bringing personal issues into the game."

"Understood. I'm a hundred percent focused when I'm in a game. I guarantee you that."

"Not what I'm seeing. A guy who's focused on the game doesn't work himself to the bone a week before the first league game. I'm not afraid to bench you. It's obvious you don't know why you're even here," he says.

"Sorry?"

"Why are you here?" His stare could knock the goalposts clear off the field.

I shift my weight from one foot to the other, my hamstrings starting to lock up from the sprints. "To play for you. Be a leader. Support the club."

He shakes his head. "Not the party line. Why are you really here? Forget the paycheck and the fact that you're a footballer. We're all here for that. I mean you. Why. Are. You. Here?"

That's the problem. I don't fucking know why I'm here.

He holds up a hand. "I don't want an answer, especially one you haven't thought really fucking hard about. But you and I both know you didn't come here to be a celebrity soccer player and get photographed all over town. So fire your douchebag publicist and work things out with your girlfriend. She adores you and she deserves better than being treated like arm candy. Smart woman—I talked to her a bit before your little theatrics." He waves his hands and rolls his eyes but the corners of his mouth edge up into a smile.

For the first time, I see the man, not the coach. I notice the piercing blue of his eyes rimmed by lines formed by years of squinting in discerning concentration at players, working out what he needed to do to make them give their best.

"You talked to her?" I know it's not the point, but the mere mention of Tatum lightens the anvil that's been sitting on my chest for days.

He rubs a hand through his graying crewcut. "Yeah, she was talking about angles and lift and trajectory—guarantee she knows more about how to bend a soccer ball than you do."

I feel the stiffness in my face crack the smallest bit thinking about her talking physics at a party—of course she was. Then the ache returns with so much force it almost knocks me off my feet. "I really fucked up there."

"She still alive?"

"Sorry?" I'm beginning to think he and Tatum have more in common than I realized. Their trains of thought go straight off the rails.

"She's still walking the planet, so are you. That means there's hope. Fix your shit. Then come back here and help me fix this team. I wasn't kidding when I said we need a leader, so get your head straight. No more bullshit."

I know when to shut up and take advice. "Understood." I pull out my cleats, but Coach shakes his head and takes them from my hands.

"You're done here today. Go work with the PT team, and get those muscles rubbed out and have them work on your Achilles before it becomes an issue. Then go home."

"Oh, I'll still be here for the afternoon session—"

"No you fucking won't. Go home and figure your shit out. Have yourself one glass of scotch and do some soul searching. Then be in my office before practice tomorrow morning and we'll talk. I'm making up the starting lineup for Saturday's opener after that."

Reading between the lines, if he doesn't like what I have to say in the morning, I'm benched. I hang my head like a school kid getting slapped on the wrist by the principal for chewing gum in class.

"Sounds good. I'll be there. Early." I don't want to meet his eyes, mainly because I don't want him to see the disappointment in mine.

His slap on my back is as much a vote of confidence as I'll get from him, but it's enough. "You're a marquee player. Your stats and reputation precede you, but far as I'm concerned, that's all in the past—on and off the field. You're here to do a job. For reasons still to be determined by you. Clean slate, what you make of it is what your reputation is going forward."

I look up and extend my hand. "Appreciate that, Coach."

He shakes it and nods, assessing me with narrowed eyes. "Doesn't mean you make up your own rules. Not ever. Means you play by mine."

"Understood." I swallow hard and watch him turn to go back into the team area. Muscles aching, I walk slowly across the field to collect my gear bag. Probably a couple hours with the physical therapists, then . . . I have no idea.

I've never been sent home early from practice, not even when I had a hundred-and-two-degree fever. And the one person I'd like to call for a late lunch date probably won't answer the phone.

Which leaves me with myself.

Fucking hell.

CHAPTER 31

onovan

THE IRRITATING HAMMERING of a pissed of woodpecker rouses me from the awful night's sleep I had after giving in and taking melatonin at three in the morning.

Damn bird.

And now it's texting me and yelling my name, pouring more chaos into my brain.

It takes me a second to accept that I need to open my eyes because the relentless bird isn't stopping. Squinting at my phone, I try to focus, but the letters all look blurry. So I throw a t-shirt over my head and stagger toward my front door. At the same moment I decipher the string of texts from Julia, I unlatch the door, throwing it open. My perky-ass sister smiles and reaches her arms for me.

Silently pulling her in for a hug, I feel the welling of a lump in my throat that suddenly makes it hard to swallow. I didn't realize how much I missed her until I felt the hug from someone who knows me better than anyone.

Finally, I work enough air into my lungs to breathe somewhat normally, then I blink back the hint of tears before they turn into something I can't control.

Julia doesn't let go first, knowing, as she always does, what I need and when I need it. But after a few moments, I pat her once on the back and release my grip. "It's good to see you, kiddo."

It doesn't matter than she's over thirty. She'll always be my kid sister, and I'll always feel protective. I take the small piece of luggage off her shoulder and hang it on my own.

She walks past me into my apartment and does a three-sixty when she gets past the entryway and into the living room. "Holy crap, Donny, this is a palace. Why didn't you tell me you could see England from here. I'd have waved." She goes to the giant window just the way Tatum did when she first saw the place.

"Cute."

I wait, hoping she'll tell me why she flew across a continent without telling me. I narrow my eyes, expecting her to turn around. "So . . . this is unexpected," I say, running a hand through my hair and trying to recall if she's told me about coming to visit and I forgot.

She casts me a look over her shoulder. "Yeah. I made the decision last-minute." She continues surveying the apartment and fingers a tassel that hangs from the tieback for my drapes. "Damask? You didn't buy these."

"No. And I'm pretty sure you didn't fly all this way to check out my curtains."

She picks up a purple pillow and hugs it to her chest as she plops into the loveseat. "Of course not. I came to talk sense into you. And wow, this couch is comfortable."

"Good to know." I cross my arms over my chest. "And who says I need that?"

She tips her head to the side like it's obvious. "Dude, I saw you almost deck a guy. Again. This needs to stop before you ruin your career."

It's my turn to sink into the seat of the comfortable furniture I didn't pick out myself. I should have known I was in deep shit when I hired a stranger to buy my couches. And there's no hiding from my sister, especially when knows me well enough to understand I need her without me picking up the phone.

"Jules . . . " Another hand raking through my hair. It's becoming an annoying habit, even to me. "I don't know what the fuck I'm doing. I'm here, a continent away from you, pretending I belong, and I'm way in over my head. Look at this place. I didn't pick out a stick of furniture myself. I have an interior designer, for Chrissake."

Without a word, Julia is up and signaling me to follow her into the kitchen, where she does a quick survey and beelines for the Nespresso setup and starts making us both coffee. I perch on the edge of my kitchen table and watch her. It's all I have the energy to do.

When the two cups are ready, Julia steers me into a chair and plops down across from me. I start to thank her but she waves a hand to shut me up.

"Let me get this out," she says before taking a deep inhale. "You need to stop feeling guilty for my choices. You didn't make me follow you to England. I trotted after you like the little sister I am, and I loved every minute of being there with you. You didn't choose the people I dated, and you aren't responsible for my bad relationships. You need to let that go."

I'm too sleep deprived to have this conversation with her right now. "Look, Jules—"

She cuts me off. "I know. We've talked about this already, ad nauseum. That's not why I'm here. I know you don't have a violent bone in your body, and the only way you'd get worked up enough to even consider laying a hand on some douchebag is if he hurt someone you love. That's why I'm here. Who is she? Talk to me, Donny."

"You're really gonna make me do this? Now?"

"Yeah, now. When else?"

"Well, I don't know. When I figure out how to fix what I screwed up?"

She leans back in her chair looking chipper and ready to hear an entertaining story. Not like she's just come off a redeye flight and hoofed it up a San Francisco hill to see her dumbass brother. When she speaks, it's with tenderness she rarely reserves for me. "Donny, you've helped me more than you'll ever know. Let me help you. You fucked up, and you're worried you've lost the love of your life. Am I right?"

I take a sip of my coffee, which tastes like liquid heaven, and give her a rueful smile. "You think you can help me with that?"

She waggles her eyebrows and grins conspiratorially, looking into her coffee cup like it contains universal truths. Then she looks up and nods. "I do. So, tell me about her, and we'll figure it out."

DESPITE ONLY TWO hours of sleep, I feel better than I have in weeks. I suppose I have my sister to thank for that. And Coach Derry. Lucky me that I have two relentless people in my life who care about me enough to put me in my place. I'm blessed, even if I hate being told I'm the asshole in the room.

Standing low in the bleachers at the training facility, I let the green turf morph in my mind, visualizing the soccer pitch in the Strikers' stadium. I can hear the roaring crowd, the vuvuzelas blasting when I get a breakaway and take it up the side for a Killer Cross.

Deep at the end of the carpet of green, I envision the keeper diving for the ball, but my touch, my angle, the bend as it flies through the air—he can't get a finger on it before it lands hard in the back of the net.

It's always been easy to see what I want. If I can see it, I can find a way to get it.

For my entire life, I've only wanted soccer.

Now I have to figure out all the ways it's prevented me from dealing with the rest of my life.

Coach Derry sits at his desk, the steam from his coffee hitting my nose as soon as I enter the office.

He watches me and waits. He's not going to hold my hand while I man up and tell him what's been eating at me since I took the job with his team.

I take a deep breath and say the words I've kept buried out of fear that saying them will give them credence, or worse, turn into a self-fulfilling prophecy. But they've been there all along, taunting me and daring me to listen and make peace with them.

"I'm here because I'm scared." I feel a chokehold on my throat as soon as the words are out, like I might burst into tears. I can't do that. Not in front of my coach.

Fuck, where's your goddamn manhood?

Swallowing hard over the lump, I take as deep a breath as I can and slowly exhale. I feel myself settle enough that I can look him in the eye.

He nods sympathetically. "I know you are. I see it." This surprises me. I have no idea what I could be doing that would make me look afraid.

"I . . . Look, I'm not big on these kumbaya moments and sharing feelings—"

He interrupts me. "What are you scared of?"

I could say I'm afraid of failing, of coming to the MLS after a storied career and failing to live up to the hype, not being deemed worthy of thirty million dollars. But we both know that's not what this is about. I still have the skill for my job.

It's about what comes after that.

"Being irrelevant to the game. Knowing it's time to hang it up." I cringe a little bit as I hear the words. Until now, they were hypothetical. Now, it feels like a solemn march of days until I look at a soccer pitch for the final time.

"Happens to everyone eventually."

My hand scrubs over my face, exhaling the anguish that comes with what I'm about to say. "Guess I went a long time convincing myself it wouldn't happen to me if I just kept playing my game. Maybe I could outrun it."

He nods, sadness in his eyes. "No one's that fucking fast."

I know he played in the Premier League a dozen years before I did but mostly he's known for his coaching. He's one of the best.

"Seems like you figured out how to stay in the game. Now you just do it on the sideline, there's your soccer longevity."

He rubs a hand through his hair, thoughtful. "I figured out how to do what I was good at. All that thinking was a hell of a lot harder than playing soccer." He sighs, looking around his office, where several league cups, awards, and plaques adorn the shelves. "I was never the soccer player you are. Not even close. Was never going to be. The best thing I ever did in my life was wise up to it before I got pushed out on my ass. Left the Premier League at the top of my game and got an assistant coach job right away."

"How'd you know you'd be good at coaching?"

He shakes his head, a dreamy expression as though he still enjoys the mystery of it. "I just knew. My instincts for players and the potential of what we could do on the field far outpaced my ability to do it with my physicality, no matter how hard I trained. I knew I was patient. And aggressive when I need to be. And a little bit of a dick. Voila, coaching material." He laughs. "And I didn't play chicken with a ticking clock."

It makes me laugh. Basic science, as Tatum would say. No one can outrun time.

His expression turns serious. "You'll figure it out. I know, it's scary as hell, but you didn't get where you are by caving to hard shit."

"I guess . . . I've just never not known what I planned to do with my life. The answer was always soccer."

"And now you see an expiration date."

"I don't know when . . . I mean, maybe I'll get a few more years in the Euro leagues after this, but there's no denying the direction I'm headed. It depresses the hell out of me." I let out a deep sigh I didn't know I was holding in.

"Does she know?" he asks pointedly.

"Who?"

He tilts his head and looks at me like I'm playing dumb. I shake my head. "I didn't want her to see that side of me, the side that doesn't know what the hell he's doing. It's a lot more fun to be the hot athlete." I force a laugh. He doesn't join me.

"And now you fucked it up. You talk to your teammates? Gotten to know them?" His change of direction surprises me, but I'm kind of glad he's not dwelling on my communication breakdown with Tatum. I'm still too raw to talk about it with him or anyone.

I nod. "Sure. They're good guys. I've studied their strengths on the field."

He leans forward in his chair, putting his elbows on his desk. His expression looks disappointed and I wonder which of my answers to his questions he doesn't like.

"Look, Donno, I like you from what I've come to know, so I'm gonna cut to the chase because I don't have time for you to work through my questions until you get to the right answer. You need to let people in. Share the demons you're facing."

His accusation has me stiffening. "I . . . do."

I don't.

And if he's suggesting I tell my new teammates I'm afraid of becoming a has-been, he's crazy to think I'll do it. They need to see me as a leader, not a guy in his golden years.

Really? Maybe they'll respect you more for being human.

My lungs fill with a welcome breath as I hear the rest of what Coach has to say, knowing with every word that he's right. "Maybe at one time, but that's not what I'm seeing here. I know you didn't play in Manchester without knowing every guy like he was your twin separated at birth. That's a gift. That's where your instinct comes from, and I don't know why . . . maybe it was the bad attention you got after that social media bullshit about the fight, but something closed you off, shut you down. And I'm telling you that's what's gonna leave you fucked when it's time to take the cleats off. Nothing else. Not the game, not your skill, not your age."

I feel my whole body slump in the chair, mostly out of relief because he's right and I needed to hear someone say the words. And because I opted not to talk about my fears when Tatum pushed me to open up. One more way I made her believe that she wasn't important enough to merit it. She trusted me, and I didn't return the favor.

Coach doesn't say anything else, but I feel his eyes on me as I digest everything he's said. We sit quietly like that for a while—several minutes—but even though we're two dudes having a moment, it doesn't feel uncomfortable.

Fuck, this man is a brilliant coach. It makes me all the more motivated to work my tail off to help earn him the championship, even though I know that's not what this is about.

For the first time since the whole social media beatdown and everything that went with it, I feel like the man I want to be. It feels like the beginning of something. I'm not sure yet what it's the beginning of, but forging a connection with my coach feeds a crack in the bedrock I've built around myself.

I thought I was safeguarding something that was slipping from my grasp. Instead, I was building a prison.

I don't know Coach well, but he doesn't seem like the kind of person who waxes poetic with his players as a rule. His mostly crusty demeanor makes me wonder what his story is.

"You married, Coach?" I'm as surprised as he looks to hear the words come out of my mouth. I'm really fucking losing it.

His amused smile turns into a gentle laugh. "I am. Be thirteen years this fall. She's smarter than me and a better person, but I know enough not to fuck it up too much because I'll never find anyone better." He watches the wheels turn in my head. Clear genius that he is, he knows he's pushed enough. He doesn't ask me about Tatum, but his advice hangs in the air—fix your shit.

I look at the time on my phone as an excuse not to meet his eye. "Okay, I'm gonna head to the field, start warming up."

"Good plan."

"Then I guess I'll start thinking bigger picture, planning for my retirement, eh?" I'm only half joking.

"First fucking step is getting out there and giving the team three more years of the best you've got. Then . . . because you're luckier than most people, you get to figure out Part Two of your life. And if you get your head out of your ass, maybe you can do it with the woman you've got wrapped around your heart."

"Understood." I leave his office knowing exactly what I need to do.

CHAPTER 32

atum

Tuesday morning comes around too fast. I've barely spent adequate time in my pajamas sulking over every rom-com I can find on Netflix and spreading Ben and Jerry's Phish Food ice cream on top of Pop Tarts. This, after the wine and cheese fest with Joan and Cherry lasted well into the evening.

After they left, I traded the proficient female card in for the heartbroken wallower. I won't apologize for it. The sadness overflowing my boundaries needed its due if I had any hope of coming back to work in one piece.

But after a cup of coffee, a shower, and a change of clothes, I at least look the part of a human being, even if my heart is still smeared around the internet like social media detritus. I can't afford to wallow at home, especially now when it's clear that my reputation is on the line at work. That is, if Paul hasn't already convinced Charlie to fire me.

Only one way to find out.

Terrance hovers near my desk with a maple bacon donut, a jumbo bag of mini Snickers, and a hug. "Wow, word travels, huh? Does everyone think I tried to sleep my way to a promotion?"

Why would they think that?" He leans against the side of my desk and folds his arms. "You didn't return my calls." He's never looked at me with the kind of disappointment I see in his eyes.

Right. He left me some messages.

I reach a hand for his arm, conciliatory. "Sorry. I turned my phone off for most of the weekend, and I didn't check my messages."

"I called you yesterday."

Why is he harping on this? "Sorry. I appreciate you checking on me. I'm fine."

"I called to tell you about Pauley," he says, looking at my face for a glimmer of recognition.

Shaking my head, I plop into my desk chair and lean hard on the ergonomic backrest. "Last thing I want to think about is that guy right now. I'm sure he's busy at his desk plotting my demise."

Terrance's smile could light a Christmas tree. "So you don't know . . . He's definitely not at his desk . . . Charlie fired his ass first thing yesterday morning. Sexual harassment."

My jaw goes slack, and I stare at Terrance for a glimmer of evidence he's messing with me. His steady gaze tells me he's not. "Seriously? Who'd he harass? I mean, other than everyone . . . who'd he get caught harassing?"

Now he looks at me like I've lost my marbles. "You . . . ? Friday night, his whole slut-shaming diatribe? Charlie has a zero tolerance policy. Canned him first thing in the morning. Out. On. His. Ass."

It takes me a moment to process everything he's saying. I'm sure my eyes look like fishbowls from the shock. "The stuff he said to me . . . that's not even that bad relative to what I've heard over the years."

Terrance shrugs. "Needed to happen. Sets a precedent. But don't say anything to anyone. I'm not sure it's public knowledge."

"Terrance, how do you know these things? You've got a line on everything Charlie does. Do you have some sort of spyware installed on his computer?"

He raises an eyebrow. "Now that would be illegal, wouldn't it?" Then he laughs. "I just pay attention. I'm not as dumb as I look."

"No one would ever accuse you of being dumb. Lazy, maybe . . ."

"Hilarious. Don't forget who keeps your sweet tooth fed."

"Okay, sugar daddy. Point taken." I turn toward my computer and start to settle in, but Terrance continues observing me.

"Can I ask? Donovan?"

I shut him down with a look. "Not right now. Thanks, but I'm fine." He doesn't move, so I cast a glance at him, hoping he'll see the fatigue in my eyes and hear what I'm saying. "Really. I've gotta work."

Nodding with a frown, he pushes himself away from the desk and waits to see if I'll change my mind. Finally, he nods and walks away.

Despite the satisfaction of knowing karma smacked Paul in the ass, I have bigger things to deal with. Even if I failed to get Donovan to participate in the VR game, I can't let myself throw in the towel.

I have one last hope of getting the job I want and the promotion I still think I deserve, so I ask Charlie's assistant to schedule me a meeting with him.

Then I proceed to get nothing done while I watch the clock and wait for her response.

When I knock on Charlie's doorframe at the appointed time, he's gazing out the window at the Santa Cruz mountains in the distance. "Come in," he says without turning around. "Have a seat." Unusual for Charlie not to shake my hand with his usual enthusiasm, but we haven't spoken since he watched my life melt down at the team event, so I'm not surprised he doesn't feel like embracing me.

I quietly take a seat opposite his desk and wait while my heart folds in on itself. Something's different—I can feel it.

Finally, Charlie turns, his eyes bright but his expression serious. "Tatum. Glad you're on my schedule. Wanted to talk with you. Like minds." He aims two fingers between his eyes and mine.

"Oh, good. I know how much you dislike extra meetings." I force cheer into my voice that I don't feel. "But I wanted to explain what happened on Friday night. You probably heard from Paul . . . " I hate saying his name almost as much as I hate the man himself, but I need to own this, whatever this is.

Charlie waves a hand dismissively, his expression sour. "I don't want to talk about office gossip. And as far as I'm concerned, that's what this is."

Air fills my lungs for what feels like the first time since Friday night. "Okay . . . " I blink a few times, trying to read between the lines. Charlie is such a closed book.

"I know I wasn't able to convince Donovan Taylor to participate in the game, but—"

Charlie puts up a hand to stop me. "Like I said, I don't want to engage in gossip about what you did or didn't do to convince him."

I close my eyes against the mortification washing over me. "I need you to know I didn't sleep with him to get him to sign on. I'd never—"

"You're not listening!" Charlie thumps his desk for emphasis.

My eyes go wide. I've never heard him raise his voice.

He continues, "If you really feel the need to go there, fine. I know what was said and I don't believe that's who you are. I won't indulge that kind of nonsense at my company."

At the risk of angering him even more, I push back. "But didn't you ask me to convince Donovan as a condition of being considered to run the project?"

He looks at me like I've grown an extra head. "Absolutely not. The two have never been connected in my mind, and if I implied they were, well . . . I apologize. If anything, I consider the fact that you're personable to be an asset and you're well-spoken about our technology—that's the extent of it. But it's a moot point now. I've decided Terrance should run the division."

His words knock the wind from me. Terrance? The worker bee who's happy to go home at six on the dot each day and who's never asked to be the head of anything? It makes no sense.

Suddenly, it doesn't matter that Paul was fired for being a sexist pig. The worse kind of sexism is being passed over for a job I can do well. With the little speech Charlie just gave, I started to believe he was different.

I try to keep my voice from shaking, but it's futile. "I'm happy for Terrance, of course. . . He deserves recognition for his work." I shouldn't say anything else. I try to push down my stupid competitiveness and just focus on being happy for my friend. Charlie stares at me, waiting for what we both know I can't resist adding. "But . . . " I'm forced to take a breath or I'll pass out. Charlie takes that opportunity to speak.

For the first time since I walked in, he smiles. "I know. Terrance has never expressed interest in running a division. That's why I need to give him a push. He's very capable and he has leadership qualities—he just needs a reason to use them."

He's right. And that's the only thing that allows a tiny smile to warm my cheeks. "He'll be great," I concede. It uses every bit of fortitude in me to take the high road. What I want to do is ask why the fuck I can't get a shot at running a division. For once.

Charlie knows I want it—I've never been subtle about my ambition.

Charlie steeples his fingers on his desk and leans his chin on them, zeroing his gaze on me. "Tell me something, Tatum. I know you're competitive and you've proven your talent and skill. But why do you want to run a game division in a sport you'd never heard of before last month?"

"I'd heard of it. I just didn't know much about it."

"That's not my point." He watches me ,and I try not to fidget. I grasp the wooden arms of the chair and look him in the eye, desperate to convince him of my seriousness. It's not just competitiveness anymore. I need to stretch and grow in order to be happy.

"Listen, Charlie, I'm a team player. For me, the point isn't to head a project only if I like the sport. I want to be a leader at this company."

"I know you do. And I know you're capable. But I don't think a VR soccer game is the right fit."

My heart sinks so quickly and with such a heavy thud that I almost don't hear the rest of what Charlie is saying. His animated grin pulls me back to the conversation.

"I've been wanting to move into new areas with VR, and I'm looking to acquire a psychological research firm that will allow us to do some good. Games are fun and they're a cash cow, but what are we really doing all of this for? It has to be for a bigger, better purpose, or what's the point? You're always talking about how the technology could be used for therapeutic purposes. Why have you never suggested running that kind of project?"

I struggle to make sense of his words and formulate an answer. "Because I didn't think it was an option."

"Well, it's an option. It's going to be a big project, bigger than the soccer game, and I'd like you to head it up. What do you say?"

Charlie is so matter of fact when he says things like "I'd like you to head it up" that sometimes I miss what he's said until a few moments later. Which is why I'm staring at him, dumbfounded, trying to parse through his words and make sure I've heard him correctly.

"You would?" It's the best I can come up with as a response.

"You'll be great. Mostly because you care about the work. We have the chance to use our technology to help people getting over trauma, veterans with PTSD, people with phobias. There's almost limitless potential."

"I agree."

"So . . . we're in agreement, then."

I stand and reach over to shake Charlie's outstretched hand. "Thanks. I'm really excited about this."

"It has great potential. And so do you."

I press my lips together and quickly bend to pretend to retie my shoe because his words choke me up a little. I hate that I need to hear his praise, but I do. And it feels good to get it.

I know my dad would be proud. I shoot Charlie a smile over my shoulder as I head for the door.

"By the way, he said he'd do it," he calls after me.

When I turn, the smug smile on his face tells me he's been holding on to the piece of information with the intent of surprising me. "Who said he'd do it?"

"Donovan Taylor. He agreed to participate in the VR game. He called me first thing this morning."

I can't hide my shock. Mouth agape, I shake my head. It makes no sense. "Why?"

"He didn't give a reason, but I suspect it has something to do with you." His eyes soften and he chews his lip. "You should probably ask him yourself."

Swallowing hard, I nod. I know I can't avoid him forever, and knowing he compromised his principles because of me sends a new kind of ache tearing through my chest. I miss him. I love him. And it may be too late for any of it. "He really didn't want to do it."

Charlie starts typing, which indicates our meeting is over. "I know. I told him we'll be fine without him. He's free to opt out."

"What? Why?" The whole point of this miserable mess was to get him on board. I feel like the rug's just been torn from beneath my feet. Again.

Charlie continues typing, but he shrugs. "He told me his reasons. If anyone understands the invasiveness of public consumption, it's me. Why do you think I hide like a hermit in here all the time? He's right to keep a part of himself sacred. I respect him even more for saying no. We can build a good game without him. We're so busy creating inhuman versions of what's real that we forget sometimes that humans are at the heart of anything we design. It's more important to me that we respect those humans than sell more games."

I stand there watching this man, my boss, who I never understood until now. Who am I kidding? I still don't understand him, but I'm a little bit closer. And my respect for him has blossomed a thousandfold. He's the mentor I've been looking for.

He's done talking to me, as evidenced by his increased typing speed and eyes that have regained sharp focus on his computer screen.

"Thank you, Charlie." I turn for the door, the wheels in my brain cranking through all the potential iterations of VR that can be used in therapy and training. So much potential.

I don't expect him to respond since I know he's long past our conversation, so it surprises me when I hear, "You're welcome. And before you head back to your desk, will you stop by the VR room and make sure no one's working in there? I'd like to run through some simulations in a few minutes."

It's a strange request. But it's Charlie. "Sure. Of course."

I head for the VR room, completely unprepared for what I see when I open the door. Donovan stands in the middle of the room, as though he's been expecting me.

CHAPTER 33

onovan

TATUM LOOKS SURPRISED, then apprehensive, which I expect.

But I'm holding out hope for something more, searching her face for a sign she's happy to see me, even a flicker, because I need it to power me through what I'm about to do.

"Hey," she says, her face an immovable mask of self-restraint.

"Hi." I've never felt more awkward in my own skin, even as a prepubescent teenager holding out hope of getting a pretty girl to see past my lanky exterior and believe something better lurked within.

She stands frozen just inside the door. There might as well be a yawning cliff drop between us, for as close as I feel to her mentally, emotionally. How did I fuck things up this badly?

Then I see it—the tiniest crinkle in her brow, a softening in her features that tells me all is not lost.

So I begin.

Standing next to the equipment cabinet, I beckon her forward with a tilt of my head and hold out a headset.

"What's this about?" she asks, her brow furrowing more. I don't expect her to sign on to whatever I'm asking her to do without an explanation, but I know she loves games, loves competition. So I'll have a better chance of getting her to listen if I play it her way.

"A VR game. I spoke with Charlie earlier, and he said we could look at a demo together."

"Donno . . . " It's the first time she's called me that. Ordinarily the nickname makes me happy, reminds me of the reputation I've built on the soccer pitch where fans scream it in a chorus of cheers. When I see the moniker on the back of replica jerseys with my number, it usually makes me happy. Crazy that I feel the exact opposite now.

Hearing her say it makes me feel like she's resigned to viewing me as the shallow player who no one really knows, least of all her. I hate it.

"Please. I know I'm asking a lot without apologizing or explaining but please, just give me a minute because I'd like to do both."

The sadness in her face mirrors what I saw the night she left the party. Her mouth tips down into a frown and she shakes her head. "I don't know what you want from me. I did what you needed, didn't I? For your career. Isn't that enough?"

"Tatum . . . " I reach a hand toward her, pleading for her to close the distance in the room, but she doesn't.

"I can't do this with you. I'm sorry." She turns to go, and I know this isn't a game of chicken. She doesn't play games.

"Wait," I call after her, even though I don't have words to convince her to stay. But if I have one chance to make things right, I can't gamble it away on a prank that might not work. The VR idea is stupid. So many new bad ideas flood my brain that I can't decipher anything, so I consider myself lucky when Tatum turns around.

"Yes?"

I don't have anything planned, so I tell her the first thing that pops into my head, feeling the lines in my forehead deepen while I agonize over the words. "Can we just talk, then? I want to apologize and explain."

She looks toward the door, torn. I know I'm cutting into her workday, and I respect her and her work . . . so I tell her. "I know I'm cutting into your workday. And I know how important your work is to you—"

"Thank you. It is important. But it's not everything," she interrupts. The surprise must show on my face because she folds her arms and explains. "I just mean . . . sometimes I get a little caught up in putting my work before everything else in my life. It doesn't . . . belong there all the time."

Carefully, so as not to scare her off, I take a step closer to her. "Listen, I don't pretend to have all the answers and I'm probably bad at relationship stuff—real relationship stuff—for lack of experience, but . . . I want to try to do better. And I want to share myself—not with everyone, but with you."

She listens and watches me. I hope what she sees conveys that I do want to share with her. Only her.

Her eyes dart to the VR sets I hold in my hands, her lips edging up into the tiniest smile. I'd banked on her limitless curiosity to buy me a chance here. From her narrowed eyes, she's interested, but wary. "So . . . let me guess. You let Charlie build an avatar of you playing the VR soccer game and we're going to face off. Do I get to be goalie?"

And . . . I've hooked her. I can't keep the smile from my lips as I shake my head. "Nope. And it's called a keeper."

Rolling those beautiful hazel eyes, she corrects me. "I've heard both terms used."

"Goalie is more of a hockey term," I challenge.

She cocks her head, accepting my verdict. "Still learning about footballers, I guess."

I don't bother correcting her assumptions, any of them. "You want to play?" I ask, holding the headset out to her and hoping, praying she'll give me a chance to undo all the ways I've fucked this up.

"Hang on." Her eyes sparkle with something I haven't seen since she walked in the room. Mischief? "Just let me . . . " I have no idea what she intended to say because she's long since lost that train of thought, now focused on the computer terminal which operates the game. The colorful screen that shows Vivi-Tech's logo and various sports figures disappears, replaced by a black screen covered with lines of code. I wait while she assesses a language I can't comprehend and types a few new lines of code.

After a few more taps on the computer, she nods and takes the VR headset from me. "Okay, I'm ready. Put me in, coach." She's still about six feet away from me, far enough to ensure minimal contact even if one of us loses balance and falls. I take what I can get and watch her eyes disappear behind the oversized VR goggles. Right before they do, I swear I can see the flecks of gold that I've desperately missed.

When I put my headset on, I see the pristine white sand beach I asked Charlie to create as a VR environment for what I have planned. The dark spiky leaves from squat juniper bushes and sage flutter along the ridges of high white walls soaring up from the sand, creating a private Greek island cove.

The water is an unreal shade of turquoise, darkening to an azure in the deeper waters as far as the horizon. And a tiny sail-boat bobs on its anchor fifty yards away.

Two lounge chairs with royal blue and white striped towels almost go overboard in making the scene look like a vacation postcard, but I don't care about any of that. I see the VR version of myself standing at the water's edge, where I hoped to take

Tatum for a virtual walk and tell her everything she ever wanted to know about me in the hours of waning sun.

But she's not there.

I pull my headset down and check. Yup, she still wears hers, standing solemnly with her controllers in her hands. So why doesn't she appear in my line of sight?

Amid the quiet flutter of barely-there waves lapping the sand, I hear what can only be described as an awkward guttural croaking sound. It's coming from my headset, though I can't imagine what Charlie programmed into the experience that sounds like a . . . beached seal?

A second later, said seal waddles over from an offscreen corner, making its awkward way along the sand, dragging its belly along on webbed fins.

I'm confused because as far as I know, seals don't inhabit the Aegean Sea.

When the flubbery mammal gets close to me, I stand rigid, hoping it will make its way to the water and swim away. Maybe it's some kind of easter egg for serious VR dorks.

But when it reaches me, the seal opens its mouth. Instead of another oarking cry, I hear Tatum's voice, "You said you wanted to talk. Let's talk."

I swallow hard. "You're a seal. Do you know you're a seal?" I pray she doesn't want to kill me for inadvertently putting her into a slippery swimming body.

"Yes, I'm aware."

Realization dawns. "Wait, you made yourself a seal?"

The seal nods.

"Why?"

She bows her head from side to side, as seals do. "Because I'm mad at you, footballer."

I take a deep cleansing breath and reset my mental game. I'm going to have to pour my fucking heart out to a seal.

You deserve a lot worse.

"Okay, fair enough." I kick off my virtual shoes and dip my feet in the cool Aegean Sea, feeling the water lick at my ankles and watching Tatum skim the surface of the water with her seal flippers.

"My name is Donovan Taylor and I'm a soccer player. I'm also new in town," I say, hoping my third introduction is the charm.

"Nice to meet you," she croaks in a deep voice. I almost lose my shit, trying to reconcile the seal's whiskers and tiny teeth with Tatum's voice.

I hold up a hand. I need her to stop talking—it's the only way this is going to work. "Let me get this out."

"Okay." She nods.

"I'm a soccer player who's scared to death of what happens when I can't play anymore. I'm a brother who sometimes doesn't do right by his sister. I'm a guy who hurt the woman who's come to mean more to me in a few weeks than I ever thought possible. I'm a mess. But I'm done trying to hide my mess from you, and most of all from myself. If I had it to do again, I'd have told you about the photographers, or better yet, I'd have fired Jordan a long time ago. But I took care of that yesterday."

"You fired him?" Tatum asks, her seal eyes blinking.

"I don't need a publicist. I don't want to be a guy with an image. I want to be a soccer player who's worthy of the woman he loves. I didn't listen when you asked me to open up about my job and my future. I didn't want to do it. And honestly, I didn't know how to do it, but I'm determined to learn. And I'm so sorry I put you through all that crap with the photographers. I put my career ahead of yours, and I wasn't honest with you. That's not the person I want to be. In no way do I think my job is more important. You impress me every day I know you with your brilliance, your compassion, and your drive, and I don't want to stifle any of those."

The seal moves closer to me and nuzzles my leg. I feel Tatum move closer to me as well, but I stay in the VR simulation.

Despite myself, I reach down and pet the seal's head. She claps her flippers together and I so badly want to end this ocean mammal charade, but she's really adorable.

"Tatum, I'm so sorry. I want to share everything with you, if you're still up for knowing the less polished parts of me."

"I am. I like those parts the best. But take your time. It's a big deal to lay bare all your deepest stuff. I can wait to earn your trust."

"You already have it. It's just . . . new for me to talk about this stuff, especially when I've done a really good job of not thinking about it myself."

"Well . . . whenever you have something to share, I'm here."

The seal goes motionless when Tatum takes off her headset. I push mine up to my forehead and stare at her, giant goggles dangling from a finger, and try to decide from her concerned expression whether she's telling me I've said enough or whether she's acting like a supportive friend.

I don't need or want a friend. If that's what we are, I'm hopeless. When her eyes meet mine, flickering with gold in a milky brown haze, I have my answer.

"I'm so in love with you," I say.

I don't even notice her closing the distance between us until her lips graze mine. She lights every nerve ending on fire with the simplest touch, and I hear her exhale a sigh that reaches inside me like a caress. Every time I hear it, she calms my shit down.

It's why I never want to let her go.

"I don't need a beach. I don't need a made-up location. I don't want to play games with you, footballer."

"I thought—"

She cuts me off with the tip of her finger against my lips, then lays the flat of her hand on my chest. I feel warmth spread under her palm and immediately feel calmer. "I get what you were trying to do and it's sweet, but . . . I don't need virtual reality when the actual reality is so, so much better," she says. "I just need you."

I tear the headset from my face and chuck it away, only realizing what I've done when her eyes grow huge. "That's like a hundred thousand dollar piece of equipment."

"Shit. Seriously?"

Her laugh fills the room. "Nope. But I couldn't resist torturing you just a little bit more."

"It's fine. I know I deserve it."

Tatum tilts her head from side to side, debating how much torture I deserve. "Not anymore. I think you've been appropriately tortured."

"It's been torture not seeing you for three days. That's a fate I hope never to repeat." I lock eyes with her because I need her to understand what I'm telling her. "Never," I say, my voice strained with intensity as I stare into her eyes.

Her gaze burns with a fire that equals mine. "So . . . what are you saying?" she asks quietly.

"I want you. With me. Forever. I want to see those gold flecks in your eyes every day—I want to be the one who puts them there. I want to tell you my secrets and hold onto yours. And I want to give you all my best moves."

She grins at that. "I love you for your moves. But I hope you understand—really understand—that I'm not with you because you're a footballer. I'm not with you because of what you are at all. I'm with you because of who you are. The more I get to know you, the more I freaking love that person. I love you, Donovan. I just do."

"Thank you for freaking loving me."

Taking my face in her hands, she lights me up with her eyes. "Thank you for trusting me with yourself."

I lavish her with a soft kiss that immediately gets hot and deep. There's nothing else I want. She's everything.

CHAPTER 34

atum

FOURTEEN MINUTES into the season opener, my stomach feels like someone loaded it full of insane honeybees without a queen to tell them to shut the fuck up.

The coffee I drank seven hours ago certainly isn't helping. The caffeine somehow got reactivated into full body jitters, and now I may explode before halftime. That would be ugly.

I shouldn't feel nervous when I'm not the one playing. But looking around the packed Strikers stadium from my perch in one of the luxury suites, I can see I'm not the only one. Fans in the hundreds of seats below the row of private boxes wave Strikers banners and dutifully show their spirit wearing the team's red and white.

Donovan tried to get his sister to stay in town for the opener, but she told him she needed to get back home for work. I met her briefly and admitted I already loved her almost as much as my own sisters, at which point she promised to book a longer trip soon. I know Donovan's a little sad she didn't move to California with him, but he understands that she can't follow him around for her entire life.

I snap a few photos of Donovan and text them to her. She immediately replies with a string of emojis and explicatives threatening retribution if Donovan doesn't pull off a win.

Amid the replica jerseys, I see that nearly half have "Donno" printed on the back. In just a week since the photos started circulating of the two of us, Donovan's public image has already rebounded, and now people seem ready to focus on his soccer abilities.

I'm one of the proud jersey wearers. I saw them in the souvenir kiosk and had to have one for myself. It's a little big, almost like a tunic over the tank top I have on underneath. I'm thinking I'll wearing it later for Donovan with nothing else.

My view from the luxury box affords a sweeping perspective on the field, almost like I'm watching it on TV. At center field, the box sits perched in a coveted spot, but I find it strange to be so far removed from the action down below, where fans are loud and less polite than the corporate types up here. People seem content to graze from the decadent spread of sushi, pub food, and full bar set up especially for the twenty-or-so of us in the private box.

I know Charlie's here somewhere in an owner's box with whomever he saw fit to invite. Knowing Charlie, he could be in there alone and be perfectly happy.

When a Strikers player does something noteworthy—a change of possession, a goal save—there are suitable high fives and fist bumps among the people in the suite.

It's too polite, almost like the soccer on the field comes in second to the party in the room. Maybe season ticket holders used to seeing several dozen games in a season don't need to watch every move the players make. But I don't like it.

Caleb Schmidt, the Strikers keeper, makes a nice save against the bullet from a Falcons forward with a strong right foot. He feeds the ball to Jordy Steiner at left back, and he plays it up the line with a hard pass to one of the midfielders.

I've watched enough soccer by now to know that most teams like to play from the back, moving the ball up the field with quick passes and footwork that makes Michael Flatley's river dancers look like they're standing still.

The Strikers' passes look tight and fast. Within seconds, they've moved the ball up the field and Donovan positions himself to receive a long pass, running to where he anticipates the ball to be, outpacing the defender, and getting his feet on the ball to take control. The crowd starts to cheer, anticipating a potential shot on goal.

Donovan's had a couple of good breakaway runs in the game, but the defense has shut him down each time he took a shot, either protecting the goal when the keeper ran up or deflecting the shot and knocking it out of bounds.

Now, with the ball shifting tightly between his feet, Donovan has what looks like his best chance at his signature move, the Killer Cross, as he dribbles the ball up the left side and looks for an unguarded moment to take the shot. I feel myself holding my breath and leaning forward, as if to will him and the ball toward the goal. "Come on, come on," I urge, even though I know he can't hear me.

But then I see the impossibility of what he needs to do. He's taken the ball so far up the side, that the angle between him and the goal is too narrow for a clean shot. The ball will have to bend in the air to have a chance of arcing into the net. And even though I know he defies the laws of physics with his shooting ability, it's a tough goal to make.

A defender chases him, angling to get a foot on the ball before Donovan can shoot, but he's not fast enough, so he slide tackles the ball instead, driving it from Donovan's feet and taking him down in the process. Donovan tumbles, but rights himself immediately as the ref calls a penalty.

I watch the defending player argue that it was all ball, and the ref goes to look at the VAR for replay. The crowd gets rowdy, booing the defender for the foul and starting to chant, "Donno, Donno."

The ref comes back and confirms the foul, eliciting howls and cheers from the crowd below. The Strikers set up for Donovan to take a free kick. The Falcons defense lines up to try to block his shot and the crowd noise ratchets down as Donovan prepares to take his shot. I find myself chewing my nails, and I've never been a nail biter, but this requires it.

The whistle blasts, and Donovan zeros in to take his shot. This is where being ambidextrous is a huge advantage. The defense has no way of knowing which foot he'll kick with, so the goalkeeper can't prepare. He'll just have to choose a side and hope he's right.

Donovan kicks a bullet to the high right corner. The keeper dives left.

Goal! The stadium erupts in cheers and more chanting of Donovan's name as he accepts the slaps and kudos from his teammates. But I know him—he doesn't want to win on a penalty shot. He wants to score again.

Behind me in the luxury box, glasses clink and joyful chatter tells me people are enjoying the game, but I don't want to join them.

Every time I look at the seats close to the field, I notice a few that sit vacant. Charlie told me some of the best seats get purchased by corporate season ticketholders who gift the tickets to clients, which means sometimes those seats go unused.

I lean over the plexiglass half wall that separates the box from the outside world and squint at the action below. The Strikers dominate the half, but a Falcons winger manages to get a nice shot off, straight at the Strikers' keeper, who catches it easily and kicks it high over the defenders to put it back in play at midfield.

Three quick passes and Donovan has the ball again. He takes it as far as he can and passes it off before he gets shut down by the defense.

I can't take it anymore. The luxury box has extra-comfy movie-theater-style seats and the benefit of attentive waiters catering to our every food and beverage need, but I don't need that. I want to be closer to the action.

With my stomach in knots, it's not like I can eat. I want to be down in front. When I yell Donovan's name, I want him to be able to hear me. My VIP pass allows me into any part of the stadium, so I use it to get to the field level, where I search out the empty seat nearest the field. I find one a few rows up from the centerline.

The field seats don't have quite the same perspective on the field as the overhead view from boxes, but I don't care. From here, the turf looks greener, the ball looks bigger, and I can smell the players' sweat. And since Donovan is a left winger, he's playing on this side of the field. I want to see the tiny blades of turf fly from his cleats. I want to watch him play.

And he plays.

Watching Donovan is like seeing a gazelle take flight. His powerful quads flex and chew up the turf as he launches into motion, gaining speed and controlling the ball with the most graceful ease I've ever seen.

"Go, go! Go, Donno," I chant, mostly to myself, eyes riveted to his body and the ball. A few months ago, I might have felt like a traitor to my beloved American football for rapturously watching this new sport with such open love. But I don't feel at all apologetic.

I've become a fan among fans, and I want a Strikers victory like I want to breathe air.

The team dominates the field, and thanks to a great assist by

Weston that gave Donovan an early goal along with his free kick, the Strikers lead by two at halftime. The players file off the field to the locker room, and I can see the fire in Donovan's expression —he's not satisfied being up by two. He wants a bigger win, and he wants to score goals.

"You a season ticket holder? I don't remember you from last year," a man a few seats over says to me, appraising my team jersey and obvious fandom.

"No, it's not my seat. Don't tell anyone."

He mimes zipping his lips and leans back to inspect my jersey. "Aha, already a fan of the new guy, I see."

"Yup, I'm a fan," I tell him. He gets wrapped up in a discussion of strategy with a man next to him, and I take the halftime break to wander to the concessions area and grab a drink. By the time I get back to the seat, the referee's whistle signals the start of the second half.

The team comes out strong, beating back the Falcons offense and taking control of the ball. Danny Weston sends a hard pass to Donovan who makes a run toward the goal, juking and using stepover moves to confuse the defender so he can get a breakaway. I watch in awe as Donovan cuts hard to the outside and uses his left foot to send the ball cleanly past the keeper and into the net.

"Gooooaaaal!" The announcer drags out the word as the place erupts in cheers of "Donno, Donno." The man next to me leans over and high-fives me along with everyone else in our row. People are pumped up about the team.

The Strikers feel it. When they reset for the next kickoff, there's a little more swagger, but only for a second. The Falcons kick off to their midfield and line up a few passes, moving the ball up the field. Every time I worry that someone will get a breakaway and run the ball up the field, the Strikers defense shuts them down.

I start to feel a little sorry for the Falcons. It's ridiculous because I know these are pro athletes who aren't going to cry into their moms' pantlegs like I did when my team got crushed in Little League.

No sooner does the thought fly through my brain then the Falcons' striker gets a great pass and shoots it over the head of the Strikers' keeper. He jumps for it and maybe gets two fingers on the ball, but he can't stop its trajectory into the net.

The small section of Falcons fans erupts in cheers and applause, but where I stand, it's quiet. "Get it back, boys!" the man next to me yells. I notice he now wears a jersey like mine with "Donno" on the back.

"Wardrobe change?" I ask, pointing.

He nods. "Figure I need to support the new guy. Want a hat trick out of him today. You think he can do it?"

"I know he can," I tell him. And somehow, I do know. Three goals in one game is a lot for any one player, but I can see from Donovan's face that he wants it.

The minutes tick by and the three-one score continues to hold. Both teams get opportunities, but their keepers shut each one down. I can see Donovan's demeanor change—he's still playing the same game, but he's more determined, more precise in his movements.

Everything he does is controlled, but now he's reading the field the way I know he does. Each pass is part of a bigger picture. He's not rushing, not squandering opportunities. Just working the ball, exhausting his opponents by making them chase him, and waiting for the right opportunity.

When he gets it, the whole stadium knows it. Weston sends him a perfect pass high on the left side and Donovan runs to meet the ball, outpacing the defender by mere inches. He moves the ball between two players and passes it back to the midfield, but I know it's not a sign of defeat.

Donovan's still running hard to the right side of the field, ready when the ball gets shot back to him. He's perfectly positioned to take advantage of a Killer Cross opportunity with his right foot. But the defense expects that so they pile on. He has to pass it off again.

Everyone's screaming, so I'm hardly alone, but somehow I feel like I'm louder. Rationally, I know Donovan can't actually hear my one voice in the crowd, but I cheer and yell as though he can.

Weston dribbles and passes to a different forward, this time right in the middle, and he takes a shot that lures the keeper out of the goal. But one of the Falcons' defenders kicks the ball away from the goal. It's what Donovan was counting on.

"Do it! Take the shot!" I don't even know if my command of soccer lingo is correct. I don't care. I scream like every drunk, face-painted football fan I always found so ridiculous and I love every minute of it.

I should paint my face. Next game. Doing it.

Of course I'm coming to the next game. I'm coming to all the games. It baffles me that until now I've limited myself to one sport.

Donovan takes two steps with the ball, heading away from the keeper, then he sends a hard straight shot right behind him and into the goal.

The crowd goes nuts. "Gooooaaaaal!" booms through the speakers again. I jump and clap and lift the jersey over my head with "Donno" facing the field. I know Donovan can't see me, but I'm caught in the thrill of his hat trick.

In my peripheral vision, I can see a few cellphones pointed in my direction, maybe even an official photographer capturing me screaming, my eyes intensely focused on Donovan, my mouth wide open as I shout his name.

It's probably a very unflattering shot, but I pay it no mind. If someone wants to post a picture of me yelling my support for a man I love more than anything, so be it. I don't care how I look or who sees it.

The final whistle signals the end of the Strikers' first season game, and the crowd goes nuts—hollers and cheers in anticipation of a new era for the team that has struggled. The dying goat sounds from vuvuzelas fill the air and the stadium sound system starts playing a celebratory rock anthem. No one's rushing to leave the stadium to beat traffic. Everyone's still too fired up.

I watch the players line up to shake each other's hands before they break off and head back to their sides of the field. Lots of back slapping and congratulating. Nothing like a big win to start off the season. My eyes never lose sight of Donovan as he moves.

He wears a satisfactory smile. He played perfectly, did everything he came here for. With three years ahead of him to do exactly that, he exudes a lightness I've been hoping to see. He's happy here. In with both feet.

He'll need to get to the press room downstairs for the postgame conference so he can say the expected words about his enthusiasm for the season, the thrill of starting out with a hat trick. No one will ask about the fight in England. It's old news now.

I look down at my phone, debating whether to send a text I know he won't see until he looks at his phone later. Sure, why not.

Me: Congrats. You looked amazing out there. And I love you.

When I look up, Donovan has stopped on the midline of the field and he's looking right at me. His smile lights up his face even more than what I saw moments before.

Maybe it's because I'm the only one in a sea of fans who stands completely motionless, utterly fixated on only one person who matters to me in this throng of people. Or maybe we have some sort of extrasensory connection that compels Donovan to look up into the stands at the exact place where I'm standing.

He walks to the edge of the field, and I weave in and out of fans to make it down the aisle to the front row of the stands. It only takes a second before someone notices him there, and he's immediately inundated with fans seeking autographs and selfies. He obliges for ten minutes or so, then stadium security starts to disperse the crowd and shuttle people up and out of the stands.

As the crowd between us dissipates, Donovan reaches for me and deftly helps me over the wall that separates the bottom row of bright red seats from the field, but he doesn't put me down. Wrapping my legs around his waist, I lean down to kiss his salty lips. I've been watching him for the past ninety minutes, so it's crazy that I've missed him so much.

"Nice jersey," he chuckles, looking over my shoulder to see his name on the back. "You know, I could have given you one of mine."

I push my shoulders back proudly. "I wanted the superfan version."

He tips my chin up and kisses me again, and I can tell he's not thinking about paparazzi because his kiss immediately becomes urgent, and in another minute we won't be appropriate for the soccer field. I pull back and he releases his hold, so I can slide down his body to the grass.

"How'd you know where I was?" Looking over to where I'd stood a minute ago, the crowd is still so thick that it seems crazy that he found me.

He smiles. "I told you, there's only one fan I care about. I think I heard you cheering. Is that crazy?"

I laugh. "I'll admit I was pretty loud." Tipping his forehead against mine, I hear him sigh. I know how he feels—lucky. When I'm wrapped in his arms, everything else disappears.

And after a minute, I become aware of the cellphones and the cameras. It's going to take some getting used to, remembering that they're there before we start making out in public. But if I don't . . . it'll be okay.

"I got a hat trick," Donovan says, guilty pleasure in his voice. The green of his eyes rivals the turf for its brightness.

"I saw. You're the GOAT."

"Ha. Not sure I'd say that. But I'm glad you know now that your sister wasn't referring to me as a farm animal." I grin at the recollection of our conversation, fully embracing the fact that he is the greatest of all time. In soccer, maybe—still to be determined. But for me, without a doubt, the greatest I could ask for.

"Want to come sit in the back of the press conference? It'll be quick, then I'll grab a shower and we can go eat."

I nod, and he takes my hand. We walk and he regales me with everything he was thinking at different moments of the game. I lap up every word, the information junkie in me thrilled to know the details.

It's light, easy. So good.

I know love isn't a game and it's certainly not a competition.

Of course, I know this.

Just like I know that falling in love with Donovan Taylor wasn't within my control. It wasn't a power move or a calculated plan. There were no metrics involved and no predictable outcomes. Once I allowed myself permission, I just fell hard and fast and completely in love.

Just Donovan. Just us. And happiness that soars beyond what I ever thought possible.

But I am competitive, probably always will be. So forgive me for saying this, but . . .

I won.

EPILOGUE

atum

THREE MONTHS Later

WHEN CHERRY TOLD me she didn't want to come to Finn's wedding without a date, I was still in the throes of wallowing, so I filed the information away in the recesses of my brain.

Fortunately, my brain functions like a game of whack-a-mole where one stray thought gets satisfied and the next one pops up demanding attention.

With Finn's wedding only six weeks away and with my heart still sailing on a cloud of Donovan bliss, I feel like it's only fair that I turn my attention to helping my sister. She's made jokes about being the last Finley standing, but I know it hurts a little to be the only sibling without a partner, so I'm determined to find her a date. A good date.

It is for that purpose that I've invited her out to dinner with

Donovan and a "surprise guest." I didn't use the air quotes when I told her because, well, I didn't tell her.

"She's going to kill you," Donovan says, pulling a navy-blue T-shirt over his impeccably-toned chest. Just as quickly, I walk over and push it up and off. He smirks. "Don't like the shirt?"

I shake my head. "Don't like any shirt."

"Well, that's going to severely limit the options for where we can go to dinner. Unless we're eating at the beach."

"Nope, no beach." I wrap my arms around the lean muscles of his back, letting my hands roam where they want. Which is everywhere. It really is hard to see him wearing a shirt when I know what's underneath.

In the months since the MLS season started, we've settled into a rhythm. When Donovan's in town, we split the time between his place in San Francisco and my Palo Alto apartment, even though we've established that his place has the better views and I'm all about the views.

Then, when he's traveling to away games, I hunker down, work ahead, and delegate tasks to my team. The new Therapeutic VR division is growing steadily, and I've loved meeting with doctors, psychologists, and trauma patients to inform them of first slate of products we plan to build.

It feels great to be working on cutting edge technology that can make a real difference in people's lives.

My team knows that when Donovan's in town, I'll probably be leaving earlier, but I'll still be available when they need me. My division is the only one in the company so far to require that employees take at least one personal day every two months. It's not a lot, but it's a start.

And Terrance tells me his division will be following our lead.

In other words, I've found balance. And I've learned compromise. Two big lessons for a Type A workhorse who never thought she'd have reason to want to leave early.

Therefore, it surprises me when Donovan—still shirtless,

thank you very much—leads me into his kitchen where he's poured us each a glass of red wine. "Aw, thank you. I thought you didn't drink during the season."

"Normally, I don't. But I wanted to propose a toast, and I'm not toasting with water. It's too important."

I have no idea what he's referring to. "Are we toasting Cherry's blind date?"

"Nope. What I hope we're toasting is this." He goes to the other side of the counter where I hadn't noticed a strange-looking heap on the counter under a red and white kitchen towel.

I hoist myself onto one of the barstools and wait while Donovan brings the heap over to the island in front of me. He dips his head, indicating I should take the towel off.

Once I do, it's impossible to hide the confusion from my face at the sight of a medium-sized, well-decorated gingerbread house. I don't want Donovan to feel bad if this is part of an inside joke I don't recall, so I smile.

"It's adorable!"

"It is, isn't it?" He grins proudly and I wonder if he made the thing. He watches me, and I know he's waiting for the dawn of recognition, but . . . I've got nothing.

Pressing my lips together, I turn toward him and meet his warm gaze. Then I lift one hand to my lips and kiss it. Yes, I'm buying time. No, my brain isn't cranking hard enough to recognize the significance of frosted gingerbread.

He starts to laugh. "What?" I ask.

"You're trying so hard to understand what's important about this." His eyes dance, and his smirk tells me he's enjoying my struggle.

So I sip my wine and say nothing. I'll wait him out.

Fine, I can't wait him out. "What? What is this? Why don't I know why I'm looking at a baked good?"

He points. "Open it."

Until now I hadn't been aware a gingerbread house could be opened. And I don't want to ruin it. Carefully, I tip the roof and notice it's loose enough to remove. Peering inside, I see a carabiner in the shape of a heart.

"It's . . . " I wrinkle my forehead and squint at him because I'm still so confused.

"Adorable?" he supplies.

"Well, it's a heart, so that's cute. And a carabiner is certainly functional, so . . . thank you."

Donovan kisses my temple and digs into his pocket, from which he produces a single key. "I figure you can use it as a keychain . . . I want you to move in with me. I want to wake up with you every day that I'm here and go to sleep with you every night. And if the commute is too horrible, we can sell this place and buy something closer to your job. The point is, no more sleepovers. I want you permanently."

Now I'm speechless because I can't wrap my brain around what he's just said. But the words start filtering through my incorrigible mind and my body does the work. So I'm nodding and grinning and jumping off the barstool into Donovan's arms.

"Yes, please. I want to be your permanent roommate. I want to be your permanent everything."

He cups my cheek and leans in, his words a delicious growl I feel in my bones. "You already are."

The deep, tender kiss from my new permanent roommate erases all other thoughts except how much I love him. Oh, and, how happy I am that he's still not wearing a shirt. My hands roam over the sculpted planes of his abs and chest. I tuck myself into the warm comfort of his body and circle my arms around his neck. "I don't plan to stop kissing you," I whisper against his lips. "Ever."

He can't respond because our mouths are fused and he's guiding me backward toward the couch. I sense he's onboard with my plan based on how insanely hard he is. And then . . . my phone pings with a text.

Cherry's downstairs.

"Ohhh, we need to go," I whimper, giving Donovan one more long, lingering kiss that promises more to come.

"Cherry can wait." He flips us over so I'm straddling him on the couch. The wild blaze in Donovan's eyes and his wicked smile draws me in.

"Who's Cherry?" He makes me forget all reason, and I love it. We're a desperate tangle of hands and tongues and I feel ready to disown all my siblings for the promise of another ten minutes here with this man.

But . . .

My phone pings again with another text.

Donovan slows our frantic pace, lifts me to a sitting position, and kisses me for another minutes until my brains feel permanently scrambled. "We will pick this up in this exact spot in . . . " He checks his watch. "Two hours. If these two haven't connected by then, they're on their own."

"You've got yourself a deal, footballer."

Reluctantly, I toss Donovan a shirt and sigh a little bit Donovan as he puts it on. On our way down in the elevator, my phone pings again. "Well, if nothing else these two are both punctual—they have that in common."

We exit the elevators and I run over to hug my sister, who's waiting in a corner of the lobby. A moment later, the door to my new building swings open and Cherry's blind date walks in with a bouquet of sunflowers in his hand.

I turn to my sister and make introductions. "Cherry, meet Charlie."

-V-

. . .

Dear Reader:

Thank you so much for reading Playing for You! I really hope you loved these characters—they owned my heart while I was writing them.

Ready for Cherry and Charlie's story? It's available HERE! Read on for a sneak peek!

ACKNOWLEDGMENTS

Readers, thank you. I'm grateful for every word you read, every kind review, every thoughtful click and comment. I could not do this without you.

Jay, Jesse and Oliver: thank you for walking the dogs and doing your dishes so I could keep writing books. Big love to you three giant men with the biggest hearts.

Amy Vox Libris and Erica Russikoff - thank you, thank you for the edits and the feedback.

Thank you, Kat, for making the cover beautiful. Thank you Jenn and the Social Butterfly team for expert advice, brilliant execution, and other superpowers. Catherine and Shan, I'm happy to have you in my corner - you make the PR part a breeze.

Bloggers and bookstagrammers—thank you for embracing my books and exposing my writing to readers. I couldn't do it without your help. Glad to have you in my village.

And to my fellow authors: you lift me up. Thank you.

ABOUT THE AUTHOR

Stacy Travis writes sexy, charming romance about bookish, sassy women and the hot alphas who fall for them. Writing contemporary romance makes her infinitely happy, but that might be the coffee talking.

When she's not on a deadline, she's in running shoes complaining that all roads seem to go uphill. Or on the couch with a margarita. Or fangirling at a soccer game. She's never met a dog she didn't want to hug. And if you have no plans for Thanksgiving, she'll probably invite you to dinner. Stacy lives in Los Angeles with her husband, two sons, and a poorly-trained rescue dog who hoards socks.

Facebook reader group: Stacy's Saucy Sisters

Super fun newsletter: https://geni.us/travisNL

Tiktok: https://www.tiktok.com/@stacytravisauthor

Website: https://www.www.stacytravis.com

Email: stacytraviswrites@gmail.com - tell me what you're reading!

facebook.com/stacytravisromance
instagram.com/stacytravisauthor
bookbub.com/authors/stacy-travis
goodreads.com/stacytravis

ALSO BY STACY TRAVIS

The Summer Heat Duet

1. The Summer of Him: A Mistaken Identity Celebrity Romance

2. Forever with Him: An Opposites Attract Contemporary Romance

The Berkeley Hills Series - all standalone novels

1. In Trouble with Him: A Forbidden Love Contemporary Romance (Finn and Annie's story)

2. Second Chance at Us: A Second Chance Romance (Becca and Blake)

3. Falling for You: A Friends to Lovers Romance (Isla and Owen)

4. The Spark Between Us: A Grumpy-Sunshine, Brother's Best Friend Romance (Sarah and Braden)

5. Playing for You: A Sports Romance (Tatum and Donovan)

6. No Match for Her - an Opposites-Attract Friends-to-Lovers Romance (Cherry and Charlie)

San Francisco Strikers Series - standalone novels

1. He's a Keeper: A Grumpy-Sunshine Sports Romance (Molly and Holden)

2. He's a Player: A Second Chance Sports Romance (Jordan and Tim)

3. He's a Charmer: A Brother's Best Friend Sports Romance (Linnie and Weston)

Buttercup Hill Series - standalone novels

1. Love You More; A Single Dad Grumpy-Sunshine Small Town Romance (Jax and Ruby)

2. Love You Anyway; A Brother's Best Friend Small Town Romance (PJ and Aidan)

NO MATCH FOR HER

SNEAK PEEK

Chapter 1
Cherry

I cast a side glance at Tatum to make sure I've heard her correctly.

After acting coy and refusing to give me any details for the past week, she's just introduced my blind date without a shred of irony or indication that we're in on the same joke.

Standing in the lobby of her modern metal and glass apartment building, she simply gestures to a plain-looking man approaching us and beams at us both.

"Cherry, meet Charlie." Three simple words with the power to change my life, doubtfully for the better.

The unbridled joy that squeaks through her voice makes me take a quick glance around to see if she's referring to someone else—someone who looks like fitness model eye candy with a brain to match. That's the level of fabulous I'm expecting from her breathless squeal.

But, no.

The man coming our way moves slowly—not fashion model

on a runway slowly—more like head in the clouds slowly. Like he might forget where he's going before he gets there. Or walk right past us because something shiny catches his eye.

Which is exactly what happens.

Charlie momentarily bypasses us to root around in the candy dish at the building's front desk until he finds what he's searching for. Then he returns to us and presents me with a bouquet of sunflowers he had tucked under one arm.

"Thank you." I clutch the long stems and wonder if they'll wilt before I can get them home and into some water.

Then Charlie holds up his newly acquired purple lollypop, turns it so it reflects the light, and slips it into his pocket. "My favorite flavor. And the color brings back the memory of building models with crystalline tiles in science class. I like how a color can instantly return us to a time and place."

As I gape at him and his non-sequiturs, I rescind my impression that he's plain-looking. I really don't know what he looks like under the shock of hair falling over half his face, the thick dark-rimmed glasses, several days' worth of scruff, and excessively baggy clothes. He's practically in disguise.

As a wandering minstrel.

And because this is Silicon Valley, home of startup companies with ridiculous valuations and stock options that multiply like spring bunnies, a man dressed like him could easily be a career-delayed, forever college student…or a wealthy serial entrepreneur.

"Cherry, meet Charlie." My sister's words echo in my head, urging me to connect the dots.

As the hamster cranks its rusty little wheels, I realize what my sister has finagled, and a feeling of annoyance settles in. Then dread.

The man standing in front of us, quietly studying me, is Charles Walgrove—the billionaire tech company owner and an investor in the San Francisco Strikers soccer team.

He's also Tatum's boss. Yes, my sister is setting me up with the man who signs her paycheck at a job she wants to keep. That can't possibly be disastrous. Especially when I'm the one sister prone to making oblivious observations about inappropriate things. Like his socks. Amid the monochromatic, dismal sky color of his clothes, he's wearing bright yellow socks, and that strikes me as strange. I bite my tongue to avoid tanking this date before it even gets started.

Staring down at my ankle length red skirt, the black spike-heeled booties, and the short black boucle sweater I'm wearing over a white t-shirt and several strings of gold necklaces and leather wrap bracelets, I sense the blush heat the back of my neck. I'm way overdressed.

As the only redhead in the family, I already look like the outcast. But now that Tatum has fallen hard for her gorgeous soccer star boyfriend, I'm also the last single sister out of five.

Unlucky in love. Really unlucky.

If the fashion mismatch isn't enough, my date is one of an elite few Silicon Valley entrepreneurs who earned their billions before age thirty. And Charles Walgrove did it with computers and algorithms.

I could not be less interested in computers and algorithms.

Even though I work for a high tech company where some people bother themselves with numbers and computer code, I spend my days working with color, design, graphics, and art. I pull swatches of fabric and create color boards. And if I can't find the textile I have in mind, I make it myself.

So forgive me if my first instinct is to appraise at the sheep-ish-looking man in front of me and decide Tatum is playing some kind of a joke.

I wait for the punch line.

Then I wait some more.

I also check the near vicinity for a tasty dessert of a man like her boyfriend Donovan Taylor. Tatum knows my type, and if ever a man fit the bill, it would be any of Donovan's teammates on the Strikers soccer team. Any. Of. Them.

Where are you, flawless man lurking nearby with an athlete's physique, a whip-smart sense of humor, and a sinfully beautiful face? Anyone?

Not finding an impish grin on Tatum's face or any other sign she's testing my sense of humor, I inhale a cleansing breath, shoot a subtle glare in her direction, and extend my hand to the man waiting patiently in front of me.

"Hi. I'm Cherry. The best sister." I've probably made that joke to half the people my siblings have introduced me to, and nearly one hundred percent of the time, it merits a smile or a laugh.

Not with Charles Walgrove.

He blinks at me a few times and presses his lips together, appraising me. He looks taken aback by my very existence, not to mention that his baggy jeans and a navy hoodie—with the hood up—make him look like some sort of stalker troll. Or the Unibomber.

Finally, Charlie seems content with the visual survey of me. He gingerly slides the hood off and reaches for my hand. "Cherry. I'm delighted to meet you." He gives my hand a firm pump, lets it go, and looks up at Donovan who's several inches taller than him. "Donno, nice to see you off the pitch. That last game was a heart-breaker, not that you need me to say it."

Donovan takes a long blink and runs a hand through his hair, no doubt reliving every disappointing moment of the most recent game. "I know. We still don't have our rhythm."

Charlie claps him on the back. "That's what it looked like." Charlie taps a finger against his lips and looks off into the distance.

I feel bad for Donovan. It's one thing to lose a game, but it's another stand in front of one of the team's investors and have to answer for it. Yet another reason why I can't, for the life of me, understand why Tatum would choose to set me up with Charlie. She and I will be having a conversation later.

"Coach has some ideas for where we've been going wrong, I'm sure you're in the loop," Donovan sighs.

Charlie waves a hand. "I'm not here to give you a hard time about a loss. But I'd love to pick your brain—I'm fascinated by the game, as you know."

"No prob, Charlie. Ask away whenever." Donovan plasters on a smile and I see his arm tighten ever so slightly around my sister's shoulder.

Her eyes question me with a subtle raised eyebrow to ask if I want them to come to dinner with us. We talked earlier about how she and Donovan might just introduce us and head off on their own. She thought it made the most sense, so my blind date and I could get to know each other without the pressure of sitting under the watchful eye of our matchmaker.

"Yeah, no watchful eyes," I told her at the time, assuming I'd want her to leave me to work my dating magic with her friend. But now that I know her friend is really her boss, I don't feel so brave. Having her as a buffer might be nice.

So I return her look with a subtle shake of my head, and she immediately nods in understanding. Picking up Donovan's hand, she pipes in, "Actually, you two can talk shop over dinner. Cherry and I thought we'd make it a foursome, just for fun."

My eyes go to Charlie's—or what I can see of them—to ascertain whether he agrees with our definition of fun. His expression is blank, save for an acquiescent rise in the corner of his mouth, and he nods. "Foursome it is."

I have mixed feelings about chickening out on a true blind date. On one hand, my sister and Donovan know Charlie, so if conversation between the two of us lags, they can pick up the slack. But if Charlie's busy quizzing Donovan about game strategy and he and Tatum start talking about work, I might feel like a fourth wheel on my own date.

These are the thoughts bouncing in my head as I survey our tidy group, thinking that we look like a motley crew. I'm accessorized to the nines with jewelry I made in a new class I'm taking, Donovan is wearing a baseball cap to keep from getting recognized, Tatum has on dark jeans and a tight black sweater I forced her to buy, and then there's Charlie, who looks like he borrowed "I've given up" attire from a three-hundred pound linebacker.

It's my own fault, sort of, that I've found myself in need of a blind date rescue operation. Our brother Finn—the oldest of our family of six siblings and the only male—has finally picked a wedding date and it's fast approaching. Every one of my sisters has seemingly found her soulmate and therefore has a date to the wedding. Each of them will gaze into the eyes of someone important on the dance floor when the bridesmaids join the wedded couple for a dance.

And unless I can find a human body to serve as my date, I will be dancing alone, and not in a Gloria Gaynor-fueled anthem about surviving on my own.

Back when Finn and his fiancé Annie announced their wedding date a few months ago, I figured I had loads of time to turn one of the first date men in my life into a sixth date wedding partner. But none of them made it past date three—not the dog trainer, the aspiring standup comedian, or the poet.

So here I am. I don't need true love. I barely need true like. I just want to be able to spend a few wedding reception hours with someone I can tolerate. Preferably someone who likes to dance.

"How do you feel about dancing, Charlie?" The bigger question is whether he's willing to put on a tux. One time, for one night.

Made in the USA
Las Vegas, NV
09 May 2024

89747106R00173